"I'll Teach You to Ski."

"You're probably very good," Shannon protested. "You wouldn't want to bother with a novice."

"It wouldn't be the first time I've taught you," Deke murmured, his eyes holding hers.

She felt a warmth stealing through her entire body. Why was he doing this? Why all the remembrances, the emphasis on the good things instead of the bad? Was he trying to seduce her with memories so she would let down her guard? Deke would do anything, use any methods to get his own way.

TRACY SINCLAIR
has traveled extensively throughout the continental Unites States as well as Alaska, the Hawaiian Islands and Canada. She currently resides in San Francisco.

Dear Reader,

Silhouette Special Editions are an exciting new line of contemporary romances from Silhouette Books. Special Editions are written specifically for our readers who want a story with heightened romantic tension.

Special Editions have all the elements you've enjoyed in Silhouette Romances and *more*. These stories concentrate on romance in a longer, more realistic and sophisticated way, and they feature greater sensual detail.

I hope you enjoy this book and all the wonderful romances from Silhouette.

Karen Solem
Editor-in-Chief
Silhouette Books

TRACY SINCLAIR
Winter of Love

Silhouette Special Edition

Published by Silhouette Books New York

America's Publisher of Contemporary Romance

SILHOUETTE BOOKS, a Division of Simon & Schuster, Inc.
1230 Avenue of the Americas, New York, N.Y. 10020

ISBN: 0-671-53640-0

First Silhouette Books printing January, 1984

10 9 8 7 6 5 4 3 2 1

Map by Ray Lungren

America's Publisher of Contemporary Romance

Printed in the U.S.A.

Silhouette Books by Tracy Sinclair

Silhouette Romance

Paradise Island #39
Holiday in Jamaica #123
Flight to Romance #174
Stars in Her Eyes #244

Silhouette Special Edition

Never Give Your Heart #12
Mixed Blessing #34
Designed for Love #52
Castles in the Air #68
Fair Exchange #105
Winter of Love #140

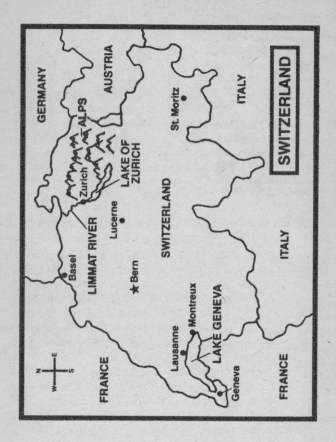

Chapter One

Shannon Shelby got up at six thirty, shivering in the icy morning cold. It was still dark outside, too early to tell what kind of a day it was going to be. Just don't let it snow, she prayed, crossing her fingers.

As she turned up the heat and put the coffee on, Shannon thought briefly of her native Los Angeles. People there took the weather for granted. The only thing they worried about in winter was whether all the tennis courts would be booked.

She sighed, tightening the belt of her bathrobe around her slender waist and pushing the cloud of raven hair away from her delicate, heart-shaped face. It felt like a million years since she had had time to play tennis. Why was she thinking about it now when there was so much work to do?

Opening the huge, commercial-size freezer, she checked the trays of hors d'oeuvres neatly stacked in rows, then reviewed the tiny cream puffs that would be filled with ice cream and transformed into glamorous *profiteroles* topped with chocolate sauce later tonight. Yes, everything was in order.

Her satisfaction lasted only until the phone rang. Glancing at the clock, Shannon's deeply fringed blue eyes darkened. Eight o'clock. Too early for the business day to begin. With a feeling of apprehension that turned out to be justified, she picked up the receiver.

"Shannon?" The voice on the other end was a hoarse croak. "It's Helen. I'm afraid I have bad news for you. I think I have the flu."

"Oh, dear! That's terrible!" Shannon cried. Helen Borchard was her best waitress, a calm, capable older woman who never lost her cool no matter how hectic things got. How on earth would she get along without her?

"I know, and I feel just awful about it, with that big reception on Long Island tonight. Maybe I can still make it if I stay in bed all day, but I thought I ought to alert you just in case."

A sense of guilt invaded Shannon. Here she was worrying about her own problems when the woman was obviously ill. "You'll do no such thing. You stay in bed and take care of yourself."

"I don't know where you'll get someone else on such short notice—and at this time of year," Helen said doubtfully.

Her fears were well grounded. The month of December was a bonanza for the catering business. Even small firms like Shannon's were booked solidly, and all the good help was snapped up weeks in advance. If this were just a small dinner it wouldn't matter so much, but the Garfield reception was the most ambitious affair they had tackled so far.

"Don't worry, we'll manage," Shannon said with a lot more confidence than she felt.

"What would you think about having my niece Rachel fill in?" Helen asked tentatively. "She doesn't have much experience, but at least she's another pair of hands."

Shannon thought rapidly. Rachel had helped out once before without covering herself with glory. She was a rather awkward teenager, not overly endowed with brains; yet as Helen pointed out, she was better than nothing. They could use all the help they could get. Shannon and her cousin Marcia had great hopes for referrals from this party tonight if everything ran smoothly. Their fledgling firm could use the business.

Since it seemed to be the only solution, Shannon attempted to put the best face on it. "That sounds like a good idea, Helen. Tell her to be at the Garfields' at five. The party starts at seven, so please impress on her that she must be prompt. I'd like time enough to give her a few pointers."

As Shannon hung up, Marcia Craddock trailed into the kitchen, smothering a yawn. "Who was on the phone this early?" she asked.

"Helen—She has the flu," Shannon briefed her. "Wouldn't you know it?"

Marcia's sleepiness abruptly fled. "Good grief! She's our best helper. Can you manage without her?"

"I'll have to." Shannon shrugged.

There was a time when a crisis like this would have thrown her into a panic. Now she prided herself on being able to handle things as they came up. Maybe Deke would finally be proud of her, Shannon thought, immediately discarding the idea with disgust. All that was over and done with long ago.

"If only there were some way I could help out." Marcia continued to worry the problem. "But that party in the city is important too, even though it isn't as big. Why did they both have to be on the same night?" She sighed.

"Stop complaining." Shannon's gamin grin made her look a great deal younger than her twenty-six years. "Remember when we would have considered that a blessing instead of a problem?"

Marcia's answering smile was reminiscent. "We've come a long way from peddling homemade cakes to the neighbors, haven't we?"

It still seemed like a miracle to Shannon, even though it had been almost five years since she showed up on Marcia's doorstep, scared and pregnant. They had indeed come a long way. The business she had sort of backed into when she was housebound and desperately looking for a way to bring in some money had mushroomed. It had grown to such an extent that Marcia finally gave up her secretarial job to become a partner.

They had always been close when they were growing up in Los Angeles, partly because they were both only children and were so close in age. Marcia was barely a year older than Shannon. Their mothers were sisters, which accounted for the strong family resemblance. Marcia's hair was the same glossy black as Shannon's, although she wore it short and curly in contrast to the glorious mane that swept her cousin's shoulders like a silken curtain. Marcia's eyes were different, too, light blue instead of deep, sparkling sapphire.

While Shannon was the acknowledged beauty of the family, there had never been any rivalry between the girls. And when their parents were killed in a horrible plane crash as they returned from a joint vacation in Hawaii, the cousins were drawn even closer. It had been a terrible wrench when Marcia married and moved to New York.

Shannon could still remember that day, because it coincided with her first meeting with Deke. She was twenty years old and feeling very alone in the world.

"It's not forever," Marcia had assured her. "Bob has this great two-bedroom apartment. You'll come to visit us often."

Shannon had bravely agreed, neither of them believing it for a moment. How could they possibly have known that in the space of two short years Marcia's marriage would be on the rocks and Shannon would be installed in the apartment, not as a guest but a permanent roommate? If it hadn't been for Marcia, what would have become of her? Shannon wondered for the thousandth time.

"You didn't wake me, Mommy." A small, dark haired boy came into the kitchen, rubbing the sleep from his eyes. "I'll be late for school."

Shannon scooped him into her arms, hugging his wiry little body with a fierce tenderness. He never stopped seeming like a miracle to her. "It's Saturday, darling. There's no nursery school today."

"I forgot." He laughed, showing pearly white baby teeth. Then the merriment faded. Saturdays and Sundays were the days his mother didn't have much time for him. "Is Mrs. Daugherty coming to take care of me?"

"I certainly hope so!" Shannon breathed a silent prayer that nothing else would go wrong. "If it doesn't snow, maybe she'll take you to the park. Would you like that?"

"I guess so." He looked up at her hopefully. "Could you come with us?"

"Oh, Michael dear, I wish I could. Maybe tomorrow," she added, seating him at the kitchen table and starting his breakfast.

He was so good about accepting the fact that she had to work on the weekends when all of the other children were doing things with their parents. Such patience in a four-year-old was heartbreaking. It also hurt Shannon deeply when Michael talked wistfully about the fathers of his playmates. Anger burned fiercely in her as she looked at her handsome son. How could his father not want him?

"We could all go to the zoo tomorrow if we go early," Marcia said helpfully. "The Tinsdale cocktail party isn't until five o'clock."

Shannon looked at her cousin gratefully as the little boy's eyes brightened. Michael's father might not care about him, but that didn't mean he was lacking for love.

On the long ride out to Long Island, Shannon's mind reverted to Deke for some reason. Why had he returned to haunt her today of all days, when she had so much on her mind? She had spent the past five years steeling herself against thinking about him. Time had taken care of the first agony of hurt, yet she still flinched occasionally when she caught sight of a tall man with an arrogant tilt to his dark head and a confident way of striding along as though he knew exactly where he was going.

From the moment they met, Deke had become a kind of obsession. After Michael was born, Marcia tried to interest Shannon in other men—without any success. At first Shannon told herself it was because she didn't have time for such things. She was too busy with a new baby and a struggling business. After reluctantly accepting a few casual dates, she was forced to face the truth: Deke Masterson had spoiled her for all other men.

From the moment of their traumatic meeting in the parking lot of Masterson Aircraft, he had taken complete possession of her mind—and later her body. Shannon couldn't help smiling when she remembered how furious he was after she crumpled the fender on his brand new Ferrari.

It was the morning of the day Marcia left for New York. Shannon's eyes were still misted with tears as she drove into the employee's parking lot at the aircraft company where she worked. She hadn't noticed Deke backing out of his privileged space. The resultant crash sounded like an explosion, although only his fender was damaged. The front of her own small car had been demolished.

Deke was out of the Ferrari in a flash, his straight black brows drawn together in a scowl, his firm mouth compressed with anger as he yanked open her car door. Shannon recognized him immediately. He had been pointed out to her on her first day at work: the thirty-year-old bachelor owner of Masterson Aircraft, the darling of the jet set, the unattainable dream of every female worker in the plant.

Her big blue eyes had darkened to violet as she gazed up at him in fear and shock. The furious words Deke was about to deliver died on his lips. He stared at her delicate, pale face without speaking.

Shannon was the one who broke the silence, her soft voice hesitant. "I . . . I'm sorry. I didn't see you." When he still didn't speak, she said, "I'll gladly pay for the damage." Even as she offered, Shannon's heart sank. The repairs would probably cost her a month's salary.

He seemed to come out of a trance. "Who are you? What are you doing here?"

"My . . . my name is Shannon Shelby. I work here."

"Why haven't I ever seen you before?" He frowned, as though disbelieving her.

"I haven't been here very long. You wouldn't have anyway," she explained. "I'm in the typing pool." At only twenty and without experience, Shannon had been happy to get the job. Now it looked as if it was going to be of short duration. Why did she have to hit the *boss's* car?

Unexpectedly, he reached out, gently brushing the

silky hair away from her forehead. Her pulses leaped at the sensuous feel of those long fingers before she realized that he was merely probing a bruise she didn't know was there.

"You've been hurt," he said.

"I . . . I'm sure it's nothing."

He took her arm, urging her out of the car. "I'll be the judge of that. You're coming with me."

He had taken her up to his office, insisting that she lie on the couch until the company doctor arrived to examine her. Shannon had never been in this inner sanctum, and her eyes widened as they surveyed the huge room that was almost bigger than her whole apartment.

Plush beige carpeting that deadened any footsteps was matched perfectly by airy draperies that cut out the sun without impairing the magnificent view of downtown Los Angeles in one direction and the Pacific Ocean in another. The huge desk was unaccountably placed with its back to the converging windows, possibly to avoid distractions. Shannon knew *she* wouldn't have been able to concentrate with the whole city spread out for her contemplation.

The doctor arrived before she had finished her examination of the bookcases that lined one whole wall and the paintings that looked to be of museum quality. The doctor was a cheerful older man who hastened to reassure Deke. "A little bump on the head is all I can find," he said. "If everyone were as healthy, we doctors would go out of business."

Even so, Deke insisted on taking her home.

"There is nothing wrong with me," Shannon had protested. "And I haven't been here long enough to qualify for sick leave. I could lose my job!" she cried.

"I wouldn't worry about that." He smiled, tucking her into the passenger seat of the Ferrari.

When they reached her apartment he made her promise to stay there and rest all day. She thought that would be the end of it; but at six o'clock Deke appeared at her door carrying two huge paper bags with delicious odors wafting from them.

"How are you feeling?" he asked, brushing by her to put his packages in the kitchen.

"The same as I felt this morning—fine. What are you doing here?" she asked, rather rudely because she was so startled.

"I brought dinner," he told her. "I would have taken you out, but I thought it would better if you took it easy today."

"You didn't have to do that," she said uncertainly. His tall, athletic body dwarfed her small kitchen, making Shannon uncomfortably aware of his blatant masculinity. "After all, you were the injured party." When he raised a dark eyebrow, she explained, "I mean, *I* hit *you.*"

He smiled easily, dismissing the damage to his expensive car. "But it happened on company property and you're an employee of mine, so you're my responsibility."

Shannon wasn't naive enough to accept that explanation. Men of Deke Masterson's caliber didn't bother with little typists like her out of the goodness of their hearts. Enough men had made amorous advances for her to recognize the opening gambit. She had ample experience fending them off, but this man made her unaccountably nervous.

She watched him rummaging around in her cupboards for plates. "You, uh . . . you don't have to bother. I'll do it after you've gone."

He looked at her in surprise. "You're not going to ask me to stay for dinner?"

It would never have occurred to her. "I'm sure you have better things to do."

His smile was so devastating that Shannon's bones seemed to melt. "I can't think of any."

Deke wouldn't let her do a thing to help. He insisted that she sit at the small table while he dished up the food, rummaging around until he found everything he needed, including a candle in an old Chianti bottle. As a finishing touch, he even put a small pot of African violets in the center of the table.

"Now be honest," he said, uncorking the bottle of wine he had brought. "Don't I cook a nifty meal?"

"You and Chasen's." She smiled, having seen the name of the famous restaurant on the cartons.

"Well, maybe I had a little help from Dave, but you have to admit I served it elegantly."

Shannon began to relax a little, aided by the excellent wine. She knew this was only a prelude to the pass that would come later on, yet she wasn't really worried. A man like Deke didn't have to force a woman into anything. There were enough women who would gladly give him what he wanted.

Shannon studied him through her long lashes. He really was amazingly handsome, the angular planes of his face giving it a rugged strength that was matched by the leashed power in his splendid athlete's body. His full lower lip hinted at sensuality; but she knew it could thin dangerously, just as his hazel eyes could go from golden to cool green when he was displeased. Shannon shivered involuntarily, not envying anyone who was the recipient of this man's wrath. She sensed that he was used to getting his own way and would be quite ruthless in achieving it.

This evening, though, he was at his most charming, amusing her with anecdotes and putting her completely at ease. Not until the evening ended did

Shannon's apprehensions return. There was something about the atmosphere that had subtly changed.

Deke's eyes seemed to take on the green glow of a predator as he looked at her and murmured, "I've enjoyed tonight, Shannon. I hope you did too."

"Yes, I . . . it was very kind of you to spend all this time with me."

"I'd like to spend more time." His hands framed her face, the thumbs making gentle circles under her chin. When she swallowed nervously, he said, "Don't be afraid of me, Shannon. I won't hurt you."

"I'm not afraid," she whispered, a tremor going through her slight body. The aura of masculinity emanating from him was almost tangible, weaving a spell that enchanted her. Without realizing it, her lips parted in mute invitation.

Deke drew a sharp breath, his head descending slowly. Then his hands gripped her shoulders, putting her a short distance away. He fumbled in his pocket for a cigarette, taking his time lighting it. "I'm taking my yacht down to Baja California this weekend," he said finally. "Will you come with me?"

The short respite had given Shannon time to come to her senses. She began to tremble, realizing how deeply she had responded to him. If just his touch affected her like that, think what would happen if he kissed her! Going away for a weekend with him was out of the question.

"I appreciate the invitation, but I happen to be busy," she explained carefully.

Deke frowned. "Can't you change your plans?"

"I'm afraid not."

"I think you'd really enjoy it," he urged. "We do a little fishing and waterskiing during the day, and the nights at sea are glorious."

Shannon didn't have to be told what the nights

would be like. "I'm sure they are," she said coolly. "But you'd better ask someone else to share them with you. I'm afraid I don't have enough experience to keep you interested for an entire weekend, Mr. Masterson."

Deke's hand circled her throat lightly, his thumb gently caressing the hollow where a pulse began to beat furiously. "You underestimate yourself, Miss Shelby. I have a feeling you're going to keep me interested for a very long while."

Shannon stiffened angrily. "I'll save us both a lot of time by telling you that I don't indulge in casual affairs."

"I'm delighted to hear it," he said gravely, although laughter lurked in his eyes. "What I have in mind for you is anything but casual."

Before she could move away, Deke's arms circled her, drawing her against his taut body. She was held immobile against his long length while his mouth took possession of hers. At first Shannon resisted, but as his lips and hands began their seduction, her struggles grew feebler. While his tongue explored her warm inner recess with a demanding masculinity, one hand slid down her back, molding her hips more firmly to his. The other hand moved to her breast, making teasing circles that caused shivers of delight to travel up her spine.

He engaged all of her senses, fanning tiny embers of desire into a roaring flame without Shannon's having the will to stop him. No other man had ever aroused her to this extent. She hadn't even known her body could feel such pleasure. Twining her arms around his neck, she ran her fingers through his thick, dark hair, sighing in complete surrender.

He could have taken her then; but for some inexplicable reason, he stopped, folding her tightly in his arms and burying her face against his shoulder. Shannon's whole body cried out in protest, and her movement against him was a silent plea. Only when Deke put her gently away did realization return. Her cheeks burning with shame, she turned away, unable to look at him.

Deke pulled her against his muscled chest, holding her when she would have broken away. Nuzzling the soft skin behind her ear, he murmured, "I'll save *you* a lot of time, my love. You're mine and there's no use struggling against it."

Shannon soon discovered that Deke was right. She had gone on the yachting trip that weekend, finding to her surprise that there was a whole party aboard. To her further bewilderment, he didn't try to take her to bed. It was a wonderful trip, although the presence of Deke's sister Chloe and her present husband—she was on her third—dampened the enjoyment somewhat. Chloe took an immediate and inexplicable dislike to her. The double-edged gibes at Shannon's inexpensive clothes and lack of experience were carefully cloaked, yet her meaning was clear: Shannon was a little nobody from the wrong side of the tracks who would never fit into their sophisticated life-style.

The other women were kinder if indifferent, while the men more than made up for any slights dealt to Shannon. It was only Deke's obvious interest in her that kept them at arm's length. He made it crystal clear that she was off limits, and no one cared to challenge him.

That weekend was the beginning. Deke danced constant attendance on her, taking her to expensive places, filling her tiny apartment with flowers and buying her extravagant gifts that she invariably refused—much to his bafflement. He took her to dinner and to lunch, even coming down to the typing pool and sitting on the edge of her desk while she tried to work.

It created a problem with the other women, since they naturally assumed she was having an affair with Deke. Many of them reacted with unkind remarks born of envy, but Shannon didn't care. She was falling deeper and deeper in love with Deke. She would have slept with him, lived with him, done anything he wanted.

When he asked her to marry him a short month later, Shannon was delirious with joy. It was more than she had ever dared hope.

The first six months were unadulterated bliss. Probably because she played Trilby to his Svengali, Shannon thought bitterly. Deke was used to being obeyed in all things, as Shannon discovered when she visited his office. It was fascinating to hear him bark out orders, to see his jaw set firmly and to watch everyone hasten to comply. He had been the soul of tenderness with her, though. And why not? She had been young enough to be pliable, and too much in love to question anything he did. To Shannon their marriage was made in heaven. It came as a shock to realize that everyone else didn't feel the same way. Other women, for instance. Deke's intense sexuality continued to be a challenge to them.

Should she have fought for him? Shannon mused, so deep in thoughts of the past that she almost missed the Sands Point turnoff. The question was really academic. The mature, confident woman she was today was light years removed from that clinging, trustful child. Shannon had grown up the hard way, yet she didn't regret it. She was completely self-sufficient now, well able to take charge of her own life. Deke and all that he stood for were part of the past.

If sometimes her body refused to forget the passionate nights in his arms, the sensuous feel of his hands and lips caressing the secret spots that could make her flame with desire . . . well, that too had to pass in time. Pushing aside the troublesome memories, Shannon got out of the car.

"I'm so glad you're here, Shannon," Mrs. Garfield gasped as soon as she walked in the door. "Nothing is going right. Tonight is going to be a disaster. I feel it in my bones!"

"I'm sure everything will be perfectly lovely," Shannon soothed her client.

"It simply *has* to be," the woman asserted. "This reception is for a *very* important customer of Mr. Garfield's. It was a coup to get him to come out here. He's only going to be in New York for a couple of days."

Shannon wasn't quite sure what business Mr. Garfield was in. There had been some mention of a factory that made small parts—for what, she didn't know. Whoever this client was, however, he was someone special—judging by the amount of trouble and expense that was going into this party.

"Are you sure we ordered enough food?" Mrs. Garfield worried. "It would be just too ghastly to run out of anything."

"We have more than enough of everything," Shannon assured her. "It's all going to go smoothly, you'll see."

"Excuse me, Mrs. Garfield. I think there's something wrong with the garbage disposal." The resident housekeeper was the bearer of those bad tidings.

That seemed to set the tone for the evening. It wasn't the disaster that Mrs. Garfield had predicted, yet everything that could go wrong seemed to. The van bringing the food and linens got stuck in traffic, with the result that the tables couldn't be set or the cold hors d'oeuvres arranged as far in advance as Shannon had planned.

Then it turned out that the florist hadn't sent enough centerpieces. At least that wasn't Shannon's fault. Mrs. Garfield had insisted on taking care of the flowers herself. It was up to Shannon to rectify it, however, which she did by a little judicious filching from each bouquet. It took time, though, minutes that she didn't have to spare.

When the help arrived, Shannon's heart fell further. Rachel was an apparition in dangly earrings and enough makeup to go on stage as Sadie Thompson. In addition, her bleached hair was arranged in an elaborate mass of sausage curls that would have looked just right at a Halloween party. Shannon took her into the bathroom, effecting a transformation with the judicious use of tissues plus a comb and brush, much against the girl's will.

Through it all, Mrs. Garfield bounced in and out of the kitchen, getting in everyone's way and tightening nerves with her gloomy predictions. Shannon gritted her teeth and continued steadily, making sure that things were put in the warming oven, seeing that the wine was chilled, checking the arrangement of the platters.

Just before the first guest was due, she took a last swing through the house to be sure everything was in order. It was reassuring. The gracious rooms looked beautiful, candy and nut dishes filled, cushions plumped up, ash trays at the ready. There was no evidence of the chaos that had preceded all this serenity. With a satisfied nod, Shannon prepared to return to the kitchen. She wouldn't leave it for the rest of the evening. Her place was behind the scenes, dishing up the food and directing her helpers.

For the first half hour, everything went perfectly.

The guests drifted in; their hats and coats were taken by the Garfield's housekeeper. After allowing time for them to be supplied with a drink, Shannon started the procession of hors d'oeuvres, carefully alternating between hot and cold. Then things started to get a little hectic as waitresses came in with empty trays and went out again with filled ones.

Intent on what she was doing, Shannon forgot all about Rachel until the girl said, "What do you want me to do now? There aren't any platters ready to pass."

Shannon was carefully piping sour cream onto tiny caviar tarts. Without looking up, she said, "You can slice those smoked salmon rolls and put them on the round silver tray with a parsley garnish. Use the sharp knife so you don't mash them."

"Okay," the girl said cheerfully.

Shannon continued with her own task, ignoring the excited chatter emanating from Rachel. She was babbling on about one of the guests who was handsomer than a movie star. A moment later there was an anguished cry. Shannon whirled around to see blood dripping from Rachel's hand onto the cutting board. She dropped what she was doing, running to aid the frightened girl. It was a deep cut that wouldn't stop bleeding. After applying first aid, Shannon called one of the waitresses out of the other room.

"You'll have to take her to the emergency hospital," she said crisply. "Here are the keys to my car. See that she gets home after they patch her up."

"But how will you get back?" the woman asked. "And how can you get along two short?"

"I'll manage," Shannon said for the second time that day.

After she had bundled them out the door, she put a small white apron over her neat black dress, her mind working overtime. Fortunately, the dinner was buffet. The guests could help themselves to some of the dishes without a serving person behind each one to do it for them. That wasn't the end of the world. The wait for dessert might be a little longer while they cleared away, but maybe it wouldn't be noticed. The excellence of the food would make up for everything, Shannon assured herself.

Picking up a platter of sliced *pâté* on thin wafers of toast, Shannon headed for the nearest group of guests. She offered it in a purely automatic gesture, her mind busily calculating the time until dinner.

"Shannon?" The astonished male voice almost made her drop the tray.

That low, slightly husky voice was tattooed on her brain, but she must be imagining it now. It *couldn't* be Deke! She looked up into the hazel eyes she knew so well. It was him. Her mind went into a spin. What weird coincidence had brought him here of all places, and on this particular night?

Mrs. Garfield, who was standing next to him, frowned. "You know Mr. Masterson?"

Shannon couldn't have answered if her life depended on it. The blood was pounding in her ears as she gazed up at the tall man towering over her. Through the haze in front of her eyes she saw that Deke hadn't changed much in five years. There were lines around his firm mouth that hadn't been there before; but the changeable hazel eyes were the same, and there was no gray in the thick, sable hair. His muscular body was still lean, and the deep tan that contrasted with his snowy linen told her that Deke still enjoyed outdoor sports whenever possible. And indoor ones too?

"What are you doing here?" he asked tautly.

His voice seemed to break the spell. Shannon's blood started to flow once more. "I'm catering a reception for you, Mr. Masterson. I trust everything is to your satisfaction?"

He bit off an oath, grabbing her arm and steering her toward the hall. "I want to talk to you," he muttered.

The slices of *pâté* teetered precariously. "What do you think you're doing? I'm not a guest here," she said mutinously. "I have work to do."

Deke wrenched the tray out of her hand, practically throwing it onto the nearest table. "You'll do as I say."

For a moment Shannon was caught in the old, familiar trap. Deke called the tune, and she danced to it without question because he was the center of her universe. Then her spine stiffened. She was her own woman now.

"Take your hands off me," she ordered. "You have no right to tell me what to do."

He might not have heard her. "I can't believe it! What are you doing here in New York?"

"I live here."

"So that's why I couldn't find you! Do you know the way I searched?"

For a moment she was taken aback. "Why would you have done that?"

"Why? Because you were my *wife!*" he exploded.

"That didn't seem to mean anything to you before. You were the one who left *me,*" she cried.

He swore pungently under his breath. "Only so that I wouldn't do something drastic. Your accusations were driving me out of my mind."

"I'm sorry if you ran out of excuses," Shannon said acridly. "It should have been a relief to you when I left."

He ignored that. "Your attorney wouldn't tell me where you'd gone."

"He didn't know. I'm aware of the power of your

money and influence," she said bitterly. "It can even suborn professional ethics."

"So you did know I'd look for you," he said accusingly.

"I once thought you might, but I needn't have worried. You could have found me if you'd wanted to."

"That's not true." His hands bit cruelly into her arms. "I ran down every lead. I searched the length and breadth of California. I even hired detectives."

Shannon was unimpressed. "You did everything except ask the one person you knew could tell you."

"What are you talking about?" he demanded.

"Your sister, Chloe," she said flatly.

"Chloe?" Deke looked at her as if she had taken leave of her senses. "How could she have known? You two hated each other."

All the agony of that far-off day came back to haunt Shannon—the day when she was forced to beg Chloe to tell her where Deke had gone. The day she discovered she was carrying his child.

"He doesn't want to have anything more to do with you," Chloe had said spitefully. "Do you have to have a house fall on you to realize that?"

Shannon had swallowed her anger. The man she loved had walked out on her; she was twenty-one and pregnant. There were more important considerations than Chloe's cruelty. "I have to tell him something," she replied carefully.

"How much you love him?" Chloe sneered. "Or how much you love his *money*? It was very clever of you to get him to marry you, but I knew it would never last."

Before her tirade could gain momentum, Shannon said quietly, "I'm pregnant."

Chloe's face turned an angry, mottled red. "You're lying! You little——" Shannon had flinched at the epithet. "You'd say anything to hang onto him."

"It isn't something I could make up. Please tell me where he is, Chloe." It cost her a great deal to humble herself, yet Shannon would have done anything at that point.

Her sister-in-law's confidence was shaken by her sincerity. She hesitated. Finally she seemed to make up her mind. "Deke told me not to tell you where he's gone, but I know how to get in touch with him. I'll tell him the big news. If he wants to do anything about it, I'll let you know."

Shannon had been forced to settle for that, since Chloe refused to disclose any further information. Several days went by—during which Shannon died a thousand deaths, aware that Chloe was enjoying her torment. Finally, Deke's sister phoned her.

"I talked to Deke and he was very upset as I knew he would be," Chloe said. "He thinks you did this on purpose."

Anger started to simmer through Shannon's misery. "I might remind both of you that he played a part in it, too."

"Oh, he isn't shirking his responsibility. Deke told me to pay you off and get rid of you."

"I don't believe you!" Shannon cried. She and Deke had had some terrible arguments, but he couldn't be that callous. No man would reject his own child.

"I'm mailing you a check. When you see his signature on it, will that convince you?" Chloe asked maliciously.

The phone slipped from Shannon's numbed fingers. Chloe's laughter was a ghostly echo, mercifully ending when she summoned the energy to replace the receiver.

The torment of that day was in Shannon's eyes as

she looked up at her former husband. "Why are you bothering to carry on this pretense, Deke?"

"Shannon, I—"

"There you are, Deke." It was Mrs. Garfield rounding up her guest of honor. "The Whitfields just arrived and they're dying to meet you."

Shannon slipped quietly back to the kitchen, finding that she was trembling uncontrollably. The shock of seeing Deke again was causing a delayed reaction. She had always wondered if they would ever see each other again, assuring herself that it wouldn't matter after all this time—but it did. Dear God, it did! The wound she thought was healed had gaped open again at the mere sight of him. Deke still had the power to stir her as no other man ever could. It was a devastating revelation. With a low moan, Shannon sank into a chair at the kitchen table, burying her face in her hands.

"What's wrong, Shannon?" George, the bartender, had just come through the swinging door.

She sat up quickly. "Nothing. I'm a little tired, that's all. We've had a few disasters this evening." That was the understatement of the year!

"It doesn't show," he consoled her. "They were all commenting on how good the canapés were. This party ought to be a real winner for you."

Well, at least it was one she would never forget, Shannon told herself bitterly.

The rest of the evening was an ordeal to be gotten through somehow. Dinner was served and eaten; the dishes were cleared away and dessert brought to the tables. Discipline took over, and Shannon was able to do her job efficiently while the part of her brain that governed her feelings remained numb. Only once was her protective shield pierced.

The guests were seated at round tables of eight

each. Shannon had assigned the most important table, where Deke sat, to one of her waitresses, carefully avoiding it herself. She was painfully aware of his eyes following her, however. What was he thinking? Was he ashamed of her? Did he see this kind of work as menial? It *isn't* menial! she wanted to shout. I provide a service that people are crying for. I'm a businesswoman, and a damn good one. I've made enough to support your son without asking you for a penny.

Dinner was almost at an end when Mrs. Garfield called her over. To the woman's credit, she thought she was being kind.

"Everything is just lovely, Shannon," she said graciously. "You did a splendid job. I'll certainly recommend you to all my friends. Good help is so hard to get these days," she informed the table at large.

"Thank you," Shannon murmured, her back ramrod straight.

The look on Deke's face was enigmatic.

Eventually the evening wound to a close. The food was all put away and the kitchen left in the spotless condition that Shannon always insisted on. The help straggled out as their chores were done, until only the van remained to be packed with the restaurant-size pots and portable warming ovens. Shannon supervised the loading, shivering in the frigid air.

"Can I give you a lift?" George asked.

"No, you go in the opposite direction," she told him. "It's all right. I'll get a cab to the station." That was really the last straw, having to take a train home at this hour. Well, it couldn't be helped, Shannon told herself wearily. It was all part of this ghastly evening.

As she turned to go inside, Deke stepped out of the shadows, tossing aside his cigarette. "I'll take you home."

She stiffened. "What are you doing out here?"

"I was waiting for you."

"What for?" she asked bluntly.

He raised a peaked eyebrow. "I should think that would be obvious. After five years we have a lot of catching up to do."

"That's for friends—which we never pretended to be," she said tautly.

Deke's eyes were unreadable in the darkness. "No, we were too busy being lovers."

Shannon turned away so he couldn't see her expression. "Please, Deke, it's late. I have to go home."

"That's where I'm taking you." His decisive tone brooked no argument.

Shannon was trembling with more than the cold. She *had* to get away from him. "Aren't you afraid someone will see you with the help?" she asked waspishly.

Deke's eyes narrowed. "Get your coat, Shannon."

After many vigorous refusals, she still found herself sitting next to him in a long, luxurious automobile. Resentment pursed her soft mouth, but the plush interior was a boon to her tired body. After a few stiff moments Shannon relaxed with her head resting on the back of the seat. Well, it beat taking the train, anyway, she thought with a sigh of defeat.

"Are you tired?" Deke's low voice inquired.

"Of course I'm tired," she replied irritably. "I just organized a dinner for seventy-five people. Your opinion of what I do for a living is painfully evident; but in spite of what you think, catering happens to be a perfectly respectable business."

He let that pass. "How did you get into it? It's a far cry from secretarial work."

Just how did he think she could go off to an office every day and still take care of their child? Since he wasn't even interested in asking about Michael, she wasn't going to mention him either, even though his indifference twisted her heart.

"When I came to stay with Marcia I had to have something to do until the . . . I needed something to do," she corrected herself. "It all started accidentally. One of the women in the apartment house asked me, as a favor, to bake a birthday cake for her husband's surprise party. Everyone seemed to like it, and then other people began to ask, so I started charging for them. From there it was sort of a logical step into catering."

Deke turned to look at her. In the soft glow of the dash lights, his expression was veiled. "I didn't know you could cook."

"There were a lot of things you didn't know about me," she said shortly. Deke had only been interested in her in one room of the house—the bedroom. She resolutely slammed the door shut on those memories.

"So it would seem," he said dryly. "For instance, I never guessed that you would run off and leave me without a word."

She bent her head. "It was what you wanted."

"You know it wasn't. We'd had an argument and we were both angry, but you must have known I didn't mean anything I said."

If only she could believe that. It would ease the sense of rejection that still tormented her. Then she remembered the check, the humiliation of being dismissed like a servant who no longer satisfied.

"Why did you marry me, Deke?" she demanded.

"You must have known I wouldn't fit into your world. Chloe did—and all those women who were sharing you and hoping to grab the brass ring."

"Why did you marry *me?*" he countered, his face grim in the half-light. "Was it for my money?"

"You know it wasn't!"

"It didn't seem to be," he mused. "Unless you were very clever. You wouldn't even accept my gifts."

"I should have," Shannon cried passionately. "Then you would have thought I was like all the rest. Why didn't you just sleep with me, Deke? I wouldn't have stopped you. With your experience you must have known that."

His mouth twisted wryly. "You underestimate yourself, my love. I wanted more from you than a few memorable nights."

Just how memorable they were rose to haunt Shannon. The passion-filled hours in his arms when he belonged only to her, his body covering hers in the darkness, his mouth trailing fiery kisses that drove her into a frenzy.

Shannon shuddered, wrapping her arms around herself. Fortunately, her torment was almost over. "It's the second apartment house from the corner," she instructed him as they turned into her street. When he followed her to the door she said, "This isn't necessary. I can get in all right."

"I'm coming up. We haven't finished our conversation."

"I can't think of anything else we have to say to each other," she said stiffly.

"Can't you?" He opened the door, flipping on the lights.

"Well, maybe one thing." He *still* hadn't asked about his son.

"What's that?"

The urge to slap his handsome, arrogant face was almost irresistible. Shannon controlled herself with an effort. "If you don't know, then I guess we haven't."

Deke raised a sardonic eyebrow. "You still have that maddening habit of talking in circles, I see."

"And *you* still have that maddening habit of ignoring anything you don't want to discuss," she replied angrily.

"As I remember, you were the one who always ended all rational conversation with a tantrum," he drawled. "I was more than willing to discuss anything."

"Even Cynthia Darby?" she taunted.

Deke's eyes narrowed dangerously. "Why does everything always get back to her, even after all this time? Cynthia Darby never meant anything to me," he said slowly and distinctly. "Not before we were married, not after."

"You really expect me to believe that? After your sister, Chloe, made sure I knew every time you were with her?"

"Do you honestly think I would have told Chloe, or anyone else, if I were having an affair with Cynthia?" he demanded.

"Maybe you thought I wouldn't care." Shannon shrugged. "It seemed to be the thing to do in your crowd. At least that's what Freddy Grimsby told me."

Deke's expression darkened. "Did he make a pass at you?"

"What difference does it make?" she asked wearily. "I was naive to expect you to be faithful."

Deke's hand caressed her cheek. "If you cared, that must have meant you loved me," he said softly.

Pain tore at Shannon as she realized that this man still had the power to hurt her. He must never know, though. If pride was all she had left, she would guard it jealously. "I was young and you were very experienced. It's easy to confuse infatuation with love."

His hands were at her hips, drawing them against his. "We also had this."

She held him off in a kind of panic. "But not anymore. That was over with long ago."

Deke's arms drew her inexorably closer, so close that his hard loins were digging into her. His mouth grazed her lips, their breath mingling as he murmured, "Are you sure, Shannon?"

"Yes! I . . . I don't . . ." she began desperately.

Deke's hand tangled in her hair, urging her face closer to his so his tongue could invade the warm recess of her mouth, entering with a male confidence that overcame all resistance. A shock of awareness went through her, accelerating her pulse-rate and starting a throbbing in her awakened body. Shannon fought against it at first, but as his hand cupped her breast, his fingers sensuously seeking out the hardened nipple and stroking it seductively, a wave of longing came over her. She caught her breath, moving against him restlessly.

"You still want me don't you, sweetheart?" he growled triumphantly, his warm mouth sliding sensuously down her neck.

"No . . . I . . ." Her protest trailed off as Deke's tongue made a delicate exploration of her ear, tracing each curve in an erotic pattern.

With a shuddering sigh, Shannon gave in to the excitement raging through her. Throwing her arms around his neck, she murmured his name over and over again, giving herself up completely to the ecstasy of being in his arms the way she had dreamed of so many lonely nights.

"Mommy, I want a drink of water."

The tiny, piping voice penetrated Deke's consciousness first. "What the devil was that?" he asked, raising his head.

Shannon opened drugged eyes. "What?"

"Mommy, I've been calling and calling."

The astonished look on Deke's face brought Shannon back to reality. He was staring at the small boy standing in the doorway blinking his eyes. "Who is that?" he asked.

Shannon's cheeks were very pink as she pulled away from Deke and smoothed her ruffled hair. Going over to the small boy, she lifted him in her arms. "I thought you'd never ask," she said shakily. "This is your son."

Chapter Two

$\mathscr{D}$eke's expression was almost comical. "What are you talking about?"

"This is Michael, the son you weren't interested in." Shannon hugged him protectively.

The little boy turned his head, looking curiously at the tall man who was staring at him as though he couldn't believe what he was seeing. "Who is that, Mommy?"

Deke's swift appraisal took in every detail: the sable hair, the hazel eyes that were the exact color of his own, the square jaw that would be the same shape as his when the baby fat disappeared. "I'm your father," he said slowly.

Michael framed his mother's face in dimpled hands. "You said my father was too busy to come and visit me."

Deke's face darkened. "You told him that?"

She gave the child a hug, setting him on his feet. "Run along to bed, honey. I'll be there in a minute with your drink of water."

His lower lip protruded pugnaciously. "I want to talk to the man."

"And I think it's time I talked to you," Deke said, squatting down in front of him. "How old are you?"

The small boy held out four stubby little fingers. "I'm four. How old are you?"

Deke laughed, sitting on the floor and gathering him onto his lap. "I'm thirty-six." The laughter died as he asked, "What else did your mommy tell you about me?"

"Deke!" The burning look he shot at her silenced Shannon.

"She said you were an ind . . . indurs . . ."

"Industrialist," Shannon murmured, scarcely audibly.

"Yes." Michael nodded his head. "Mommy said you lived far away and you had a whole bunch of business to take care of, so you couldn't come to see me, but you loved me lots."

In the tiny silence, Shannon couldn't look at Deke. His voice was husky as he said, "Your mommy was right, son."

"Are you going to come live with us now?" The sweetly pitched little voice was hopeful. "Derek Johnson's daddy lives with him."

"I have a better idea," Deke said casually. "How would you like to come and live with me?"

Shannon uttered a strangled cry, which Deke ignored.

"I don't know how to get there," Michael said with simple directness.

"I'll take you on an airplane," Deke told him. "Would you like that?"

The child's eyes widened with excitement. "Oh, yes! I've never been on an airplane. Can I go, Mommy?"

"Certainly not!" Shannon snapped, shooting a dagger-filled look at Deke. "It's time you were in bed, Michael."

As the small boy's face crumpled, Deke winked at him. "Leave it to me, son. We'll talk about it in the morning. Right now you'd better do as your mother says." He rose to his feet. "How about a piggyback ride?" He swung the little boy to his broad shoulders, where the delighted child clutched Deke's hair with one hand, stretching the other arm above his head.

"Look, I can almost touch the ceiling! Mommy can't hold me this high. She used to give me piggyback rides, but she says I'm too big a load to carry now."

Deke's eyes held Shannon's. "Your mommy has been carrying a load far too long. She's about to lay down her burden," he added ominously.

Shannon's blood chilled as she watched them leave the room. Was that a threat? Surely Deke couldn't be serious about taking Michael to live with him! It was hardly likely, after ignoring him completely for more than four years. Still, Mike was a beautiful child, a son any man could be proud of. Maybe seeing him had triggered some latent paternal feeling.

Choking panic rose in Shannon's throat. Deke had always taken what he wanted, as she knew by bitter experience. But he wouldn't take her child away from her on a whim, would he? It wasn't as though Michael meant anything to him. After the novelty of having a son wore off, he would turn him over to governesses.

Shannon's nails made deep crescent marks in her clenched palms. If Deke thought he could walk in and take Mike without a struggle, he was due for a surprise. She was no longer the compliant, lovesick little fool she used to be. She would fight like a leopardess for her child! Brave words, yet a cold shiver ran down Shannon's back as she realized what she was up against—the power and money of the Masterson empire.

"Why didn't you tell me I had a son, Shannon?" Deke's low voice came from the doorway.

She whirled around, eyes blazing. "Is that what makes the difference—that he's a boy? I suppose you never inquired because you didn't want to find out you had a mere daughter."

"What the hell are you talking about?" He advanced into the room to tower over her.

"You can't deny you haven't shown any interest in him before now."

He ran his fingers through his thick, dark hair. "How the devil could I? This is the first I knew of his existence."

"You're lying!"

The ugly words seemed to reverberate in the quiet room. Deke grasped her shoulders and shook Shannon until her long silken hair flew into wild disarray. "You've evidently forgotten a lot about me. Whatever other faults I have, I don't lie," he grated through clenched teeth.

She flung her head back, looking up at him defiantly. "What would you call it, then? I happen to know Chloe told you I was pregnant that weekend you and Cynthia Darby went away together."

He was momentarily diverted from the subject. "I never took Cynthia away—at any time."

"Why are you bothering to deny it? Chloe made sure I knew."

"Chloe again!" he bit out savagely.

"It wasn't only her," Shannon said desolately, the fight suddenly going out of her. "That last party we went to, I heard some of the women talking. They said Cynthia had no intention of letting a little thing like our marriage stand in her way. She told them you were tired of me but I was so madly in love with you that you couldn't just turn me out. You had to wait for some kind of pretext to get rid of me." Shannon's head bowed as the pain of that revelation returned.

Deke raised her chin with a long forefinger. "And you believed them?" he asked incredulously. "Was that the reason for the big blowup we had that night? Why didn't you just tell me, instead of accusing me of everything else under the sun?"

"I couldn't," she whispered. "I was afraid you would admit it."

He gathered her in his arms, pressing her head against his hard shoulder. "Do you know where I went that weekend? Up to our cabin in Arrowhead —alone. Your accusations were driving me up the wall and I had to figure out what to do about them. You were so young, darling." He smoothed her long hair tenderly, laughter lightening his voice. "I even thought of buying you a dog or a pony to take care of. I thought it was too soon for a baby."

That brought Shannon back to earth with a thud. For just a moment she had allowed herself the luxury of believing him, the incredible joy of being in his arms again softening her brain.

She pulled away, putting distance between herself and that virile male body that still had the power to turn her liquid inside.

"If all of that were true, why didn't you come back when you found out about the baby? Why did you send your sister to get rid of me?" As Deke started toward her she backed away. "Don't try to deny it, your signature was on the check."

"What check?" he exploded.

"The ten thousand dollars that was supposed to pay me off."

"What ten—" He checked himself, an intent look

replacing the anger on his face. "Wait a minute! I vaguely remember something about that amount."

"I thought you might," Shannon said cynically.

Deke snapped his fingers, his eyes looking into the past. "Yes, it was that same weekend. I remember now, because I was furious at Chloe for bothering me with minor matters when I was so desperate about your disappearance. She said she had lost it in Las Vegas and they were dunning her to pay up. Chloe was always a fool about money; it's the reason all of hers is tied up in trust. She's forever coming to me to cover her extravagances; that's why I didn't think anything of it."

Shannon looked at him uncertainly. "But she wouldn't . . . even Chloe couldn't do a thing like that."

A pulse was throbbing at Deke's temple. "I'll kill her when I get my hands on her," he gritted.

Shannon's legs abruptly gave out and she sank into a chair. "I thought you didn't want the baby," she murmured.

"How could you think that?" he asked huskily. "The only thing that makes me feel a tiny bit better is that at least you weren't destitute."

"I didn't take the money, Deke," she said simply.

Anger and pain crossed his face. "Oh, God! If Chloe knows what's good for her, she'll stay out of my way for the rest of her life. To think of you struggling to take care of a baby all alone, without any money . . ." He took a deep breath to calm himself. "Well, that's over now. It's time for a new start."

"What do you mean?" Shannon asked warily.

"We'll get married as soon as I can get a special license."

For a moment it was a terrible temptation. Then

sanity returned. Five years had passed—five years during which she had changed but he hadn't. He still gave orders and expected them to be obeyed. What would happen when she refused to follow them? She could no longer be Deke's plaything, living for the moment when he would make love to her, content just to be with him.

"You've given me a son, Shannon," Deke said softly. "Do you know how that changes my life?"

If she had any doubts, his words dissolved them. It wasn't Shannon he wanted, it was his son. Where were the tender protestations of love, the wonder at the miracle of finding her again? He didn't even ask how she felt about him after all this time. Mike was the one Deke wanted. It had been a relief to discover that he hadn't callously ignored his child; now it was a danger.

"You're welcome to see him anytime you like," she said, picking her way carefully.

Deke's eyes narrowed. "What's that supposed to mean?"

Shannon swallowed painfully. "This whole thing has been an . . . um . . . unfortunate misunderstanding."

"Is that the way you'd describe it?" he snorted.

Heeding the warning signals, she proceeded cautiously. "I can understand that you'd want to get to know your son."

"It's good of you to realize I have rights as his father," he said sarcastically.

Shannon didn't like the way this was going at all. "I didn't say that!" When his mouth thinned dangerously, she became defensive. "Well, none of this was *my* fault, you know."

"Wasn't it?" Deke's voice was deceptively soft. "Didn't you see it as a way to punish me for my supposed infidelities? Why would you believe Chloe when you knew she would do anything to undermine our marriage? You didn't try very hard to tell me you were carrying my child."

Tears misted Shannon's eyes. She could understand how it would seem that way to Deke. Everything he said was true up to a point. Yes, she distrusted his sister, and Chloe was aware of it. She was the clever one. She knew Shannon would never believe her without proof—Deke's signature on the check. That, coupled with their final argument and the things Shannon had said to him, convinced her she had killed his love.

As he looked at her bowed head his eyes softened. "Well, it's all in the past. We'll try and forget it. How soon can you be ready to leave for the Coast?"

Her tears dried swiftly. "I'm not going with you, Deke. You're right about one thing; the past is over and done with."

"Are you saying you won't marry me?"

"That's correct." Shannon was amazed at the steadiness of her voice.

"Where does that leave Michael?"

"I told you that you could have visitation rights."

"I intend to have a hell of a lot more than that! He's my son and I want him."

"You can't have him," she cried. "He's mine."

"I had a little something to do with it," he said dryly.

"But he doesn't even know you," she pleaded. "How could you even consider taking him away from me? He's only a little boy."

"You have an alternative," he said implacably. "You can come along."

"A package deal, is that it?" she asked bitterly. "Two for the price of one—a sleep-in governess."

He raised a skeptical eyebrow. "You'd regard being married to me as a job?"

"What else would it be?"

"Anything you cared to make it. You've already demonstrated that you still feel something for me. Shall I prove it to you again?"

Shannon hated him at that moment. Hated his supreme male confidence and her own weakness. As he moved toward her with a cruel smile, she backed off in a panic. Her protests were cut off by his firm mouth taking possession of hers. He jerked her against his lean length, running his hands down her back and grinding her hips against his. Her struggles only made her more aware of him, of the masculine power in those muscular loins.

While his mouth subjugated her completely, his hands wandered over her body, trailing paths of fire. When his fingers moved to the buttons at the front of her dress, Shannon's attempts to stop them were halfhearted. Deke took his time, exploring each area of satin skin as it was exposed to his questing hand. His head bent to her swelling breasts, his mouth burning through her lacy bra until she longed to tear it aside, to feel his lips on her bare, quivering skin. When he touched one rosy peak with his tongue, Shannon moaned her tormented desire.

"Why are you doing this to me, Deke?" she cried desperately.

He ignored her plea, caressing her thighs suggestively. "Remember . . . ?" His husky voice murmured soft words in her ear. "You'd like that, wouldn't you, darling?"

Her whole body throbbed with remembrance. How could she go on resisting? Clasping her arms around his neck, Shannon drew Deke's head down to hers, surrendering totally. She was now the one who rained kisses on his face and neck with urgent abandon, her body clamoring for his possession.

Deke raised his head, gold flecks spangling his hazel eyes. "I repeat, when will you be ready to leave?"

Shannon gazed at him for a moment in bewilderment before hot shame colored her cheeks. How effortlessly he had broken through her defenses! That was just a sample of the humiliation she would suffer if she ever put herself in his power again. All it would take would be one night in his arms, and she would be back in bondage once more. Except that this time it would be worse. Deke no longer even pretended to love her. The only thing remaining between them was sex.

Shannon took a deep breath, vowing not to let her body betray her. "I meant what I said. I'm not going with you. What happened just now doesn't mean a thing except that you still appeal to me physically. But that's no basis for a marriage. It wasn't then and it isn't now."

"Do you mean that you never loved me?" he demanded. "Even in the beginning?"

"I thought I did. As I told you, I was very young and you were a sophisticated older man."

"How about those passion-filled nights in my arms?" he asked mockingly. "When you declared your undying love and said you couldn't live without me?"

"I learned to, obviously," she stated flatly. "And I intend to go on doing it."

Deke's eyes were hard. "Then you'll do it without Michael."

Shannon stiffened angrily. "You can't frighten me, Deke. Everything I've done has been for him. No court would take a child away from his mother."

"Not completely," he conceded. "But you'll certainly have to share custody with me."

"You live three thousand miles away," she cried. "How can you expect him to go that far for week-ends?"

"You forget that I'm in the aircraft business," Deke pointed out sardonically. "I could send a plane for him. But I'm not talking about weekends. I intend to have him six months out of the year."

Her worst fears had been justified. Shannon felt like a small, cornered animal. Maybe if she explained it to Deke. Tears filled her violet eyes. "Mike is my whole life," she pleaded. "He's all I have."

His expression softened as he looked at her lovely heart-shaped face. He reached out and touched her cheek gently. Then his hand dropped and his manner hardened. "It might turn out to be the best thing in the world for you—give you time to take up your own life. You've been too long without a man, Shannon," he said lazily. "It's made you very vulnerable."

He was standing so close that she could smell the woodsy scent of his after-shave and the clean male odor of him. She started to tremble, knowing he was using his masculinity to taunt her, to force her into line.

"My sex life is no concern of yours," she flared.

"True, but we both know what a passionate woman you are," he said mockingly. "I hate to see all that ardor go to waste."

"I thought your concern was for your son," she said coldly.

"It is. I've been thinking about what you said— that he doesn't know me. You're perfectly right there, and it has to be rectified immediately. I'm taking a party of friends to Switzerland for skiing over the Christmas holidays. This would be a perfect time for Mike and me to get to know each other."

The casual way he proposed spiriting her son

halfway around the world infuriated Shannon. "I'm acquainted with your friends, remember? They aren't the sort I want my child to be around."

He eyed her dispassionately. "It's a good thing I turned up. With that kind of attitude, you'd keep him in short pants until he was ready for college."

"I'm not an overprotective mother, if that's what you're implying," she said stiffly. "I'm merely concerned about my son's welfare."

"And you think I'm not?"

"That remains to be seen. I *demand* to know who's going to be there!" she cried.

"You don't have to demand, all you have to do is ask," Deke said coolly. "I'll be happy to oblige. To begin with, Jim and Helene Deighton are coming with their daughter, Stephanie. I believe you remember them?"

"He's your attorney, isn't he?" Their estate was next to Deke's in Beverly Hills, and Shannon remembered Jim Deighton as being a man in his late forties, a rather humorless person. His only interest was business; he was uncomfortable at social functions. His wife was not. Helene was a nonstop talker and something of a social climber. Shannon had spoken with her only at large parties.

Actually, Shannon knew Stephanie a lot better. The young girl used to come over to use their tennis court, often staying on for dinner if Deke and Shannon had no engagement. She seemed to enjoy being with them, especially with Deke, whom she worshiped openly. Stephanie had been about fifteen then, a brown-eyed honey blonde who gave promise of great beauty. She was a rather rebellious child, yet Shannon really couldn't blame her. Her father had too little time for her and her mother had too much.

"The other couple are Marlee and Rustin Stevenson," Deke continued. "You don't know them; they live here in New York. Rustin and I went to Princeton together. He's a stockbroker, and Marlee was once a famous model. She now runs a well-known modeling school." Deke's face took on a sardonic smile. "Is that a complete enough dossier for you?"

"Quite adequate, thank you," Shannon said formally.

"I also intend to entertain now and then. Unfortunately, it won't be possible to send you the guest list ahead of time for approval," he said sarcastically.

Shannon refused to allow her anger to show. "That won't be necessary. I'm sure you're not planning any orgies with a small boy and an impressionable young girl in residence."

Deke's eyebrows rose. "That 'impressionable young girl' could give you cards and spades in experience," he said with a chuckle.

"She's still in her teens." Shannon frowned.

Deke shook his head. "She's twenty . . . going on thirty." Shannon gritted her teeth at the look of male appreciation that colored his expression. "I'll have to declare her out of bounds for Jeff if I expect to get any work out of him. Oh, by the way, there is one more member of the party—Jeff Collins, my assistant. He came after your time, but I assure you there's nothing to worry about there, either. Jeff is straight out of a G-rated movie: twenty-eight, clean-cut, altogether a perfect role model for Michael."

Shannon's anger got the better of her. "You think this is all a big joke, don't you? That's because you've been an absentee father all these years. You didn't have to be responsible for Mike."

The humor fled from Deke's face. "Don't make me remind you that you were the one who deprived him of my guidance. You had only to pick up the phone to provide him with two parents."

"I'm glad now that I didn't!" she cried, standing up to him furiously.

Deke's jaw tightened. "Walk softly, Shannon. You're on very dangerous ground. Just have Mike ready to leave early Monday morning. I'll be by to pick him up."

"So soon!" Shannon gasped, her belligerency evaporating. "But you can't . . . he won't . . . he doesn't even have the right clothes to go skiing."

"I'll buy him everything he needs."

There was a steely quality about Deke that told her it was useless to argue further. Still, Shannon made one last try, twisting her slender fingers together. "He's so little, Deke. And he's never been away from me before, not even for one night."

"You can come too, if you like," he said casually.

"I can't. We're all booked up. I couldn't possibly get away now, even if I wanted to."

He shrugged. "Too bad. I'll have Mike call you on Christmas Day. So long, Shannon."

She sank slowly down onto a wing chair, pressing her cheek against the nubby fabric, unaware that Deke had paused in the entry. As he looked at her dejected pose, compassion flooded his strong face. He started toward her, only to check himself. With a thoughtful look he softly closed the door.

Shannon was enveloped in such a cloud of misery that she was in actual pain. How could she give up Michael for half of every year? Children changed so rapidly at this age. She would miss precious stages of his development. It wasn't fair! To whom? a small voice inside her asked. Michael had talked so wistfully about a father—Did she have the right to deny him his? It was no use telling herself that he would be unhappy without her. Children adjust easily, and Mike had accepted Deke with instant delight. Had he felt a deeper lack than she knew? Was Deke right, did a boy need a father as he grew older? Maybe she could fill that need herself now that she knew about it, Shannon thought desperately. Maybe she could play baseball with him, or . . .

Her head drooped dejectedly on her hand as she realized the futility of such plans.

"Shannon?" Marcia was standing hesitantly in the hallway leading from her bedroom. "I couldn't help hearing."

"It's all right," Shannon said wearily. "I'm glad you did. It saves having to go over it again."

"Are you really going to let Mike go?"

"What choice do I have? Oh, I could stop him now. I could make Deke get a court order. That would delay things, but it wouldn't change them. Deke is correct—he can get partial custody. Right now he's willing to settle for that. If I make things difficult for him, who knows what he'll ask for?"

"I guess that's sensible." Marcia looked at her cousin uncertainly. "Have you thought about accepting his offer—going back to him, I mean?"

Shannon shook her head. "I couldn't possibly. I've worked hard for my independence. I can't just turn my life over to Deke again. And that's what I'd be doing."

Marcia hesitated. "There isn't any love left at all?"

Shannon's long eyelashes lowered. "I don't know if I ever truly loved him. Perhaps it was all just sexual attraction." She jumped to her feet, pacing the floor with her arms wrapped around her body. "Deke is a very physical man and he has vast experience."

"I can imagine." Marcia smiled. "If things were different I wouldn't mind having a go at him myself."

"You'd have to stand in line," Shannon said shortly.

"I'm not so sure." Marcia looked at her cousin contemplatively. "I believed him when he said there had never been anything between him and that Cynthia whatever-her-name-was. There was something convincing in his voice. Besides, there wouldn't be any point in his lying about it now."

"What difference does it make?" Shannon shrugged.

"A lot of difference. If you were wrong about her, maybe you're wrong about all the other women."

Shannon's expression was hopeless. "It doesn't matter. You heard Deke. He's only interested in getting me back as Michael's mother." She sighed deeply. "At least he cares about his son. I guess that's the important thing."

"I can't believe you're really going to let Mike go without a struggle. That isn't like you, Shannon."

"Oh, Marcia, I don't know *what* to do. Maybe I've been selfish all these years," she said slowly. "Deke is a very wealthy man. He can give Michael things I can't."

"That child has never gone without anything," Marcia said indignantly.

"No, he's had plenty of love; that's all a baby needs. But he's growing up, Marcia; he's going to need a father's companionship too. Deke can do things with him that we can't. And no matter what you say, I don't have the right to deprive him of the material things. Deke can send him to the best schools, buy him a car when he's old enough to drive. Mike will learn to play tennis at the country club."

"What's wrong with the public courts? That's where we learned."

"We didn't have rich fathers, and he does," Shannon said quietly. "If you love someone, you don't deny them the advantages they're entitled to for purely selfish reasons. Look at this place." She gestured toward a large desk and filing cabinet filling a corner of the small living room. "Half of it is given over to business. There isn't any yard for Mike to play in. I can't take him for outings on the weekend unless we get home early, because that's our busy time."

"He understands that. He's never complained."

"You know what I'm saying, Marcia." Talking it out had clarified things. As soul-rending as it was, Shannon realized what she had to do. She could never live with herself if she put her own desires ahead of her son's welfare. "It's going to be like tearing the heart out of my body, but I have to let Mike go with his father for six months of the year."

"And suppose he's so dazzled by the swimming pool and the private airplanes and everything that he doesn't want to come home?" Marcia demanded. "He's only four, you know."

"I'll face that problem if it comes up," Shannon said resolutely, but her eyes filled with tears.

Marcia threw her arms around her cousin, her own eyes filling. "Oh, Shannon, what are we going to do without him?"

Shannon wondered the same thing on Monday morning when Deke came to pick up his son. The little boy was in a white heat of excitement.

"Daddy says we're going in an airplane all the way across the ocean! And he says there's a dog at his house that I can play with. A sam . . . sam . . ."

"A Saint Bernard," Deke said, smiling.

"Yes, and he says he's going to teach me to ski," Mike said excitedly. "What does that mean?"

"Oh, Deke," Shannon murmured. "You will watch him carefully won't you?"

"Do you doubt it?" he asked gently.

Looking up at the tall man who exuded such an air of confidence, Shannon didn't doubt it. He would take care of his son. She even had a moment of pride when Deke's big hand enveloped Mike's small one. Her two handsome men. Shannon bit her lip and turned away as she realized she was only half right. Only one belonged to her.

The enthusiasm with which Mike had accepted his father, coupled with his eager willingness to leave her, had hurt Shannon deeply. But when departure time came, the little boy had second thoughts.

"Maybe I better stay home with you, Mommy," he said uncertainly.

To her surprise Deke remained silent, his eyes narrowing on her. It cost Shannon a lot, yet she knelt beside her son, putting her arms around him. "You wouldn't want that dog to be lonesome would you? If you don't go with Daddy, he won't have anyone to play with."

There was approval in Deke's eyes—and something else. "Your mother's right, son. You must always listen to her."

After they had gone, the apartment was unbearably quiet. Shannon picked up Mike's teddy bear, hugging it to her as though she could still feel the imprint of his little fingers.

"It's only for two weeks," Marcia consoled her.

Shannon looked at her with despair. It might as well be an eternity. Already she missed Michael so much she ached.

Chapter Three

$\mathcal{A}$ ctually it was less than two weeks until Shannon saw her son again—It turned out to be only five days.

The day he left was the worst. Mondays were traditionally Shannon and Marcia's day off since there was rarely a party on that night. They used the time to get the house and themselves back in shape, resting up for the coming week. Tuesday it was back to work, shopping and making canapés to stockpile in the freezer.

Shannon walked through the chores like an automaton. She did all the necessary tasks by rote. It was almost a relief when Wednesday brought a party to cater. Thursday was also busy. She was so tired by evening that she fully expected to sleep soundly for the first time since Michael had left.

The telephone woke her out of a deep slumber. At first Shannon buried her head under the pillow, trying to ignore the intrusive noise—until it dawned on her that it was the phone.

"Shannon?" Deke's deep voice on the other end of the line brought her instantly awake.

The darkened windows told her it was the middle of the night. "What's wrong, Deke?"

"I don't want you to get upset. It isn't anything serious."

Icy fingers traveled up her spine. "It's Michael, isn't it? What happened?"

"He had a little skiing accident."

Fear threatened to smother her. "Is he alive?"

"Of course he's alive!" Deke's reassuring voice hummed across the wires. "How could you even think such a thing? He got knocked down and he has a slight concussion."

The relief was so great that Shannon felt limp. It was soon replaced by burning anger. "What do you mean a *slight* concussion? You should have watched him better! How could you let a thing like this happen?"

"Calm down, Shannon, he's fine. He didn't even have to be hospitalized."

"You didn't call a doctor?" she cried.

"Naturally I did, and he said it was only a little bump on the head. He just has to stay in bed for a few days."

"Deke, how *could* you? You promised you'd take care of him."

"I didn't have to tell you, Shannon." He sounded annoyed. "He's perfectly all right. I just thought you'd want to know."

"Of course I do! Can I talk to him?"

"Well, he's sleeping now. It's a quarter to seven here. You wouldn't want me to wake him, would you?"

"No," she said reluctantly. "I'll call back. How soon do you think he'll be awake?"

Deke hesitated. "Would it make you feel better if you could see him, Shannon? I can arrange for a ticket for you."

"Oh, Deke, would you?"

"Sure. I'll call you back within the hour. Stand by."

As though she would budge from the phone! In spite of Deke's reassuring words, Shannon was cold with apprehension. Mike was such a little boy.

"I heard the phone. Is anything wrong?" Marcia appeared in the doorway.

Shannon told her, running shaking fingers through her sleep-tousled hair. "Deke is making arrangements for me to fly to Switzerland." She threw the covers back, jumping out of bed and going to the closet to drag a suitcase from the top shelf. "I'd better pack so I'll be ready when he calls."

"Do you want to borrow my red cashmere sweater?" Marcia asked. "It's nice and warm."

"Yes, and maybe your—" Shannon broke off, a stricken look crossing her face. "I completely forgot about all the work we have lined up. How can I leave you alone at a time like this?"

"Don't be an idiot! I can cope."

"I don't know how." Shannon was torn by indecision.

"For one thing, Helen is back on the job. She's a Rock of Gibraltar. But even if she weren't, you shouldn't be thinking twice about it. Mike is the main concern right now."

Shannon was forced to agree, allowing Marcia's brisk efficiency to overcome her guilt feelings.

As the plane leveled off after its majestic ascent, Shannon watched Manhattan recede in the distance. The first-class section was completely filled with happy people going on vacation. It was a tribute to Deke's influence that he could get her a seat at such short notice the week before Christmas. The planes must all have been fully booked ages ago.

It was going to be a long day. Although it was only 9:00 A.M., it felt much later. Shannon hadn't gone back to sleep after Deke's call. There wasn't time, actually, since she had to check in so early.

She should have been able to sleep, but she couldn't. Nor could she eat, her stomach protesting at the mere thought. All around her people were drinking champagne or wine with their endless meals —the flight attendants kept up a constant flow of food and drinks. Shannon refused everything, staring out the window with a desperate concentration as the day slowly turned into night. Somewhere out there her child needed her.

Eventually the empty world of sky and water gave way to land. Mountain peaks jutted up like icy pyramids with small towns nestled at their bases. Then the jet started its descent to a lovely city by a lake.

Shannon was met at the Zurich airport by a pleasant older man who informed her that he had been sent to meet her plane. She knew it was foolish to expect it, but she couldn't help feeling disappointed that Deke hadn't come himself.

The man introduced himself as Paul Biedermann, explaining that he and his wife, Gretel, were year-round caretakers at Deke's chalet in the mountains. Gretel did the cooking and housekeeping, while Paul acted as chauffeur and man of all work. Shannon gathered that life at this vacation house was less formal than at Deke's many other establishments, although there were still evidences of luxury. After collecting Shannon's luggage, Paul led her to a long black limousine.

It was almost eleven o'clock in the evening, Swiss time, when the powerful car arrived at the small mountain village where Deke's chalet was located. In spite of her tension and fatigue, Shannon had been fascinated by the impressive scenery. She was looking forward to seeing the awesome Alps by daylight. In the headlights of the car they loomed up majestically, massive, snow-covered, with little clusters of lights dotted here and there like Christmas-tree ornaments.

Shannon was stumbling with weariness when Paul helped her out of the car. It didn't seem possible that she was finally here. The large two-story timbered house looked welcoming, with lights streaming out of every window and faint strains of music hanging in the frigid air. The melodious sound of sleigh bells in the distance lent the finishing touch to this idyllic setting.

From the entry hall Shannon could see into a long room dominated by a huge stone fireplace that was ablaze with crackling logs. There were a few people standing in front of it with glasses in their hands, while others occupied the long couches or stood around a piano in the far corner of the room. It seemed that a party was going on. Shannon was swept with unreasoning anger. Her child was lying in bed ill, and she was the only one who cared.

Deke approached with outstretched arms. "Shannon, darling, I thought you'd never get here. Was the plane late?"

Her eyes glittered like sapphires. "No, it was on time. And you don't seem to have been suffering for lack of company," she said coldly. "Thank you for remembering to send someone to meet me."

His arms dropped to his sides. "I wanted to come myself, but I thought you'd prefer for me to remain here in case Mike woke up," he said quietly.

Her eyes grew enormous in her white face. "Have there been complications?"

"Of course not! He's fine." Deke took her cold hands in his warm ones.

A tall, good-looking young man in his late twenties joined them in the hall. "Oh, good. She finally got here." His friendly brown eyes were smiling. "Deke has been wearing a path to the door watching for you."

"This is Jeff Collins, my assistant," Deke told her.

Somehow Shannon acknowledged the introduction before turning urgently back to Deke. "Can I see Michael now?"

"Sure." He put his arm around her shoulders, guiding her toward the steps. "He's sleeping, but I know you'll feel better after you've looked in on him."

The room was lit by a night-light, so Shannon could see Mike curled up in bed. He was clutching a large stuffed animal, his cheek resting on its plush stomach. Shannon knelt at his bedside, her heart filled with gratitude as she gently smoothed her son's dark hair. His breathing was even and he was rosy with sleep. When she touched his hand, Mike's chubby fingers curled around hers as they used to do when he was a baby.

After a while Deke put his hand under her arm, trying to urge her to her feet. "You're exhausted, Shannon," he said in a low voice. "Let me show you to your room now that you've satisfied yourself that Mike is all right."

"*No!*" She lowered her voice hurriedly. "Let me stay, Deke, please."

His eyes were concerned. "You look like you're ready to fall apart." When she gazed up at him mutely, Deke sighed. "Okay, I'll leave you alone with him. I know that's what you want."

Shannon sat on the floor in the semidarkness

watching her son. She couldn't seem to get enough of him. She leaned her head against the bed and gave thanks. Deke hadn't lied to her; it wasn't anything serious. Gradually her eyes closed as the long day took its toll. Her breathing became measured and she slept.

Deke found her like that sometime later. He looked down at the sleeping pair, his eyes tender, then he picked Shannon up in his arms. She sighed, fitting her head into the curve of his neck and nestling close. Deke's arms tightened, his lips caressing the soft hair at her temple.

He carried her into a bedroom. When he tried to put her down on the bed, she clung to him, frowning, so he sat down with her on his lap. He undressed her as he would a child, except that his hands gently smoothed the satin skin as it was revealed. Reluctantly sliding her between the sheets, he leaned over and kissed her full mouth. Shannon smiled and murmured his name. Deke waited expectantly, but when she slept on he sighed and left her, closing the door softly.

The sun was high in the heavens by the time Shannon awoke. For a moment she stared out of the window in puzzlement at the strange scenery. Then memory returned and she jumped out of bed. It was a shock to discover that all she had on was a pair of satin panties.

Who had undressed her and put her to bed? Bright color stained her cheeks as she realized who it must have been. How dare he? She would have something to say to Deke Masterson about that! Shannon rapidly changed her mind when she envisioned the amusement that would light his hazel eyes, the suggestive things he was apt to say. If she knew Deke, he hadn't missed a thing. Shannon's pulse quickened as she experienced a moment's regret that she hadn't awakened, quickly suppressing the vagrant thought with disgust.

Someone had brought her suitcases up while she slept, and Shannon rapidly riffled through the contents until she found a long, fleecy pink robe. She went out into the hall, locating Michael's room easily by the voices coming from it. It was the one next to her own.

The sight that greeted her made Shannon pause in the doorway. Unconsciously she had been expecting to enter a sickroom. Instead, she found Michael playing cards with a young girl in blue jeans who was sitting cross-legged on his bed. Her heavy, honey-blonde hair was parted and caught over each ear with a scarlet ribbon, making her look like a child herself.

"I don't have any eights," Mike was saying gleefully. "You have to go fish."

Stephanie Deighton saw Shannon before her son did. "Look who's here, Mikey."

"Mommy!" The little boy held out his arms to her, clutching her tightly when Shannon gathered him close. His lower lip quivered as he said, "I fell down and got hurt. I was terrible sick."

"You little faker," Stephanie said, laughing. "You've been enjoying all the attention."

"Are you all right, darling?" Shannon asked anxiously.

"I got a bump here." He bent his head, pointing to the back of it.

"He did get quite a crack, but it wasn't anything serious," Stephanie assured her. She reached out and ruffled his hair. "Tell your mother what a big brave boy you were, tiger."

He beamed at her. "I didn't cry hardly at all, did I?"

Stephanie winked at Shannon. "Only three tears," she said solemnly. "I counted them."

"Daddy said he was proud of me," Mike informed his mother.

Before she could comment, Stephanie said, "It's good to see you, Shannon. Remember me?"

"Of course. It's been a long time, hasn't it?"

Stephanie grinned. "Here comes the line that goes, 'My, you're all grown up now.'"

"Actually I was thinking that you haven't changed." Shannon smiled.

"You should see me when I try." Stephanie uncoiled her long legs and stood up, displaying a figure that had indeed changed.

Her high, full breasts, unconfined under the tight T-shirt, could only be described as voluptuous; the rest of her figure equally so. Gazing at the skin-tight jeans that appeared to be painted on, Shannon could only wonder how she had gotten them on over those rounded hips. Now that she had seen the girl, Shannon understood the look on Deke's face when he described her. Stephanie was a knockout.

"I was sorry to hear about the divorce," Stephanie said in the direct manner of youth.

Shannon appreciated it. It made a lot more sense than the attitude of some people who pretended it had never happened. Or else referred to it as "your trouble," or something equally asinine. As though you had a terminal disease.

"It was just one of those things." Shannon shrugged.

Stephanie flopped into a chair, draping one leg over the arm. "Funny, I always considered you and Deke as the perfect couple."

Shannon's smile was devoid of humor. "That's because you were fifteen."

"I thought you were an awful chump for walking

out on him." Stephanie's long-lashed brown eyes regarded her reflectively. "As a matter of fact, I still do."

Why had she ever thought that candor was refreshing, Shannon wondered in annoyance. "You're entitled to your opinion, I suppose," she said coldly.

"Well, I mean, just look at Deke. He's gorgeous; he's rich; he's sexy. Do you know how many women there are who would love to climb into his bed—with or without benefit of clergy?"

"Yes, I believe I do," Shannon said tightly.

"Then like I say, you're a chump. You had him neatly tied up in ribbons and you blew it."

"At the risk of sounding rude—"

"Okay, I'll cease and desist," Stephanie interrupted. "Tact was never my long suit. The only reason I brought it up was because I've always admired you—and I *adore* Deke. The thought of one of those man-eating cats of his making off with him drives me right up the wall!"

Michael looked up from the intricate house of cards he was building. "What kind of cats, Steffy?" He turned puzzled eyes on his mother. "Does Daddy have cats that eat people?"

"No, of course not, darling." Shannon crossed swiftly to the bed, putting her arm around him while she looked warningly over his head.

"I get the message," Stephanie said. "Little pitchers have bigger ears than I realized. I just want to say one thing before I go: Deke is too big a prize to go unclaimed forever. If you've really declared yourself out of the running, you'd better not be surprised at anything that happens."

Shannon stared after her departing figure. That sounded like a warning. But of what? Surely the child didn't consider herself in love with Deke? Even as she rejected the idea as absurd, Shannon realized that Stephanie was no child. She had always been precocious, and that body of hers definitely belonged to a woman. Deke certainly thought so.

Did Stephanie want to be the next Mrs. Masterson? The notion was totally repugnant to Shannon. It wasn't that she felt any personal involvement, she assured herself; it was just that Stephanie was much too young. For one thing, there was Mike to consider. If Deke persisted in his plan to have Michael for six months out of the year, what kind of an influence would Stephanie be? And how much attention would a newly married man pay to his son? Something occurred to her: If Deke did marry Stephanie, maybe he wouldn't insist on having Michael for such a long period. The idea didn't bring as much comfort as it should have.

Shannon's head started to throb. Damn Deke Masterson anyway! The last thing she wanted was to get involved in his affairs again. She had her own life back in New York, and the sooner she got back to it the better.

When Deke came into his son's room a short time later, Shannon was spoiling for a fight.

"Daddy!" the little boy crowed, driving a spike into her heart. Deke had certainly carved a place in the child's affections speedily.

"How's the invalid today?" He smiled.

"I want to get up," Mike told him. "I'm all well."

If Shannon had been in charge Mike would have deviled her unmercifully, yet a firm refusal from Deke was accepted without protest.

"Do you feel more rested this morning?" Deke asked, turning to Shannon.

"Yes, thank you. I guess I went out like a light last night." Her long eyelashes brushed her flushed cheeks.

Deke's strong fingers kneaded the tense neck

muscles under her long, silky hair. "You had a grueling day."

"You should have wakened me," she insisted, not looking at him. It was as close to a rebuke as she dared go.

"I didn't mind acting as lady's maid. I've done it often enough in the past." There was laughter in his voice as he added, "Although the rewards were greater then."

Shannon jerked away from his tantalizing touch. "There is something I'd like to discuss with you," she said stiffly.

"At your service, my love." He was enjoying her discomfort.

"I was wondering if you got me a round-trip ticket. I know how crowded the airlines are now. If you haven't made my return reservation yet, I think you should."

Deke's eyebrows climbed. "You just got here."

"You're not going home, Mommy?" Tears threatened in Michael's hazel eyes.

"Well, not exactly yet, honey, but I'll have to leave soon."

"I don't want you to go!" He climbed into her lap, throwing his arms around her neck. "Don't let her go, Daddy."

"Don't worry, son, I won't." When Shannon started to protest, Deke said firmly, "You've earned a little vacation."

"But I left Marcia with all the work. We're completely booked—Everyone is depending on me."

He cupped her chin in his hand, his fingers cool on her flushed face. "It's time you started thinking about yourself for a change."

After he had gone, Shannon thought desolately, I *am* thinking about myself. I don't think I can stay here and watch you take my son away from me with one hand while you give my name to another woman with the other. There was no answer, though. She couldn't go home until Deke arranged it.

Shannon spent the whole day with Michael, so it wasn't until dinner that she met the rest of the house party. Jim Deighton was exactly the same. He gave her a friendly kiss on the cheek and indulged in a few pleasantries. It was Helene's attitude that was the revelation. Her greeting fulfilled the requirements of etiquette, nothing more. Now that Shannon was no longer Deke's wife, she didn't merit attention. It amused rather than annoyed Shannon, as she had never made the mistake of considering Helene Deighton a friend.

Turning her attention to the Stevensons, Shannon recognized Marlee's lovely face. Some years ago it had graced the cover of every high-fashion magazine at one time or another. Her figure was a little fuller than in the matchstick days of her modeling career, but it was still elegant; and Marlee's beauty would always be arresting. Her tilted green eyes looked out serenely from an exquisitely boned face crowned by russet hair.

"I'm so glad to meet you finally, Shannon," she said warmly. "Deke has told us so much about you."

Shannon felt immediately drawn to this woman. "I almost feel as though I know you after seeing your picture so often," she told her. "You've given me an inferiority complex for years."

Marlee's laughter had a silvery sound. "I can't imagine why. With your looks, I could make you a top model."

"May I join this mutual admiration society?" Rustin Stevenson asked. He was a charming, distinguished-looking man with a sprinkling of premature gray at his temples that gave his strong features added character. Together they made a stunning couple. "I'm happy to meet you, too, Shannon. Deke always said he was going to marry the most beautiful girl in the world." He put his arm around his wife. "Lucky there were two of you."

Marlee gave her a merry look. "It's blatant flattery, but I love it."

Shannon sat next to Jeff Collins at dinner. "I think I owe you an apology," she said when they had a moment to talk. "I barely acknowledged our introduction last night."

"Not to worry." He smiled. "You had a lot more important things on your mind. Do you feel a little better now that you know Mike is okay?"

"*So* much better."

"Good, then you can relax and enjoy yourself."

"Not really. I have to be getting back, as long as I'm not needed here."

Deke overheard their conversation. "I've been trying to convince Shannon to stay on at least until after Christmas," he said.

"You really should," Stephanie advised her. "We have all kinds of nifty things planned."

Her mother frowned. "Perhaps Shannon has someone special waiting for her."

"My cousin Marcia," Shannon said shortly. "She's doing her job and mine too."

"You're working?" Helene Deighton's eyebrows rose as though she had said an indelicate word. "What do you do?"

"I have a catering business. We do all kinds of parties."

"How neat!" Marlee exclaimed. "Will you do some dinner parties for me when we get back?"

"I'd be happy to."

"Rustin and I both love to entertain at home, but I can never manage the cooking in addition to my job, and I can't seem to find anybody to do it for me."

"That's always a problem," Helene agreed. "Household help is so hard to get, and they demand the world nowadays."

A gathering storm darkened Marlee's normally limpid eyes. "What a strange way to refer to Shannon's profession. That's like describing John Steinbeck as a typist."

Helene's face reddened. "I certainly didn't mean any offense. You didn't take any did you, Shannon?"

"Not really, I'm used to it. Any damage to my sensibilities is cured when I present my bill." A mischievous smile curled her lips. "As you say, we charge the world nowadays."

Rustin raised his glass to Shannon, neatly turning the gesture into a request for more wine. "This zinfandel is excellent, Deke."

Deke's expression was sardonic. "Yes, some things improve with age—and some don't."

"The only thing you get with age is older," Stephanie said impatiently.

Marlee laughed. "Spoken like a twenty-year-old."

"Well, it's true. That's why you shouldn't waste time on unimportant things."

"If this is another bid to quit school, forget it," her father said tersely.

"I didn't bring it up, you did. But now that you mention it, college is nothing but an anachronism today!" Stephanie cried. Turning to Shannon she asked, "Did you go to college?"

"I had just finished my freshman year at U.C.L.A. when I had to quit because my parents died," Shannon said wistfully. "I always hoped to go back, but . . ."

"But you got married instead," Deke finished for her when her voice trailed off. "Why didn't you tell me that's what you wanted, Shannon?" He was looking at her as though they were the only two people in the room. "You could have gone back at any time."

"There, you see!" Stephanie was triumphant.

Jeff joined the conversation for the first time. "Shannon was just starting. You have only a year to finish; that's the big difference," he said quietly.

"You heard Deke," she said angrily. "I could always go back for a degree later if I felt the need. Right now *I* consider other things more important."

"Such as what?" Her father's voice was heavy with irony. "As far as I can tell, the only things you think about are the next rock concert and what you're going to wear to it."

Stephanie lifted her chin. "Really? What would you say if I told you I'm thinking about getting married?"

"Stephanie!" Helene gasped. "This is the first you've even mentioned such a thing. Why didn't you tell us?"

"Because you'd be sure to find some objection. Either he'd be too old or too young, too poor or too rich, too—"

"That's enough, young lady," Jim interrupted sternly. "We'll discuss the matter later. This is neither the time nor the place."

Stephanie subsided into a sulky silence, shooting Jeff an angry look for his lack of support. Because he was closer to her age than the others, she had probably counted on him to back her up.

Conversation around the table became general as everyone sought to gloss over the embarrassing moment. Shannon didn't join in. Her thoughts were in a turmoil. Stephanie's parting words in Mike's room this morning meant exactly what they sounded like. She must be more involved with Deke than

Shannon realized. Had they actually discussed marriage? A sense of loss that was totally incomprehensible shot through her.

All these years that she had been out of contact with Deke, the possibility that he might have remarried occasionally crossed her mind. Now that their lives had become unavoidably entangled once more, Shannon discovered that she hated the idea. It was ridiculous to feel this sense of possessiveness for a man she didn't even want, Shannon chided herself. She became aware that Jeff was speaking to her.

"I'll bet you can't wait to get out on the slopes tomorrow," he commented.

Shannon forced all the conflict out of her mind. "I'm afraid I never learned to ski," she said.

"Really? Well, we'll have to remedy that," Jeff smiled. "I give lessons by appointment."

Deke frowned. "Business before pleasure, Jeff. They're waiting for the cost analysis on that new Turbot four-eighteen. Shannon will have to settle for group instruction."

Stephanie's eyes narrowed as she stared at the two men. Her displeasure at Deke's interference was evident. Did she hope that Shannon and Jeff might hit it off, thus removing her from competition for Deke in case she was having thoughts of reclaiming him?

After they had all moved to the living room for coffee, Stephanie said, "What shall we do tonight?"

"I thought your father and I would have a rubber of bridge with Rustin and Marlee, if they're willing to put up with us. It's a treat to play with such superior players." Helene's ingratiating manner was a transparent effort to get back in their good graces.

The Stevensons exchanged an amused look. With an imperceptible shrug of her elegant shoulders, Marlee said, "Why not?"

"There's no accounting for tastes," Stephanie commented. "Why don't the rest of us go over to the lodge and see what's doing?"

Shannon would have bowed out, but the others wouldn't hear of it. Even Stephanie added to the urging. After Shannon had run up to check on Michael, finding him sound asleep, the four of them set out.

It was a star-filled night, so crisp that their breath floated in white puffs in front of their tingling faces. Fortunately, the lodge wasn't far, because Shannon soon found herself shivering in her inadequate clothing.

"We'll have to get you a warm parka tomorrow," Deke said.

"That won't be necessary, since I'll be leaving so soon," she told him.

"We'll see," he murmured.

Before she could argue the point, they arrived at the lodge. The main room, whose focal point was a huge, glowing fireplace, was filled with men and women in casual but elegant wool pants and intricately patterned sweaters. Most of them were drinking *gluhwein*, the hot mulled wine for which the lodge was famous.

Deke and his party were well known, as evidenced by the greetings from all sides. Stephanie and Jeff gravitated over to a group around a small spinet in the corner, leaving Deke surrounded by a crowd of well-wishers. Since Shannon didn't know any of them, she wandered over to the wide windows, looking out at the village.

In a matter of moments Deke was by her side. "Why did you run away? I wanted to introduce you around."

Shannon knew his offer was merely dictated by good manners. "You needn't bother. I'm perfectly happy looking at the view. It's like a Christmas card out there."

It was an apt description. The tall Alps completely ringing the small town were like protective arms enclosing a toy village full of gingerbread-trimmed chalets and slender church spires that were miniatured by the stately mountains. As she gazed out the window, a horse-drawn sleigh full of laughing people went by. Bells jingled on the horse's harness, ringing out a merry melody as he snorted and tossed his head. It was the finishing touch somehow. Shannon pressed her nose against the window, trying to follow the sleigh's progress down the snowy street.

"Would you like to take a walk and see something of the village?" Deke asked.

"I don't want to take you away from your friends," she said hesitantly.

He didn't even bother to answer that. "Wait here. I'll borrow a parka for you and be right back."

Shannon was a lot more comfortable in the down-filled parka Deke located for her. It was scarlet, contrasting nicely with Deke's navy one. Under it he wore a navy turtleneck sweater and slacks. In the casually elegant clothes he looked like an Olympic contender, his athletic body lean and fit. Shannon hadn't been surprised at the number of women who left their escorts to come over and greet him.

They strolled leisurely down the main street, with the snow crunching underfoot, stopping every now and then to look into lighted shop windows. Every kind of merchandise pertaining to skiing was displayed, interspersed between little gift shops filled with enchanting handmade wares. The surrounding hilly streets were dotted with chalets decorated for the holiday season with winking colored lights like strands of precious jewels. The absence of cars gave the scene an enchanted, fairy-tale appearance.

"I feel like I'm in Santa's village," Shannon marveled.

"Now aren't you glad you came?"

"I really am. I can see why you wanted a house here." She looked up at the tall man beside her. "Do you come here often, Deke? I didn't even know you liked to ski."

His face was somber as he gazed down at her. "There were too many things we didn't know about each other." When Shannon would have moved away, he reached out and took her hand, leading her down the street. "To answer your question, I have banking affairs in Zurich, so I come over quite often. By combining business with pleasure I salve my conscience."

"You're the boss; you don't have to answer to anyone."

"Meaning I don't need a conscience?" He smiled.

"I didn't say that." After a pause Shannon asked, "Does . . . do the Deightons come with you very often?"

Deke stopped to look at a tiny pair of binoculars, smaller than the palm of his hand. "This is the first time Helene has been here," he replied absently.

"I see," Shannon murmured.

Actually she didn't see at all. Was it the first time Stephanie had been here too? Or did she accompany Deke regularly? Shannon was as much in the dark as ever about how far their affair had progressed. It looked serious, though. She knew from the old days that Deke didn't have a very high opinion of Helene. Did he invite her for the holidays because she was his prospective mother-in-law?

"What do you see?" Deke had turned his attention back to her.

Before she could answer, a streak of fire shot across the sky. "Oh look, Deke, a shooting star!"

He glanced over his shoulder, then back at Shannon. "You have to make a wish."

She stared up at the heavens, her eyes wistful. For one heart-stopping moment, Shannon wished for the impossible—to go back to a time when she felt secure in Deke's love and life had no hard edges or thorny problems. Then the fire in the sky died out and sanity returned. Squeezing her eyes tightly shut, Shannon made her wish: Please don't ever let me be separated from Michael.

She opened her eyes when Deke's warm hands framed her face. "I wonder if we wished the same thing," he murmured.

"I don't think so," Shannon answered in a low voice.

"Tell me what yours was." His head descended to hers, blotting out the light until all she could see was his face. It filled her consciousness.

"You can't tell, or it won't come true," she managed with difficulty because her heart was racing so loudly she thought he must surely hear it.

"Whatever it is, I have a feeling it's going to come true, my darling."

Deke's lips touched hers lightly, his breath mingling with hers. She could smell the clean male scent of him, mixed with the surrounding odor of pine and wood smoke. His firm hands on her shoulders urged her gently forward, and Shannon moved into his arms in a dreamlike state. Anything that happened in this magical setting had to be right. Somewhere close at hand a church bell chimed as though in benediction, and Shannon put her arms around Deke's neck, relaxing trustingly in his embrace. His warm mouth was tender on hers, like the caress that lovers exchange after passion.

He kissed her closed eyelids and the hollow of her throat. His hands smoothed her hair gently at first, then tangled in it as he gripped the back of her head, holding her for his deepening kiss. Shannon could feel his muscular chest even through their double parkas; the hardening of his body as a flame leaped between them. An answering hunger gripped her, and she clung to him, their bodies merging into one person.

They were completely oblivious to the world around them, locked in their own mystical place, until the sleigh that had passed earlier returned. Laughing comments finally penetrated their consciousness.

Shannon opened dazed eyes. Snow was falling lightly, powdering Deke's dark hair and filling up their footsteps. It was like a lace curtain that would become thicker and thicker. She had a mad impulse to stay right here and let the snow form a protective cocoon around them, shut them off from everyone else. Loud voices from a chalet up the hill brought her to her senses. Shannon bit her lip, knowing it was only this fantasy atmosphere that made the impossible seem possible.

"We'd better go back," she murmured.

"Yes, I suppose we had," Deke agreed reluctantly.

Stephanie was waiting for them, a pinched expression on her face. "I was wondering where you two had gotten to."

"Deke was showing me the little village," Shannon said, not looking at him.

"Well, it took you long enough," Stephanie snapped. "This place is dead; I want to get out of here."

"Jeff could have taken you," Deke pointed out.

Jeff joined them at that moment, looking slightly grim. Stephanie had evidently taken her jealousy out on the poor man, Shannon reflected.

"I didn't want to go with him; I want to go with you," Stephanie said, taking Deke's arm and pointedly leading him away from the other couple.

"I'm sorry," Shannon said, not quite sure what she was apologizing for.

"That's all right." Jeff helped her exchange the borrowed parka for her own coat. "Our Steffy is a mite spoiled, as you may have noticed." His well-shaped mouth tightened. "It's about time she found out that she can't always have her own way."

Shannon looked at the couple disappearing through the door, Stephanie clinging to Deke's arm, her goodwill restored now that she had him back. She even glanced over her shoulder to be sure that Shannon noticed she had resumed possession. Jeff was wrong about Stephanie. She would get her own way sooner or later.

Chapter Four

$\mathcal{D}$eke was seated at the dining room table having a solitary breakfast when Shannon came down the next morning. She hesitated in the doorway, feeling self-conscious about being alone with him after last night. The romantic setting had been solely responsible for that madness in the snow, Shannon assured herself, yet it didn't lessen her embarrassment. If she couldn't control her emotions any better than that, she'd better leave.

Deke put down the paper he was reading, giving her a welcoming smile. "Good morning, early bird."

"Am I the first one down?" Shannon asked, envying him his ability to act as if nothing had happened. Then she reminded herself—nothing *had* as far as he was concerned.

He stood up to help her into a chair. "The others are taking advantage of their vacation to sleep late." He looked critically at her delicately boned face and slender figure. "That's what you should be doing. You look like you could use a rest."

Shannon shrugged. "I'm so used to getting up early that I wake automatically."

"We'll try to break you of that habit while you're here." He smiled.

It was the opening she needed. "That's what I want to talk about, Deke. It was very thoughtful of you to arrange for me to come. I know the money doesn't mean anything to you; it's your consideration I'm grateful for. But as long as Mike is all right, I really do have to go home."

Deke frowned. "I don't understand all the rush. Mike would be terribly disappointed if you weren't with him for Christmas."

"He didn't expect me to be anyway," she pointed out.

"But you're here now; that changes things. I don't think he would understand why you left."

"Mike knows I have to work." Shannon's eyes were on her napkin, so she didn't notice the pulse that throbbed suddenly at Deke's temple. "He's always been very good about it."

"I have an idea. Why don't you call Marcia and see how she's making out? If everything is going smoothly there's no reason why you shouldn't stay for the festivities." Before Shannon could object, Deke said persuasively, "I really need your help. I don't even know what to put in his Christmas stocking."

Shannon's face was stricken. "Oh, Deke, I don't have anything to give him! I expected to mail his presents, and then when I left in such a hurry I didn't even think to bring them."

"No problem. I have to go into Zurich today. You can come along and we'll go shopping."

That, at least, seemed like a good idea. If she did go home Michael would still have some packages from her under the tree.

Deke rose, pulling Shannon to her feet. "Come on, we'll call her right now."

The connection was so good that her cousin sounded as though she were in the next room. After she had inquired about Michael and been assured that he was fine, Marcia asked, "How's Switzerland? I'll bet it's exciting."

Shannon stole a look at Deke who was standing over her, his rangy body exuding masculinity. She gripped the receiver tightly. "It . . . it's very nice."

"Is that all you can say?" Marcia snorted. "If a gorgeous man like Deke spirited *me* off to his chalet I'd be able to whip up a little more enthusiasm."

Shannon changed the subject, hoping Marcia would take the hint. "You must be going out of your mind with all the work I stuck you with." She was conscious of Deke moving his broad shoulders impatiently under the perfectly tailored tweed jacket.

"No, we're doing fine," her cousin assured her.

"How could you possibly be? You don't have to put on an act for me."

"Honestly, Shannon, everything is going great. Helen is back on the job, and she has a cousin visiting from Columbus who is helping out too. She's even better than Helen, if you can believe it."

"It's good that you found reinforcements, but I know you must need me. I'm coming back as soon as I can make arrangements."

"Don't be crazy, Shannon! It would be ridiculous to take that long trip for only a couple of days. Stay and have Christmas with Mike."

"I just wouldn't feel right about it," Shannon insisted. "I should be—"

Deke took the phone out of her hands. "Hello, Marcia, it's good to talk to you again. I hope you were able to reassure Shannon. She's been worrying about you."

"I told her that was silly. Everything is under control here."

"I'm glad to hear it, because I think she needs to relax and enjoy herself." He ignored Shannon's protesting noises.

"She doesn't sound like she's doing it," Marcia said shortly. "Have you been tormenting her?"

"What do you mean?" Deke asked carefully.

"Shannon is like a sister to me and I know when something is bothering her. Does it have to do with Mike?"

"No, she told you the truth. He's fine."

"I'm not talking about that whack on the head. Does she have something more serious to worry about? Have you been threatening to take him away from her completely?"

"Of course not!"

"It broke Shannon's heart to let Mike go with you—as you damn well know! I don't mind telling you I tried to talk her out of it, but she said she couldn't deprive him of all the fancy goodies you can provide. If you're trying to bully her into giving him up entirely, you'll have to fight both of us!"

"I can assure you that isn't the case." Deke's strong voice was warmly reassuring.

Marcia hesitated before saying soberly, "I want what's right for both of them. Don't hurt her, Deke; she isn't as tough as she tries to be."

Deke looked at Shannon's troubled face, lingering over the shadowed blue eyes. His voice was husky as he said, "Don't worry, that's the last thing I would ever do. In spite of what you think, our goals are identical. Just trust me, Marcia."

"I don't know why I should," she said frankly. "But you know something funny? I do!"

"What was that all about?" Shannon asked as Deke handed her the phone. "Marcia, what's going on?"

"Deke and I were just getting acquainted," Marcia said breezily. "Stay for the holidays and have a wonderful time, Shannon. I think this trip is just what you needed."

The line was disconnected before Shannon could argue any further.

"Well, that's settled," Deke said with satisfaction. "Let's go up and say good-bye to our son, and then we'll be on our way."

Michael was not so pleased as his father. "You're *both* going?" he wailed.

"I'll tell you a secret." Shannon put her arms around him. "We're going into town to buy you some Christmas presents."

With his good humor effectively restored, they were able to leave with a clear conscience.

It was a sparkling day, but the air was frigid. Shannon wrapped her arms around her body, waiting for the car heater to warm up.

Deke glanced over at her black wool coat, his brows drawing together in a slight frown. "Don't you have anything heavier than that? You're going to freeze."

"I'll be fine," she assured him. "I wore this all last winter in New York."

He was unconvinced. "In this weather everyone wears furs."

Shannon raised her chin. "I'm sorry if you're ashamed to be seen with me."

Deke's teeth clicked together in annoyance. "Do you have to misconstrue everything I say?" He slowed down for a curve, taking it competently. "We'll get you a fur coat in Zurich."

"We'll do nothing of the sort," she replied angrily. "I never wanted anything from you before and I'm certainly not going to take anything now."

His firm mouth thinned with displeasure. "I suppose you'd rather catch pneumonia?"

"Oh, for heaven's sake!" Shannon heaved a sigh of exasperation. "I'm not some delicate little blossom. The last time I was in a hospital was when I had Michael."

Deke's strong hands gripped the wheel, his face paling under its tan; Shannon had a moment's compunction. He seemed to take it as a reproof, reminding him that he hadn't been there, which was not her intention.

She remembered how much it had hurt when they wheeled her to the glass-fronted nursery after Mike was born. All around her, fathers and mothers were waving and cooing to their babies while Shannon had been alone with hers. It was hurtful at the time, but Deke's pain now must be even greater. He had missed something infinitely precious. For the first time she realized what that would mean to a father.

Seeking to change the subject, she said, "Will you be going back to California after the holidays?"

"I'm not sure. It depends on a couple of things," he answered briefly.

Deke seemed preoccupied, so Shannon stared out the window at the truly breathtaking scenery. The road wound through Alps that were awesome in their timeless grandeur. They towered like giant sentinels, silent and majestic under their lavish cloaks of dazzling white snow. From a distance the tall pine trees that dotted the slopes looked like little bushes decorated with fluffy cotton.

On the outskirts of Zurich on the hills above town, they drove by small plots of ground that puzzled Shannon. They were marked out in precise rectangles, and each one had a little structure on it, something like a large playhouse.

"What are those used for?" she asked Deke. "Surely people don't live in those tiny houses, do they?"

"They're summer places," he explained.

"But they can't have more than one room," she protested. "And the ground is about the size of a garden."

"That's exactly what it is. In the summer the owners come out for the day to tend their flowers or vegetables. They don't live there. Those little buildings are just used to store tools, and maybe a chair or two. At the end of the day they go back to their city apartments. These places are greatly in demand," Deke told her. "The waiting list can stretch into years."

As they started down the slope, Shannon turned her attention to the city spread out below. Zurich proved to be different from anything she had anticipated. Knowing that it was a world-famous banking center, she expected it to be full of modern skyscrapers. Instead, it was a charming metropolis that managed to look like a small, old-world town.

A broad river ran through the center, dividing it into old and new Zurich, although the newer section managed to maintain its aura of antiquity. Tall spires rose on both sides of the Limmat River that was spanned at intervals by low, curved bridges.

Deke pulled over to the curb on a broad, tree-lined boulevard. "The Baur au Lac Hotel is two blocks down." He pointed to the right. "Meet me there in an hour. We'll have lunch before we shop."

"That isn't necessary. You said you have business to take care of."

"I do have an appointment, but it won't take long."

"If I hurry I can be all through by the time you are," she insisted. "That way we can start back without wasting any time."

Deke raised one eyebrow. "It isn't very flattering

to hear that you consider having lunch with me a waste of time."

"You know what I mean," she muttered, refusing to admit the real reason why she wanted to cut the trip short. Shannon was beginning to enjoy the day almost too much.

Deke reached across her, opening the car door. "This is a no-parking zone," he said impatiently. "I'll see you shortly."

After he left, Shannon walked down the Bahnhof-strasse, looking into the shop windows. Every kind of merchandise imaginable was displayed: exquisite handmade lace handkerchiefs, French shoes and delicate Swiss watches, among other things. It was all beautiful and expensive-looking, although she didn't know the rate of exchange. Belatedly, Shannon remembered that she didn't have any Swiss francs, so it didn't make any difference. Whether she liked it or not, she would have to wait for Deke to go shopping.

After looking in the windows for a while, Shannon wandered a few blocks down to the harbor where immaculate white boats plied their way on the busy Sea of Zurich. A broad park lined the waterfront, and she strolled through it, sitting on a bench awhile to watch the activity. When the cold started to seep through her cloth coat Shannon retraced her steps, not realizing how far she had strayed. By the time she walked up the tree-lined drive of the Baur au Lac, she was shivering with cold.

The warmth of the quietly elegant lobby made her skin tingle, and Shannon pulled off her gloves, blowing on her fingers to warm them. Deke appeared, eyeing her disapprovingly.

"I told you that you'd be cold," he said. "Now will you stop being stubborn?"

"I'll be fine as soon as I have a drink," she said hastily. "It's just a little brisk outside."

"Switzerland in winter is more than brisk. I'm going to buy you a fur coat whether you like it or not."

Shannon was acutely conscious of the interested employees, even though they pretended not to be listening. "Please, Deke," she murmured. "Can we have lunch? I'm starving."

The manager appeared at Deke's elbow. "You are going to lunch with us, Mr. Masterson? Would you prefer the dining room or the solarium?"

They had to brave the cold outside to get to the solarium, which Deke chose, but once inside it was worth it. The separate, glass-enclosed building was like a large garden house, with an unobstructed view of the water and the surrounding grounds. Their table faced the snow-covered gardens where tiny winter birds were foraging for food.

"This is lovely, Deke," Shannon exclaimed.

"Worth wasting time over?" he teased.

A bubble of pure happiness enveloped Shannon at the beautiful setting and the afternoon that stretched ahead. What was so wrong with enjoying herself for just one day?

"You aren't ever going to let me forget that, are you?" she said, laughing. "I didn't know you had such a fragile ego."

He covered her hand with his. "I'm beginning to discover that neither of us knew enough about the other. It's something we'll have to rectify."

Shannon's long eyelashes fell. "It's too late for that, Deke."

He gave up much too easily. "We can still be friends," Deke said casually.

Shannon looked at this man whose body she had

known intimately. He had experienced every part of her too, although they had never managed to explore each other's minds. Could they really be friends? Was that even what she wanted?

Shannon traced intricate patterns on the linen tablecloth. "There's been so much bitterness between us. We've said terrible things to each other."

"Unfortunately, that's true. But you can't deny that we were happy in the beginning." Golden sparks lit Deke's eyes as he held her gaze hypnotically. "Do you remember the day we took the yacht to Catalina, just the two of us?"

How could she ever forget? The notoriously rough water had been calm that golden California day, the sun a burning smudge in the glowing blue sky. They had decided to fish from the top deck. Shannon was used to a light rod and reel, but that day Deke said he was going to teach her to use the deep-sea equipment. There were two swivel chairs fixed to the deck, with stanchions to hold the heavy-duty rods when a big fish struck.

Shannon had gotten the first bite. Her line gave a high, thin hum as it went taut, almost whipping the pole out of her hands. Deke secured it quickly, showing her how to play the fish so it didn't snap the line, but he refused to take over for her. He stood by, giving advice for over an hour until both she and the monster were winded. When its blunt head finally cleared the water and she saw the razor-sharp teeth of a shark, Shannon squealed and made him cut it loose. Laughingly he had complied, telling her she was too squeamish to be a fisherman but he was proud of her anyway.

Then Deke had gathered her aching body in his arms and carried her down to their cabin. He ran a warm tub for her while he gently undressed her, but the water was cold before she ever got around to it.

They made love in the golden afternoon, glorious, fulfilling love. Deke used all of his expertise and knowledge of what especially pleased her, first setting her body on fire with his hands and mouth until her passion mounted almost unbearably, then satisfying her as only he could, his body merging with hers in a rite of ecstasy.

Afterward, Shannon curled up in Deke's arms, soothed to sleep by the gentle rocking of the ship and the reassuring hardness of his bare shoulder beneath her cheek.

Shannon found that her nails were curved into her damp palms. Drawing a shaky breath she said, "Memories are for fools."

"On the contrary. The ability to remember the past is one of the things that distinguish us from animals."

"Maybe so, but it's still a waste of time. What's the good of looking back?"

"Perhaps to relive an especially beautiful moment —like our honeymoon, for instance." A smile played around Deke's mouth as his eyes looked into the past. "You were so virginal I was almost afraid to touch you."

Shannon refused to allow herself even to think about that enchanted time. It was too dangerous. "I seem to remember some rather heavy passes *before* we were married," she scoffed.

"That was just to keep in practice." He chuckled. "I never intended to take you until our wedding night. I wanted to do everything right with you, my love. I even left you to get undressed alone like a proper bridegroom should. When I saw that nightgown, though, it almost scared me off."

An unwilling smile twitched the corners of Shannon's mouth as she remembered the voluminous long-sleeved, high-necked garment she had worn on her wedding night. Deke's expression had indeed been dismayed; and looking back now, Shannon couldn't blame him. With her long black hair streaming over her shoulders and her eyes wide with apprehension even though she adored this man with every fiber, she must have looked like a sacrificial maiden about to be offered to some pagan god.

"I was pretty preoccupied at the time, but all these years I've been wanting to ask where the devil you found an outfit like that," Deke said.

"It belonged to my grandmother."

"I don't doubt it for a minute!"

Shannon smiled reminiscently. "It was a tradition in my family. Each new generation of brides wore it on her wedding night; then it was supposed to be put away for her daughter."

"Let's hope all of your subsequent children are boys," Deke said fervently.

A sharp pain stabbed viciously through Shannon as she realized there wouldn't be any more—boys *or* girls. How could she let anyone but Deke father her child? "You'd think we were a hundred years old, the way we're wallowing in the past," she said lightly. "If you're finished with your lunch, I'm really anxious to go shopping."

Deke called immediately for the check, and soon they were on their way. Over her protests, the first stop was a boutique that sold ski clothes.

Deke was adamant. "You can't come all the way to Switzerland without going skiing at least once. I doubt if the Swiss would even let you out of the country if they found out. It's erratic behavior."

"Be sensible, Deke. That stuff is expensive, and I won't have any use for it back in New York."

"Consider it a Christmas present."

Nothing she could say would change his mind. Shannon found herself being outfitted from head to toe. Deke and the saleslady consulted, choosing a buttercup-yellow quilted anorak and matching pants. The outfit was completed by a sleeveless jacket in the same color, plus a blue sweater that matched her eyes.

Looking at herself in the full-length mirror, Shannon had to admit that it was an excellent choice. "I feel like such a fraud, though," she complained.

"Why is that?" Deke asked.

"I feel like those women who wear little tennis dresses to the supermarket, although they've never been on a court."

"If that's all that's bothering you, I'll teach you to ski."

"You're probably very good," she protested. "You wouldn't want to bother with a novice."

"It wouldn't be the first thing I've taught you," Deke murmured, his eyes holding hers.

Shannon felt a warmth stealing through her entire body. Why was he doing this? Why all the remembrances, the emphasis on the good things instead of the bad? Was he trying to seduce her with memories so she would let down her guard? Deke would do anything, use any methods, to get his own way. Wouldn't it be nice if he wanted her back for some other reason than just as Michael's mother, Shannon thought wistfully.

"I'll see that these things are delivered to your chalet this afternoon, Mr. Masterson." The saleslady's competent voice broke the spell.

An exclusive fur store was next door to the ski shop. Shannon braced herself for another argument with Deke. She was surprised when he merely glanced in the window and continued walking. The sound of carols was a faint echo in the crisp air.

"There's something right about snow on Christmas," Deke remarked with satisfaction.

"That's true. I always enjoyed the holidays in New York, no matter how much I missed California the rest of the time."

He turned enigmatic eyes on her. "What was there to miss?"

She refused to look at him. "Well, I was born there, after all." Before he could pursue the matter, Shannon said hastily, "What do you have planned for Christmas? I mean, are you having a party or anything?"

"Not on Christmas Eve. I thought we'd trim the tree and fill Mike's stocking after he goes to bed. A real family evening." He reached out and took her hand.

To force down the happiness that rose within her, Shannon commented, "That would give your old crowd a laugh."

"I'm sure you know how little that troubles me," he remarked dryly.

Yes, Shannon knew. Deke wasn't bothered by the insecurities that plagued ordinary mortals. He was a law unto himself. "You don't have to give up your whole holiday because of Michael," she persisted.

He gave her a slow smile. "What makes you think I'm giving up anything?"

"You know what I'm saying. If you want to have a party or . . . or anything . . . I'll understand."

"It's the 'or anything' that interests me," he teased. "You never used to be so forbearing."

She tried to pull her hand away, but he wouldn't let her. "I no longer have the right to sit in judgment of you," Shannon said stiffly.

"I don't think that's going to stop you." He grinned. "Actually, I'm flattered. If I engaged in as many bedroom calisthenics as you attribute to me, I wouldn't be able to get up in the morning."

She didn't want to contemplate the picture that conjured up. Turning her head, Shannon stared into a shop window. "Oh, Deke, look at that adorable cap. I have to get one for Mike!"

The bright blue knitted stocking cap had a small, brown stuffed mouse sitting on the button top. In his tiny paws was a felt piece of yellow cheese.

Inside the store were other unusual things, and Shannon happily selected several items. A problem arose when she went to pay for them.

"Will you lend me some money, Deke?" Shannon asked. "I don't have any Swiss francs."

"That won't be necessary," he told her. "I'll pay for it."

"I don't want you to," she insisted. "All I want is a loan."

"You don't honestly think I'd let you pay, do you?" Deke frowned.

Shannon set her chin stubbornly. "If you don't, then I'm not going to buy anything."

"Oh, for God's sake, Shannon!" Deke exploded. "We're here to buy gifts for Mike. He doesn't care who pays for them, and I'm certainly not going to tell him." He looked at her with narrowed eyes. "Is that what's bothering you? You think I'm trying to lure him away from you with bribes?"

"No, of course not!" Her response was too vehement. It betrayed her inner turmoil, the doubts that beset her.

Deke's face was austere. "What other reason is there?"

How could she explain that she didn't want to be obligated to him? That she recognized it as the first step inside the trap he was setting. Shannon refused to be merely a convenience to this man who had once loved her.

"You can buy him anything you like," she said obstinately. "I'm going to pay for my gifts with my own money."

Deke smothered a curse. Reaching in his pocket, he pulled out a wad of bills. "Here! Now you won't have to ask me for anything."

She looked at the thick roll helplessly. "How much is this? I want to keep track."

"Would you also like to pay me interest?" he inquired sarcastically.

Shannon's cheeks were very pink as they walked out of the store. She could just imagine what the clerks were saying. Deke's dark face wore a scowl and his hands were jammed in his pockets. Well, it was just too bad if he was annoyed! Shannon lifted her chin. It was time he realized that she had a mind of her own. No longer would she dance when he pulled the strings.

They were approaching one of the wide, curved bridges that led to old town. Across the river were stores and quaint restaurants housed in ancient stone buildings that looked as though they had been standing during the time of the crusaders. Traffic on the wooden bridge was brisk as people crossed back and forth, using the time-honored means of transportation. On the other side Shannon was enchanted to discover narrow cobbled lanes twisting up a hill.

"Could we . . . would you mind if I took a peek up that street?" she asked diffidently.

Deke's stern expression softened and he reached for her hand once more. "Come on, we'll go exploring."

In the back streets they discovered all kinds of funny little shops, silversmiths and heraldry artists jumbled in among apothecaries and antique stores. Shannon was fascinated by the aura of antiquity, stopping to examine each window carefully. She was only marginally aware of the biting cold piercing her inadequate coat until Deke remarked on it.

"You're freezing," he said. "We'd better stop in for some hot coffee."

"I'm fine," Shannon denied, trying to stop her teeth from chattering.

Deke's eyebrows rose. "Does your nose always turn blue when you're in tip-top shape?"

She closed her fingers over it and he laughed, guiding her into a small restaurant. It wasn't very fancy. The red-and-white checked tablecloths were of dubious cleanliness and the menus were a little gravy-stained, but it was deliciously warm. Shannon's fingers and toes started to throb as her blood began to circulate. Deke ordered steaming coffee and a wonderful pastry that was meltingly flaky and permeated with rich Swiss chocolate.

"Mmm." Shannon's eyes swept the ceiling. "How I'd love to have this recipe."

"Maybe the chef will oblige."

"I don't know." She looked dubious. "Recipes are guarded closely."

"Perhaps a suitable payment would unlock the safe." Deke smiled.

Anger warmed her chilled body. He was so patronizing about it! Was he trivializing her profession? "I have a flash for you—Money can't buy everything," she flared. "Someday you'll find that out."

"I've known it a great deal longer than you," Deke said quietly. "I've been surrounded all my life by sycophants, people who want something from me. Would you believe that you were the first genuine woman I ever met?" His mouth twisted wryly. "And in spite of my irritation at your . . . independence . . . I want you to know I admire you for it."

Shannon's anger turned into shame. No matter

what his motives, Deke had treated her with generosity and consideration, while she was constantly paying him back with a spiteful tongue.

Eyeing the downcast lashes on her pale cheeks, he said gently, "For this one afternoon, why don't we declare a truce and just enjoy each other's company?"

"I'd like that," she said, meaning it with all her heart.

After that, the rest of the day turned into a delight. Deke ordered her another pastry, and the chef came out of the kitchen to join them at the table. He and Shannon spent a happy half hour discussing the intricacies of baking.

"But if you add the eggs to the hot mixture, won't they curdle?" Shannon asked, her eyes intent.

"No, no, no, madame." The chef became animated. "The secret is in the wire whisk! You beat, beat, beat, while you add the eggs ever so slowly."

Shannon nodded, looking absently at Deke. His expression surprised her. He looked fondly approving. When their time together stretched on, the proprietor started hovering in the background. Finally, the chef got reluctantly to his feet. Deke rose also, extending his hand. For one terrible moment Shannon was afraid he was going to tip the man, something she sensed would be a terrible affront to his pride. As usual, she had underestimated Deke.

Gripping the man's hand he said, "It's a pleasure to meet a man so knowledgeable about his craft."

"And you are equally blessed to have a wife who is not only beautiful, but also very competent."

"I'm well aware of that." Deke smiled, his eyes holding a secret as they rested on Shannon.

There wasn't any point in correcting the chef's misconception, so she went along with the fiction that she was Deke's wife. Strangely enough, instead of irritating her, it gave Shannon a warm feeling.

After leaving the cafe, they wandered through the cobbled lanes until Shannon finally realized they must go back to the main street to find a toy store. The one they discovered was a child's dream. She was sorry that Mike wasn't with them, although it would have defeated the purpose.

Deke's eyes lit up when he spotted a huge stuffed giraffe, almost as large as Shannon. "This is definitely in order," he declared.

"That's a grandfather toy," Shannon laughingly told him. "One of those wildly impractical things they fob off on doting elders who have more money than brains."

"Insults will get you nowhere, young woman," Deke said sternly. "Mike will love this."

"I can't wait to see how they wrap it." She giggled.

Deke waved that away. "Mere details."

They wandered around the store picking up games and toys. Then Deke spied an electronic basketball game on a large table. "Look at that!" he exclaimed.

"You can't be thinking of it for Michael," Shannon said, laughing. "Your future athlete isn't tall enough yet to reach the knobs."

"Well, it wouldn't hurt to try it out," Deke said. "Do you want to be the red team or the blue?"

"The red, naturally. It matches my sweater."

Positioning themselves at opposite ends of the table, they started the game lightheartedly enough. Soon the tempo changed imperceptibly. As he pushed the levers that moved his team across the field, Deke's eyes narrowed in concentration. His lean body coiled into a deadly spring. Deke was playing to win—as he always did.

Suddenly it became terribly important to Shannon

to see that he didn't. Without bothering to examine
the reason, she knew it would prove something if she
could best him just this once.

The game turned deadly serious. People passing in
the aisles smiled at the tense couple, not realizing
that, on Shannon's side at least, there was something
at stake.

The score mounted steadily as each pushed his
advantage. Shannon was fiercely glad that Deke was
showing her no quarter; she would never have
forgiven him if he had. It had to be a clean victory or
none at all. Just before the clock ran out, Shannon
saw an opportunity and took it. She moved her man
in for the winning basket as a bell signaled the end of
the game.

Turning a triumphant face to Deke she cried, "I
did it! I won! I beat you!"

The taste of victory was heady, like champagne
bubbles in her veins. How would he take defeat? His
reaction surprised her. As soon as the game was
over, Deke relaxed. There was no hint of injured
male pride, nothing grudging in the congratulations
he offered. Was it possible that he played to win
because that was his nature, not because he needed
to dominate? Although she was sure it seldom
happened, he could take defeat in his stride.

The feeling that she had misjudged this complex
man, plus the suspicion that she herself wouldn't
have been as good a loser, made Shannon defensive.
"I want you to remember today the next time you
get to feeling you're invincible."

"Go ahead and gloat," Deke said good-naturedly.
"I'll have my revenge when I get you out on the
slopes tomorrow. Then I'll get my due respect."

"No way," Shannon declared. "You have years of
experience on your side."

Deke took her chin in his hand, lowering his head to hers. His warm breath fanned her cheek as he murmured, "Count your blessings, little one."

A clerk approached. "Would you like to purchase that game, sir?"

"I think not," Deke said, laughing. "My wife is too good for me. We'll just take the other things we picked out."

When the man had gone for his sales book, Shannon focused her eyes on the knot in Deke's tie. "You shouldn't tell people I'm your wife," she reproached him.

"Ex-wife sounds so unwieldy."

"You don't have to tell them anything," she pointed out.

Deke raised a derisive eyebrow. "When a man and a woman go shopping for toys, it can be safely inferred that there's a child in the picture somewhere. Would you rather have him think I was cad enough not to make an honest woman of you?"

"There could be any number of reasons why we're here together," she argued. "I could be your sister or . . . or your girl friend."

"Do I have a choice?" He grinned. "I pick girl friend, definitely. The feelings I have toward you are anything but fraternal." Bending his dark head, he brushed her closed lips with the tip of his tongue.

"Deke! Not here." Shannon looked around nervously.

Putting an arm around her shoulders, Deke guided her behind a stacked column of cartons. His arms went around her in a possessive embrace, urging her against his lean body. When Shannon lifted her head to protest, Deke's warm mouth covered hers. At first she was rigid in his arms, but as his lips caressed hers seductively, a slow flame ignited in her midsection.

The uncontrollable shudder that rippled through her slim body signaled the weakening of her defenses. Deke was quick to take advantage of it. Molding her body to the length of his, he deepened the kiss, compelling a response she was powerless to withhold. Time and place slipped away. Her awakened body remembered only his hands and lips, the male possession he had taken so often.

"Oh, there you—" The salesman's cheery words ended on a note of embarrassment.

Deke's only reaction was annoyance, which he managed to mask. "You want my signature, I imagine."

Shannon turned her back while he scribbled his name, agonizingly aware of the hot color that made her cheeks look like wild roses. When the salesman left, she turned on Deke in a rage. Before her hot words could spill out, he grinned infuriatingly. "Now aren't you glad I told him you were my wife?"

"You . . . you . . . how *could* you?" she sputtered.

"Very easily," he teased.

Whirling away from him, Shannon marched out the door, her head held high. She kept her eyes straight ahead as they walked down the street; she ignored his attempts at conversation. Finally Deke propelled her into a doorway, his hands firm on her shoulders.

"Wait here," he commanded.

Now what was he up to, Shannon wondered. In a few minutes he was back carrying a small paper bag.

He offered it to her gravely. "A peace offering." Inside were dark-chocolate-covered peppermints, Shannon's favorite kind of candy. Deke remembered after all these years. As she looked up at him mutely, he grinned. "Now am I forgiven?"

"Oh Deke, what am I going to do with you?" She sighed.

"I don't think I'd better answer that question," he murmured. "Eat a peppermint."

"I couldn't possibly. I'm still stuffed with all that pastry. Are you trying to make me fat?"

He eyed her critically. "That's something you'll never have to worry about. Steffy might very well have a problem, but not you."

Shannon's blood chilled slightly. Did he think of them in the same connection? She glanced up uncertainly, further confused by his warm smile.

They stopped to look at a window full of music boxes. "Would Mike like one of those, or are they only for girls?" Deke asked.

"Not necessarily, but we have so much for him already," she protested.

"We can go in and look around anyway," Deke coaxed.

Inside the shop, a cacophony of sound greeted them. Dozens of tiny figures revolved on boxes of various shapes, each playing a different tune. The result was a merry sort of curiosity-shop madness. Deke and Shannon wandered around happily, bending down to distinguish a particular song.

After they had selected a toy for Michael that had two children bobbing up and down on a seesaw, Deke noticed a lovely round porcelain box with a delicate, dark-haired ballerina that revolved with exquisite grace. He touched the tiny painted face gently.

"This looks like you," he said huskily. "Eternally beautiful." Picking up the box, he closed her hands around it, his own strong fingers cradling hers. They stared into each other's eyes as something intangible bound them together. Shannon felt her resistance fading along with her doubts. Today Deke had been the man she first met, the laughing, tender lover she had fallen so hopelessly in love with. Could they possibly start over?

"Isn't that one adorable?" A saleslady's voice intruded jarringly.

Deke stared at the woman in bemusement, having difficulty placing this interruption. His eyes swept over her frowningly.

She was carrying a music box, which she held up for their inspection. "This one can't compare, but it's rather amusing, don't you think?"

A chubby, dark-haired child was reaching for a string of toys suspended over her head. As the box revolved she reached up and pulled each toy down to her level.

Deke started to laugh. "I have to buy that one for Stephanie. If ever I saw a girl who wanted it all and went after it, it's my Steffy."

As Deke followed the woman to the desk, Shannon bowed her head. You can't go back, she realized. Too much had happened in between. Deke still desired her physically—that was something that had always been a powerful force between them. But whether he realized it or not, he was more than halfway in love with Stephanie. The only real hold Shannon had on him was Michael—and it wasn't enough.

The music box in her hand had run down, and she absently wound it up. The tinkling tune gradually penetrated her consciousness. "The party's over. It's time to call it a day."

"Do you want to take it with you, Shannon, or should I have it sent?" Deke called.

She wandered over to the counter. "I'd like to take it."

There was something in her face that made Deke's

eyes narrow. His glance went to the tiny ballerina. As it revolved more slowly, the sad little tune became more poignant.

Deke heard it for the first time. He muttered something under his breath. "You don't want that thing," he said sharply.

"Yes, Dcke, I do," Shannon said clearly.

Chapter Five

The trip home from Zurich had been uncomfortable. All the teasing banter was gone. They made polite conversation instead, while Shannon, at least, mourned their lost camaraderie. Deke seemed preoccupied, his thoughts on something other than her.

For that reason Shannon was purposely late coming down to breakfast the next day. She had resolved never to be alone with Deke again if she could help it. And if her resolve should ever weaken, there was always the music box to remind her.

Everyone was assembled around the big dining-room table when she arrived. Without looking at Deke, Shannon said a general good morning.

"Did Deke wear you out yesterday?" Rustin asked sympathetically. "The man's energy is awesome."

"I wish I'd been with you," Marlee remarked. "It must have been fun browsing around all those nifty shops."

Shannon avoided Deke's eyes. "Yes, it was very nice. We got a lot done."

"Did he take you to that darling little place that

serves *raclette?*" Stephanie demanded. Turning to Deke she said, "If you went there without me you're in trouble."

"What's *raclette?*" her mother asked.

"It's gorgeous," Stephanie said. "Boiled potatoes in their skins, and this huge hunk of cheese that's kept hot. You scoop off the melted part and put it over the potatoes. Deke and I adore it."

Helene looked speculatively from her daughter to Deke. She couldn't have been more transparent if her head were made of glass. Evidently, it had just occurred to her that this might be the man Stephanie intended to marry. How would she take it, Shannon wondered. Helene's reaction wasn't long in coming.

"It sounds like a delightful dish." Trying to mask her growing excitement, she inquired casually, "Have you and Deke been there often?"

"As often as he'll take me." Stephanie grinned. "How about a return engagement?" she asked Deke.

"I'll have to think about it." He grinned back. "You'll get fat and then I won't love you anymore."

"Too bad. Then I'll just have to find someone else to lavish my affections on." She fluttered her eyelashes at Jeff. "Will you love me if I get fat?"

"Why not?" He chuckled. "I've put up with you in every other guise."

"See there!" Stephanie crowed triumphantly. "Be forewarned, Deke Masterson, I am hereby transferring my affections to another man." She twined her fingers with Jeff's and they smiled warmly at each other.

"Let go of his hand and let the poor man eat his breakfast," her mother said, frowning.

"You're too prosaic, Helene," Marlee drawled. "Haven't you ever heard of living on love?"

"Don't be ridiculous!" the older woman snapped.

One corner of Stephanie's mouth curled cynically. "Mother believes in living on dividends—after a proper church wedding with twelve bridesmaids. All from the right families, of course."

"Will you stop talking to your mother that way?" Jim Deighton said irritably.

He was right about the edge to Stephanie's voice. Shannon wondered why that should be, when she and her mother wanted the same thing. She supposed it was Stephanie's normal reaction to Helene's lifelong meddling.

"Did you get everything you wanted in Zurich yesterday?" Rustin directed the question to Shannon, diplomatically changing the subject.

She managed a smile. "I think we bought one of everything. Mike will be opening packages until New Year's."

"What did you get for yourself?" Marlee asked. "They have such heavenly furs here. Did you happen to go by Landler's?"

Before she could reply, Deke remarked dryly, "Shannon has her independence to keep her warm."

The air was momentarily charged, and Marlee looked uncomfortable. "I just wondered if you'd looked in the window. Their prices are outlandish, of course."

"Since when did that ever stop you?" Rustin's head was bent over his plate, and for once he wasn't his perceptive self.

As usual, Helene blundered in with both feet. "It's different with Marlee. Shannon wouldn't have any use for fancy furs."

Marlee's mouth thinned with annoyance. It tightened even further when Deke drawled, "No, Shannon doesn't have time to be soft and feminine."

Jeff rode to her rescue. "You're out of your mind.

She couldn't be anything else. Shannon would be gorgeous in a gunnysack." He was unaware of Stephanie's indrawn breath.

"Thank you, Jeff." Shannon gave him a tight little smile before directing her angry words at Deke. "Considering that you're a connoisseur of women, I suppose I should be crushed by your derogatory opinion. Strangely enough, I expect to survive."

"What makes you think I have a derogatory opinion of you?" Deke taunted.

"I know your feelings about women who can take care of themselves," she said hotly. "You like yours to be dependent on you for everything."

There was a little smile about Deke's firm mouth as he hooked his arm casually over the back of the chair. "Not everything, Shannon. But even you must admit there are some things only a man can supply."

"*Any* man," she said scornfully.

Impish laughter lit Deke's hazel eyes. "Have you been conducting a survey?"

"Why not?" Shannon was goaded into saying. "Women today have as much right as men."

Helene frowned as she glanced from one to the other. The electricity that crackled between them penetrated even her thick skin. "Personally, I think that one good man is enough for any sensible woman," she interjected primly.

"Yes, yes, I'm sure that's true," her husband said impatiently. Inadvertently, he was the one who broke the tension. Jim considered the whole conversation frivolous and was anxious to get down to the only thing he was interested in. "After breakfast, Deke, I'd like to review those contracts I brought along."

His wife gave an exclamation of annoyance. "I

thought maybe you'd drive Stephanie and me into Zurich. As long as we're here I might as well get her some of that beautiful handmade lingerie."

"Why, Mother, it sounds like you're assembling my trousseau," Stephanie gurgled.

Helene was unperturbed. "I'm sure you'll be getting married someday."

"There's no rush, for heaven's sake," Jim said irritably. "Deke and I have work to do."

Deke smoothed the troubled waters. "Paul can drive you in," he told Helene.

"Couldn't Jeff take us?" Stephanie suggested.

Deke shook his head. "He has that cost analysis to finish."

"Then how about you?" Stephanie wasn't one to give up easily.

"I have some work to do too," Deke told her.

"You took Shannon," she reminded him sulkily.

"And I brought you a present, remember?" He reached over and ruffled her hair. "You're an ungrateful little muppet."

"I know." She gave him a rueful smile. "I just like to be with you."

Shannon shoved her chair back abruptly. "If you'll all excuse me."

Deke stopped her. "What are you going to do today, Shannon?"

"I'm going to spend the day with Michael," she said coolly. "It's the reason I came."

Deke started to say something, then let her go without further comment. Only later did Shannon remember that he had promised to take her skiing today. He was probably going to make some excuse, and then realized he didn't have to.

She wouldn't have gone with him anyway. His outspoken opinion of her at the breakfast table was bad enough; she wasn't going to reinforce it by making a fool of herself on the slopes.

Michael's greeting was balm to her wounded sensibilities. "Mommy! I've been waiting and waiting for you!"

She gave him a warm hug. "How's your head today, darling?"

"It's all better. I want to get up."

Shannon knew how to get around that. "We'll have to ask Daddy."

The little boy gave in with a sigh. "Did you bring me anything?" he asked hopefully.

"Lots of things, but they're all for Christmas."

"Daddy always buys me something when he goes to town."

A chill of foreboding ran up Shannon's spine. "Then you don't need more toys today," she managed to say lightly.

His next words deepened her uneasiness. "It's nice having a daddy. I'm glad he's not too busy for us anymore."

It was the opportunity Shannon needed to prepare Mike for the change that was coming in his life. She had avoided even thinking about it, but common sense warned that it couldn't be put off forever. Forcing a cheerful smile, she said, "I think you're going to be seeing a great deal of your father from now on. Would you like that?"

"Oh, yes!" He bounced up and down in bed. "Are we all going to live here?"

"Not exactly. Perhaps you'll go to stay at his house in California for a while," she explained carefully.

"Oh boy!" Before the pain of his enthusiastic response cut off her breath entirely, Mike said, "Will you come too, Mommy?"

"I can't, sweetheart. I have to work."

That was something the little boy understood. "Then maybe Daddy could live at our house."

"I . . . No, I'm afraid he can't."

"Why not?" he asked with simple directness.

"Because we . . . well, we don't have a room for him."

He considered this for a short time, coming up with the solution. "He could sleep in your bed." While Shannon grappled with the paralyzing prospect, Mike eyed her dubiously. "Except that he's kind of big. You'd have to sleep all scrunched up together."

"That's right." Shannon gulped. Before he could get any more ideas, she said, "Daddy has a great big house in California. He'll teach you how to swim and everything." Memories of her son's recent accident clutched at her heart. "But you must be very, very careful, Michael."

He recognized the barely concealed panic in her voice. "Don't worry, Mommy. Daddy will take care of me."

Shannon couldn't help it. The bitterness shone through. "As he did on the ski slope?"

Michael hung his head. "That wasn't Daddy's fault, only I wasn't supposed to tell you."

"What do you mean?" she asked sharply.

His clear eyes were apprehensive. "Daddy went to help a little girl on account of her ski came off. He told me to stay right where I was, but I got tired of waiting. I wanted to go down the hill by myself, Mommy." His little voice was plaintive. When she didn't comment he said, "I bumped into a lady and we both fell down." His small, white baby teeth sucked in his lower lip as he looked up diffidently through long eyelashes. "Are you mad at me?"

Shannon's thoughts were in a turmoil. Deke hadn't been careless, as she had immediately supposed. Michael's accident wasn't his fault. "Why did Daddy say you weren't to tell me?"

"I guess he didn't want you to be mad at me. You aren't, are you, Mommy?"

Deke must have known that she would seize any chance to blame him, yet it was more important to shield his son. Remembering how she had berated him, Shannon was deeply ashamed. She had automatically assumed that this whole winter holiday was a spur-of-the-moment fancy, that Michael was just a passing diversion to Deke. Now she knew differently. The knowledge caused a bittersweet pain.

"Mommy?" The little boy's anxious voice recalled her.

"No, I'm not angry, darling. But now you know why it's important not to disobey." He looked so miserable that she hugged him tightly. "How about a game of Chinese checkers?"

Mike's room was stocked with games that they played all morning. When his early lunch tray appeared, Shannon read to him while he ate.

After lunch Shannon announced that it was time for his nap. She was surprised when this brought no protests. Michael had always been a good child, but naps and bedtimes were usually met with resistance. He invariably complained that he was too old for the first, and the other came around too early. As Shannon tucked him in, she reflected that Deke had performed a miracle in a very short space of time.

After she left Mike, Shannon wandered down to the kitchen, finding that she was hungry. She hadn't eaten much breakfast, what with one thing and another.

Gretel was bustling around the large, homey room that was big enough to accommodate a fireplace and a round oak table and chairs. She looked up with a smile from the bowl she was stirring.

"What can I get you, Miss Shannon? I was not planning lunch for an hour yet, but if you are hungry I will be glad to fix you something."

"Please don't bother, Gretel, I can wait."

"Nein, nein." The plump woman's glance swept Shannon's slim frame with disapproval. "You ate not enough at breakfast to keep a bird alive. I will fix you something. You like quiche?"

"That's too much trouble," Shannon protested. "Some bread and cheese will be just fine."

In the end they settled on a bowl of soup to accompany the freshly baked bread and local cheese. The portions were much too large. Shannon viewed them with dismay while Gretel hovered over her with implacable purpose.

To distract her, Shannon said, "Paul told me you live at the chalet all year around. How lucky you are! It's so lovely here."

"Yes, it is nice. Very quiet and peaceful."

Shannon made a face. "Except when Deke descends on you with all his guests."

The Swiss woman was unperturbed. "Paul and I like company. It makes things so lively—the excitement, the parties."

"And all the endless meals," Shannon finished ruefully. "I'm in the catering business. I know how much extra work that is."

Gretel was momentarily distracted. "You know how to cook?" It was clearly a surprise to her.

Shannon experienced a certain wry amusement, imagining Deke's usual companions. He didn't pick his women for their homemaking abilities. "That's how I make my living," Shannon assured her. She hesitated a moment, not quite sure of her ground. "If I could help out in any way, I'd be happy to."

The housekeeper wasn't insulted, as Shannon had

feared, but she rejected the offer. "You are a guest, Miss Shannon."

"Well, I just thought . . . with Michael confined to bed and all the trays and everything . . ."

Gretel's round face was wreathed in smiles. "Ach, that beautiful child! It is the boy who has made the difference. Every year we have parties. Mr. Deke brings many different women—and men," she added hastily, her clear complexion coloring with embarrassment. "Only this year it is a *family* Christmas. A whole different kind of . . . of . . . atmosphere."

Shannon concentrated on her soup. "I know what you mean." She understood exactly, not wanting to think about those other holidays and all the women who had shared Deke's bed in this lovely mountain retreat.

Gretel pressed her advantage, not realizing the implications. "I have never seen Mr. Deke so happy as he is with his son beside him." She eyed Shannon obliquely. "I think he has been a very lonely man."

Shannon forced a smile. "Come on, Gretel. Didn't you just tell me about all the women he brings here?"

The housekeeper turned toward the sink, wiping its spotless surface aimlessly. "My English is not always so good. Sometimes I do not use the right words."

"I got the picture perfectly," Shannon said bitterly. "I know what you're saying, but you're wrong. Mr. Deke has the best of two worlds—his freedom and his son."

Gretel looked unhappy. "He loves the child very much." She hesitated, concern winning out over propriety. "It would be cruel if you took the boy away now." The words came out in a little rush.

Shannon wanted to tell the woman how badly

twisted her priorities were; that it was her cherished employer who was turning *Shannon's* life upside down! However, it wasn't the sort of thing you discussed with a stranger, no matter how well-intentioned.

"I'm sure Michael will be coming here often with his father," she said gently. "And I'm happy that you don't consider him a bother."

"Never!" Gretel seemed to be struggling for the appropriate words. She glanced obliquely at Shannon. "All of Mr. Deke's loved ones will be welcomed here by Paul and me."

Shannon stared down at her plate, a vicious pain twisting her midsection. Gretel meant well, heaven knows. She wanted Deke to be happy, and in her simple mind that meant being married. Well, her dream was closer to realization than she knew. It was only a matter of time until Deke replaced his changing string of women with a beautiful new bride.

Jeff's arrival was a welcome interruption to Shannon's somber thoughts. Sticking his head around the door, he closed his eyes and took a deep breath. "I followed my nose and it led me straight here. What is that ambrosia you're cooking, Gretel?"

Jeff was evidently a favorite of hers. Shrugging her shoulders, she said disparagingly, "Only my mushroom barley soup. You have had it a million times."

"And always came back for more. How about a big bowl for a starving man?"

The housekeeper looked worried. "Maybe I planned lunch too late? I was not going to serve for an hour yet. Mr. Deke and his friend are still working in the den—"

"Not to worry," Jeff assured her. "What Shannon is having would hit the spot."

He managed to quiet her apprehensions about the

simplicity of the food and the fact that they were eating in the kitchen. When Gretel went to dish up his soup, Jeff turned to Shannon. "How's Mike today?"

"Raring to go. Only Deke could keep him in bed for the required week." She shook her head in wonder. "He even settled down for his nap with only a token protest."

"Good. Then you can collect on that skiing lesson I promised you."

"I thought you had to work on a report."

"All finished," he informed her. "And after slaving over a desk all morning, I crave some exercise."

"Oh, I don't know, Jeff. It wouldn't really be any fun for you. Why don't you ask Rustin and Marlee?"

"They went to Zurich with Steffy and her mother. Any more excuses? Pretty soon I'll think you don't enjoy my company," he said plaintively.

Shannon laughed. "You know that isn't it. It's just that I don't think you know what you're letting yourself in for."

"I've taught a lot of beginners," he said confidently. "Don't worry, we'll start on the nursery slopes. I'll teach you how to walk first so you get the feel of the skis."

Suddenly the prospect of some exercise was irresistible. Shannon wasn't used to being this sedentary. "Okay, you've convinced me. But take heart, you won't have to start at the very beginning. My father taught me the rudiments."

"Why, you little fraud! Telling everyone you didn't know how to ski."

"It was ages ago," Shannon protested. "I probably don't remember a single thing."

"Of course you do. It's like riding a bicycle. Your body doesn't forget."

"I seem to recall falling down a lot," Shannon

said, laughing. "I hope my body's memory is selective."

Anticipation accompanied Shannon to the slopes. It was exciting going up in the ski lift, in spite of her apprehensions about the descent. The beautiful white world spread out below was peopled with brilliantly colored stick figures darting in undulant curves like restless dragonflies. A limitless vista of white icing sprinkled with sparkling sugar crystals glistened in the bright sun.

Raising her ski tips so they wouldn't catch on the edge of the ramp as they approached the top was an automatic gesture. Jeff took note of it, raising a sardonic eyebrow. "Just a beginner, huh?"

"Little things are beginning to come back to me," she admitted.

"Don't hand me that. You were probably going to let me explain every little thing, and then schuss right by me straight down the fall line, executing a perfect christy at the bottom."

"Don't I wish!" Shannon laughed. "Stand by to give moral and every other kind of support."

Her first efforts were indeed clumsy. Shannon hadn't been lying about being a novice, but her natural grace made up for inexperience and lack of practice. After some initial failures and a little instruction from Jeff, she was able to perform quite creditably.

It was exhilarating when she finally mastered enough technique so that Jeff didn't have to hover over her. Shannon's cares lifted magically as she swooped down the icy surface, her mind intent only on sending signals to her limber body. Her cheeks were rosy with cold that didn't penetrate her down ski suit. All Shannon felt was pleasure at being young and healthy and alive.

Inevitably, overconfidence was her undoing. Failing to execute a sharp turn, she landed in a heap in a snowdrift, her eyebrows and lashes coated with white.

"You look like a snow woman," Jeff said, laughing before concern got the better of him. "Did you hurt yourself?"

"Only my dignity," Shannon announced cheerfully.

He hauled her to her feet, dusting her off. "How about stopping for some hot chocolate? I'm getting winded."

She knew it was his tactful way of showing concern for her, but a hot drink did sound good.

Easing herself into a chair in the crowded restaurant a short time later, Shannon groaned. "I just remembered you're supposed to do warm-up exercises when you're as out of condition as I am."

"It would have been a good idea." Jeff grinned suddenly. "If you think you're stiff now, just wait until tomorrow morning. Deke is going to have my hide."

Only then did Shannon realize that she hadn't thought of Deke all afternoon. He wasn't a welcome intrusion. "I'm sure it won't matter to him one way or the other how I feel," she said coolly.

Jeff lifted his steaming cup, giving her an oblique look. "I think you're wrong."

"Then you don't know him very well." She took an unwary gulp of her hot chocolate, scalding her tongue.

"I've worked for the man for over six years," Jeff said gently.

"You deserve a medal. Deke isn't the easiest man in the world to please."

"Because he demands your best effort? Have you

ever thought that we gain as much from that as he does? Believe me, Shannon, he's a kind and generous man."

"He can afford to be." Shannon stubbornly refused to acknowledge what she knew to be true.

"I'm not talking about money, although he gives that freely too. Did you know that in addition to his big donations to the organized charities, Deke has dozens of private philanthropies—all anonymous. Other people establish foundations in their own name; Deke doesn't need that kind of recognition."

Shannon couldn't help but feel remorse. "That was churlish of me. I do know how charitable he is, Jeff."

"Not only with money. Deke gives of himself. Look how good he's been to Steffy."

Shannon felt her goodwill dry up. "I imagine most men find that easy," she said stiffly.

"Come off it, Shannon. You know what I'm saying. That mother of hers would drive anyone up the wall, and her father isn't much better. The only time he notices the kid is to tell her not to do something. No wonder she spends all her free time at Deke's."

The naiveté of men never ceased to amaze Shannon. Her mouth pursed in annoyance. "You mean she's one of his charities? The poor little rich girl from the mansion next door?"

"Okay, kid around if you like, but I'm telling you that Deke has given her stability and a sense of values. God knows how she could have wound up without him." Jeff looked thoughtfully at his cup. "At least in this instance he's getting something in return."

Shannon snorted in a decidedly unladylike way. "I was wondering how long it would take you to figure that out."

He gave her an absent stare, his mind clearly not on her words. "Neither of them has ever had a real home life." When Shannon straightened abruptly in her chair, Jeff reached out and took her hand. "Excuse me, Shannon, I didn't mean that the way it sounded. You were together for such a short time, though, and Steffy has *never* known the closeness of a family. She and Deke complement each other."

"You and Gretel are two of a kind," Shannon said impatiently. "She worries about him too. Gretel has the weird notion that Deke is lonely."

"He is," Jeff said quietly.

"And you think Stephanie fills the void by being his surrogate family?"

"Without question."

"Have you ever thought that she camps on Deke's doorstep for some other reason?" Shannon demanded.

For the first time Jeff looked ill at ease. "Steffy is young and impulsive. She gets a lot of ideas in her head. The trick is to be sure she knows what she really wants."

"That doesn't exactly answer my question, but I'll let it go," Shannon said dryly.

There wasn't any real point in talking about it. They both knew how things stood. If Jeff was trying to reassure her that wedding bells weren't imminent, he was wasting his time. It was demeaning enough to have him think she cared.

To change the subject she said, "I didn't realize you'd been with Deke that long."

"Yes, I started right after he went back to work."

She looked questioningly at him. "What do you mean?"

"After that long layoff he took in Europe. I didn't know then how uncharacteristic it was. I just thought his friends were delighted to have him back."

A frown creased Shannon's smooth brow. "When was this?"

"Right after the . . . uh . . . divorce, I guess."

It was indeed unusual for Deke to leave the hub of his empire for a prolonged period of time. "Maybe he was putting together a deal somewhere," she said slowly.

"Perhaps that was it." As they drank the last of their chocolate, Jeff said casually, "You haven't changed much in all these years."

"Thanks for the compliment," she said, smiling. "But how would you know that?"

"From your photograph, the one taken on Deke's yacht." He looked at her steadily. "He keeps it in his desk drawer."

Shannon felt a small rush of pleasure at the news. She knew it was foolish to attach any importance to it, yet the thought that he had kept a snapshot made her heart sing. Adopting an offhand manner, she said, "I never could get Deke to clean out that messy desk. I see he hasn't changed his habits."

Jeff smothered a sigh, pushing his cup away. "Yes, well . . . are you ready for another session or do you want to call it a day?"

"No, please let's go on!" Stopping to rest had been a mistake. It allowed the insoluble problems to return for more jabs with their sharp pitchforks. Shannon wanted to recapture the mindless happiness that she had found for such a brief time in the snow.

It was almost twilight when Jeff finally called a halt. "Tomorrow is another day, Shannon. I swear, for a little slip of a thing, you can wear out ten strong men."

"Just one more run," she begged.

"Okay, but don't blame me if you can't get out of bed tomorrow." He grinned.

All except the most inveterate skiers had given up. They had the exhilarating experience of having the slope almost to themselves. As they reached the bottom, Shannon turned a triumphant face to Jeff, expecting to be complimented on her smooth stop. Before she could demand praise he held up a warning hand, his head held in a listening position. Shannon gave him a puzzled look. There was nothing to hear but silence.

Then a series of shrill whistles came clearly through the increasingly frigid air. Six short blasts followed by silence again. Jeff fumbled in his pocket. He drew out a little silver whistle and gave three blasts in return.

"Someone is in trouble," he explained. "We'll have to go to them. Stick close to me, Shannon."

"How do you know?" she panted, having difficulty keeping up. Jeff had left the piste and plunged into an uncharted field that was heavily dotted with trees. "Maybe somebody is just fooling around."

He shook his head. "Six shouts or whistles followed by a minute of silence is the international mountain distress call. The answer is three of the same. It's something you should know." They had stopped under a tree, waiting for a repeated call to give them the direction.

"How do you think he got way over here?" she asked.

"Some hot dog who thinks he's too good to stay on the piste," Jeff exclaimed disgustedly. "He probably isn't even smart enough to look for a shelter."

Shannon glanced up at the dark, snow-laden tree above her. "These wouldn't give much."

"I meant an emergency shelter. They're scattered over the slopes in case someone gets caught in a storm. Little cabins equipped with food and blankets."

"What a good idea!" Shannon exclaimed.

"That's another thing you should know, although you won't ever be skiing alone."

The short whistle-blasts came again, sharply to their right. Jeff dug his poles into the deep powder, maneuvering expertly while Shannon struggled to follow his path.

A short time later they reached the stranded skiier. It was a man, half-covered with snow, his leg twisted at an unnatural angle. "Thank God," he breathed. "I thought for sure I was a goner."

As he struggled to raise his body on his elbows, Jeff pushed him gently back. "Don't try to move. You're okay now. I'll go for help."

The man clutched fearfully at his sleeve. "You're not going to leave me alone?"

"You'll be all right," Jeff assured him.

"I'll stay with him," Shannon said quietly. "You'll go faster without me."

"That would be best if you're sure you don't mind."

The prospect of waiting in the freezing cold with inactivity stiffening her sore muscles wouldn't have been her first choice, but Shannon pinned a smile on her face. "Just don't forget to come back."

"What, and lose my job?" he teased. "Deke would have me out looking for you with a candle."

It seemed like an eternity before he returned. The man, who turned out to be an American, insisted on explaining to her that he had skiied all over the world without an accident.

"I've been down mogul fields like you wouldn't believe," he complained. "You'd think in a place like Switzerland they'd mark an obstacle."

"You're supposed to stick to the pistes and stay within the markers," Shannon remarked primly.

"The Alps are a little more formidable than our mountains at home."

This only served to provoke another flood of testimonials to his expertise, and to the laxness of other countries. By the time the stretcher bearers arrived, Shannon was heartily sick of the man.

"Well, we did our good deed for today," she told Jeff as they started home. "But I'm not sure that character even appreciated it. All he could talk about was that it was somebody else's fault."

"They do say that virtue is its own reward," Jeff said, grinning.

"I guess so. And we did save a life. Somebody out there must love him, unlikely as it seems."

"Remember, one man's escargot is another man's snail." Jeff's laughter stilled. "I hope today was a good object lesson for you, Shannon. You must never take chances."

"I won't," she promised.

He looked at her searchingly. "I could tell you were enjoying yourself today."

"Oh, I was! I'd forgotten what a marvelous sensation it is to go sailing down a mountain like a feather in the wind."

"You got back in the swing of it amazingly fast, but you're not a pro," Jeff insisted. "Overconfidence can land you in the kind of mess that wimp was in today—or worse."

Shannon tried to allay his fears. "Don't worry. The way I feel now, I wouldn't even attempt the nursery slopes."

They were approaching the chalet. With the light streaming out, turning the snow to gold, it looked like Eden and Shangri-la and every other magic, unattainable place. The last few yards seemed like a mile. Shannon's legs had turned to rubber. With the darkness came bone-chilling cold that seeped inside her ski suit like a thief, robbing her body of warmth.

Jeff smiled down at her. "Cheer up, we're almost there."

"I'm not sure I can make it." She sighed. "If I drop right here, send out the Saint Bernard with a keg of brandy around his neck."

"You'll enjoy it a lot more in front of a roaring fire." He laughed. Putting his arm around her waist, he urged her the last few feet.

Shannon let her head drop to his shoulder, snuggling close to absorb some of his body heat.

Suddenly the door flew open. Deke stood in the doorway like the Prince of Darkness—tall, taut and menacing. "Where the hell have you been?" he thundered.

Jeff took his arm from around her waist and she let loose her grasp of his chest. Each waited for the other to speak. When neither did, they both answered at once.

"We were out on the slopes."

"I went skiing with Jeff."

"Until this hour?" Deke demanded, his face contorted with some strong emotion.

"There was an accident," Jeff explained diffidently.

Deke sucked in his breath sharply. Drawing Shannon into the hall, he examined her searchingly. "Are you all right?"

"It wasn't me," Shannon said inelegantly. She was dimly aware of Stephanie frowning over Deke's shoulder.

"Somebody got into trouble and we had to help out," Jeff said.

Deke transferred his narrowed gaze to his assistant. "What were you doing out there with her in the first place?"

"Well, Mike was taking a nap, and I thought Shannon could use a little break."

"You're not a gigolo. I don't pay you to romance my women guests."

Shannon gasped. She had never heard Deke talk to *anyone*—employee or even enemy—in that cold, insulting way. After the shock came anger. He had no right to treat them like that when they hadn't done anything.

Flinging her head back, she looked up at him stonily. "Jeff finished your precious report this morning, if that's what's bothering you. Isn't he entitled to a little relaxation, or is slavery a common practice in Switzerland?"

Jeff put his hand on her arm. "It's all right, Shannon," he said gently. "I think Deke was just worried about you."

"That's a laugh! You're the one who's valuable to him." Turning to Deke, she said furiously, "Did you think I spirited your trusted aide off to a motel for the afternoon?"

Stephanie's indrawn breath sounded like a hiss. She insinuated herself into the conversation, taking Deke's side. *"Is* that what you did?" Her challenging gaze went from Shannon to Jeff.

"Oh, for—" Jeff smothered a curse. Grabbing Stephanie by the arm, he dragged her down the hall. "Come on. I don't think our presence is helping anything."

Left alone, Deke and Shannon glared at each other. A muscle jumped in his jaw. "I'm still waiting. Where were you all afternoon, Shannon?"

"None of your business." She started toward the stairs.

He gripped her shoulder, pulling her so close that she could sense the violence he was barely restraining. He forced the words past his clenched teeth. "I don't intend to ask you again."

She was shaken in spite of herself. "I . . . I told you. We went skiing."

His fingers tightened, if that were possible. "It was a mighty long lesson."

"No, you don't understand," Shannon said breathlessly. "I'm not a rank beginner."

"I'm aware of that," Deke grated. "I was your first teacher, remember?"

As the enormity of his words reached her, pure rage flooded her veins, giving her strength. Flinging her arms wide, she broke his paralyzing grip. A hard push on Deke's chest put distance between them.

"Don't you *ever* put your hands on me again," she said distinctly. "You have no right to question me about anything."

"You're the mother of my son," Deke glowered, although he didn't touch her. "I expect a certain standard of behavior from you."

"Oh! You . . . you . . ." For a moment Shannon was incoherent. Pulling herself together, she cried, "You have a lot of nerve! How about *your* behavior? How about all those women you bring up here? Why is it any different if I indulge in the same pleasures?"

Deke restrained himself through a heroic effort that left him clenching and unclenching his hands. "I already know your views on women's rights. I don't want to hear them again."

"I wouldn't bother. The only rights you care about are your own. You're a rotten, spoiled male chauvinist!" Shannon was so carried away that she actually stamped her foot. The resultant jar made her wince as a pain shot through her sore calf muscles.

"What's the matter?" Deke asked sharply.

Shannon had an inspiration. Smiling sweetly, she

said, "I guess I'd forgotten that making love was so strenuous."

The smile faded as she glimpsed the black fury on Deke's face. His rage was truly awesome, transforming him into a man possessed.

She whirled around and ran for the stairs, looking fearfully over her shoulder. As Deke reached for her she stumbled, landing painfully on her back with the edge of the steps digging into her. Her legs tangled with Deke's and he fell on top of her.

Immobilized by his weight, Shannon was helpless. What would he do to her? It didn't help to know that it was her fault for goading him past the breaking point.

His dark head was directly over hers, his hands at her throat. They stared into each other's eyes. Slowly the fury left his face. Deke's thumbs revolved over the hollow in her throat where a pulse beat wildly. His fingers stroked the length of her slender neck. Shannon's apprehension turned to fear of another sort as Deke's warm breath fanned her cheek.

"I was so worried about you," he groaned, his mouth grazing her skin. "I thought you'd wandered off and gotten lost in the mountains."

"Gretel could have told you where I was," she whispered with difficulty. Deke's taut body covering hers was making it hard to sustain her anger. "She knew we went skiing." Shannon didn't realize her words had the ring of truth. She had told Deke what he wanted to know.

It didn't seem important to him anymore. He was examining her face as though it were something infinitely precious. His fingertips traced the feathery line of her eyebrow, the tilted curve of her small nose. His mouth was so close that their breath mingled as he murmured, "It was Gretel's afternoon off."

Shannon didn't feel the steps digging into her spine. The quickening of Deke's body drove everything else out of her mind. His hardened loins pressing into hers sparked an answering response from deep inside her. This was the intimate embrace she had experienced so often in her dreams. It evoked a wild longing that was almost uncontrollable. Shannon drew a shuddering breath, moving restlessly beneath him.

Deke misunderstood. Moving his weight to the side, he drew her into his arms. "I'm sorry, darling, I'm hurting you."

Her respite was short-lived. His hands moved sensuously down her back, drawing her so close that she could feel the heat he was generating. Shannon made a supreme effort. Lifting her head, she pleaded with him, "Please, Deke."

His lips grazed hers in a feather-light caress that was tantalizing. "Please what, my love?"

She had to force the words out. "Let me go."

His arms closed around her convulsively as he buried his face in the scented cloud of her hair. She was crushed so tightly against his tense body that they were all but joined. "After today I don't ever want to let you out of my sight. You don't know the things I was imagining."

She touched his cheek tentatively, delighting in the firm texture of his skin, the subtle male smell of him. "Were you really worried about me? Was that why—?"

"Worried?" His voice was husky. "If you only knew!"

Deke lifted his head to stare at her, his eyes warmly topaz. As his mouth descended, Shannon's lips parted with a sigh. How could she fight something she wanted so much? Her arms moved around Deke's neck just as a discreet cough sounded above them.

"Sorry, old chaps." Rustin's rueful voice floated down. "You really should have built a back stairway in this place, Deke."

Sanity returned to Shannon, bringing with it a choking sense of embarrassment. Giving Deke an outraged look, she tried to scramble out of his arms.

He didn't share her guilt. "All I can say is, Rustin, you picked a helluva time to be punctual for dinner."

"Actually, I wouldn't have disturbed you for anything that mundane. Gretel forgot to replace our towels and Marlee wants to get out of the bath."

Shannon succeeded in freeing herself from Deke's possessive arms. Scrambling hurriedly to her feet, she raced up the stairs toward the safety of her room, averting her flaming face from Rustin.

She would never, *never* forgive Deke for this latest indignity. He seemed to feel he could make love to her whenever and wherever he liked. Well, this was absolutely the last time he would get away with it, Shannon promised herself.

That whole scene on the stairs was suspect, anyway—Deke's towering anger turning so conveniently to phony passion. He recovered fast enough when Rustin appeared, didn't he?

Shannon slammed the bedroom door with all her might, trying to ignore the fact that her own body still ached with the need Deke had created.

Chapter Six

The horrendous scene with Deke and its traumatic ending had driven everything else out of Shannon's mind. Alone in her room, she was still too charged up to realize that every bone and tendon in her body ached. After she had paced the floor for a time, engaging in imaginary conversations with Deke—exchanges that she invariably won—Shannon began to be aware of her physical discomfort. Muscles she never knew she possessed were protesting her recent activity. A hot bath was definitely in order.

Her usual tidiness was abandoned as she shed her clothes in a heap, not even bothering with a bathrobe. After sprinkling bath salts with a lavish hand, Shannon lowered her weary body into the steaming tub. As the warm water relaxed her aching muscles, she reviewed the scene with Deke, carefully avoiding its conclusion.

What on earth had put him in such a rage? Was it really worry over her safety? It seemed like an inordinate amount—after all, she wasn't a child. Deke had always treated her like one, though, and he hadn't changed. He just couldn't get it through his head that *she* had. Even without Stephanie, there was no future for them. It would be a constant clash of wills. Shannon had fought too hard for her maturity to allow Deke to envelop her once more. Shannon's heart felt as heavy as her body felt weightless.

That's ridiculous, she told herself sternly. You don't need a man to make you happy—and certainly not that man! Think about all the upbeat things in your life. The business was growing to such an extent that they really needed another van. And they should rent space and buy modern equipment: radar ovens and a larger freezer at the very least. That would mean taking out a bank loan, though. There would be the pressure of monthly payments, and what if business fell off?

Shannon sighed, putting her head back. Why was everything such a problem? She wished herself back to the slopes where nothing filled her mind but the beauty of nature and the incredible joy of gliding down a mountain. Her mouth curved with remembered pleasure as her eyelashes drooped lower and lower before coming to rest on her cheeks like feathery wings.

"Don't you know you shouldn't fall asleep in the bathtub?" Deke's voice brought her eyes wide open.

Shannon sat up indignantly, then ducked back under the water just as hurriedly. Discovering that the bubbles had all but dissipated, she grabbed for a washcloth. "What are you doing here? Get out of my bathroom this instant!"

"So you can go back to sleep?" To her outrage, he dipped a hand into the water. "Just as I thought, the water's almost cold. How long have you been in there?" He eyed her appraisingly. "You're as wrinkled as a raisin."

"You don't have to look at me," she stormed. "If you had any decency, you wouldn't be here."

"And if you had any sense, you wouldn't be lying in a cold tub." Deke pulled an oversize towel off the heated bar.

Shannon attempted to cover herself with the inadequate washcloth. "I'll get out as soon as you leave." She was in no position to argue with him further.

"You'll do better than that." Deke reached in and scooped her out of the water, wrapping her mummy-fashion in the big towel.

"Wha . . . what do you think you're doing?" she gasped.

"I'm drying you before you catch pneumonia." One arm was around Shannon to steady her while his other hand briskly rubbed her back from shoulders to thighs.

His movements were firm without being rough. Her skin started to tingle, and in her flustered state Shannon wasn't sure if it was from the friction of the towel or the man who was wielding it. But when he started to dry her breasts she flinched away from him.

"Stop it! You don't have any right to do this to me," she cried.

Deke's hands ceased their impersonal patting. His eyes held hers with a glowing intensity as a subtle change came over him. "Because I no longer have a piece of paper that gives me permission?" Cupping the roundness of her breasts, he traced their shape, bending down to rub his cheek against the gentle swell. "What difference do a few words spoken by a stranger make? Do you think the other paper that took away that right obliterated my memory? I've experienced every inch of your velvet skin. I know your body as intimately as you know mine. And I know how to please you, Shannon. It's something you can't deny even if you want to. Not when your nipples change from satin to coral," he said huskily, stroking them lingeringly.

Deke's words and actions were evoking remembrances that set her body on fire. How *could* she deny it? The primal need that he inspired stripped Shannon of her defenses. Every part of her clamored for his possession. Every erotic zone remembered the touch of him. She started to tremble uncontrollably.

Deke drew a shuddering breath, containing himself with an obvious effort. "You're cold. This isn't the time, is it?"

Shannon couldn't answer. As he knelt in front of her, she clutched at his shoulders to keep from collapsing. Deke's hands on her stomach, her thighs, her legs, were stoking the flames that threatened to consume her. By the time he straightened up she would have surrendered completely, but Deke had gotten himself in hand.

His face was impassive as he said, "Now I'll give you a rubdown."

"No, Deke, please, *no!*" she moaned.

He stripped away the wet towel, wrapping her shrinking body swiftly in a dry one. Lifting her in his arms, he carried her over to the bed where he deposited her gently on her stomach. "Don't play the stoic with me. If we don't loosen up those tight muscles, you're going to be limping around here for a week." He picked up a tube on her bedside table, unscrewing the cap.

She attempted to roll away from him, looking for any excuse. "I hate that stuff—it smells awful."

His hand pinned her inexorably to the bed. "Not this. It's something new."

Deke pulled the towel down, exposing her body to the point where her slim thighs joined her torso.

Before Shannon could complain, he squeezed a ribbon of ointment down her spine. The slight chill made her flinch.

"That's cold!" she complained, other emotions momentarily forgotten.

"Just for a minute," he soothed.

"I'm going to smell like a medicine cabinet," she said weakly. Deke's hands were making slow sweeps up and down her back, circling her buttocks with a lingering motion that was generating its own heat. A haunting scent of lilacs assailed her nostrils.

"Would I do that to you?" he teased. "I told you this was something new."

He stripped away the towel before she knew his intentions. Shannon half turned, then lay hurriedly back on her stomach. "You put that towel back immediately," she raged.

"Don't you think it's time you dropped this false modesty?" Deke inquired lazily. He separated her legs, massaging her upper thighs with firm strokes.

"Forgive me if I'm not as sophisticated as you are," Shannon stormed, closing her legs and succeeding only in trapping his hand between them. "In my circles, a man doesn't take these liberties."

"All I'm trying to do is loosen you up. If there isn't anything going for us anymore as you claim, why does it bother you?" he asked innocently.

"It doesn't bother me," Shannon lied. "I . . . I just want you to stop."

Deke's hands moved mercifully to her calves, kneading the tight muscles. "You'll thank me tomorrow."

"I won't ever thank you!"

"That's good," he said calmly. "Gratitude isn't an emotion I ever wanted to generate in you." His long fingers moved to her back, tracing the tapering line from her underarms to her slender waist, slipping in to tantalize the curve of her breast. "You have such a beautiful body, Shannon. It never changes." His warm mouth trailed down her spine, leaving a burning path in its wake.

Shannon twisted away from his seductive lips, sitting up in a convulsive movement. In her need to escape from one peril, she hadn't reckoned with another. Deke's eyes glittered as he looked at her smooth body, the tender curves of her white shoulders and breasts giving way to the flat plane of her stomach. His fingertips slid sensuously down, caressing, exciting, reexploring remembered paths.

"Why are you doing this, Deke?" she moaned.

"Don't you know?" he murmured before his mouth closed over hers.

She was powerless to resist. Deke's expertise combined with her own vulnerability were too much for Shannon. Her lips parted before his onslaught and her arms went around his neck. Weaving her fingers through his thick hair, she clutched him close, accepting the male dominance of his tongue as she arched her soft body against his hard one.

Deke pressed her into the pillows, his hand going beneath her to urge her pliant body against his rigid loins. "You belong to me," he muttered. "Don't you, my love?" When a last vestige of caution kept her silent, he moved down her body. The excitement of his mouth made her gasp. Raising his head, Deke's eyes blazed triumphantly. "Let me hear you say it!"

Shannon was completely in thrall. As her trembling lips formed the words of surrender, a small voice broke the spell.

"Mommy! Mommy, where are you?"

Deke reacted even before Shannon. "I'll go to him," he murmured, kissing her tenderly.

It was a testament to her confusion that she

allowed it. Always before, a call from her child had brought immediate response. Now Shannon's reflexes were slow, her mind foggy. Throwing off this unaccustomed lethargy, she blamed herself bitterly. How could she let anything come before Michael? Scrambling into a robe, she rushed into her son's room. Deke was holding him in his arms.

"I was calling you, Mommy," Mike complained.

"I know, darling. I'm here."

Deke relinquished his place on the bed and Shannon took Mike in her arms. He leaned heavily against her shoulder. "I can't sleep. Will you stay with me?"

Although he had only had a bad dream and he was already half-asleep, Shannon didn't hesitate. "Of course I will, sweetheart." Sliding under the covers, she cradled his little body against hers, finding comfort in its warmth.

Surprisingly, Deke made no protest. He tucked them in, kissing them both on the cheek. The look in his eyes was unfathomable as he paused at the entry for a long moment before closing the door softly.

The morning light seeping around the edges of the drapes awakened Shannon. For a moment she was disoriented by the unaccustomed surroundings. Michael's warm body fitted into the curve of her own brought back the events of the night. A peek at the clock informed her that it was only a little before six.

Shannon eased herself cautiously out of bed, wincing as her sore muscles reminded her of yesterday's activity. Jeff was right. She was paying a price for her pleasure.

Going into her own room, Shannon stripped and got into a hot shower, staying under the steaming water until her body grew limber. She steadfastly refused to think about last night's events, willing her mind to remain blank. It was the only way she could face the day.

After dressing warmly and taking her parka, Shannon went downstairs. She longed for a cup of coffee, but the house was quiet and she didn't want to wake anyone. Maybe there was a cafe open, although at this hour she doubted it.

Slipping quietly out the door, she breathed deeply of the fresh, icy air. As Shannon expected, the little village was deserted. After traversing the length of the main street, she turned toward the gentle slopes above the charming town.

Her footsteps were the only ones in the fresh snow except for small animal and bird tracks that she tried to decipher, bending down for a closer look. Shannon was so sure she was the only one up and about that it surprised her when she came on freshly made human footprints. Rounding a bend, she discovered two men cutting down trees. They were equally surprised to see her.

"Are you lost, m'amselle?" The French accent placed the burly lumberjack as being from the west of Switzerland, perhaps Geneva or Lausanne.

Shannon knew that the various regions had different languages and customs. The huge man who greeted her was definitely Gallic, right down to the appreciative look in his dark eyes as he surveyed her trim figure.

"No, I'm just out for an early-morning stroll," she told him.

"It is the best part of the day," he told her approvingly. "Most tourists miss it."

"This is my first, and maybe last trip to Switzerland. I don't want to miss any of it." She smiled.

"Surely not your last visit." The other lumberjack

joined them, extending his hand. "I am Jacques Thibeau, at your service, m'amselle."

The first man was Rene Delange. He joined his friend in protestations. "Switzerland is a small country but, still, you cannot do it justice in one encounter."

"It wouldn't be by choice, I assure you," Shannon told them. "I'd like to see every part of it—especially the Matterhorn. I've heard so much about that."

"Ah yes, the sphinx of the Alps." Jacques nodded. "It is indeed a wondrous sight, rising like a great Gothic cathedral above Zermatt."

"But you must not get the idea that Switzerland is only mountains and snow." Rene took a Thermos out of a large canvas knapsack lying on the ground. He looked at Shannon questioningly. "You will join us in coffee, m'amselle?"

"Please call me Shannon. And yes, I'd love some."

After pouring her a steaming cup, he brought out a package of flaky pastries. Jacques joined them and they all sat on a fallen log that Rene brushed free of snow.

Shannon licked a crumb from the corner of her mouth, sighing ecstatically. "These are absolutely marvelous—like everything else I've tasted here. The other day I had *raclette* for the first time."

"It is good," Jacques agreed. "But for me, I prefer the fondue."

"Only because of the benefits." Rene grinned.

"Yes, I suppose it is healthy," Shannon said. At their own informal parties, she and Marcia often served fondue, a blend of melted cheese, wine and spices kept warm in a chafing dish. It was easy to serve because guests helped themselves by spearing chunks of bread on long-handled forks and dipping them into the mixture.

Both men laughed. "I was not referring to the health benefits," Rene teased. "In Switzerland we have a custom. When a man and a woman share this dish, the one who loses the bread off the fork owes the other a kiss."

Jacques' eyes danced with merriment. "Anyone beyond kissing age must buy the party a bottle of wine, but so far that has never been known to occur."

"I see." Shannon decided it was time to change the subject. "It's interesting that you both have French accents. Everyone I've met so far speaks German."

"We have four national languages," Jacques explained, "French, German, Italian and Romansch."

"It seems strange in a country as small as ours," Rene expanded. "Just as it surprises many people when they encounter palm trees in Switzerland."

"Now I *know* you're putting me on," Shannon exclaimed.

They assured her they were not. "At Lugano for one, near the Italian border to the south."

The time fled by as the two men, finding an enthusiastic listener, extolled the wonders of their country. They painted vivid word pictures of Switzerland in the summer when wild flowers replaced the snow in alpine meadows, and rainbow trout flashed in countless streams and rivers.

Shannon was entranced by tales of Zurich during the spring Festival of Sechselauten. At the height of the festivities, a giant dummy stuffed with fireworks is touched off in the square for a mammoth display that's meant to represent Old Man Winter being publicly put to rout.

Those and other stories kept her glued to the log, completely unaware of the cold. It was with great reluctance on all parts that she finally let the men go back to work.

Deke was just coming down the stairs as Shannon let herself in the front door of the chalet. He looked at her in amazement. "I thought you were still sleeping."

She had trouble facing him, the memory of last night setting up a wild clamor in her veins. "I . . . I woke up early."

He walked over to where she stood rooted at the entry. "How do you feel this morning?" he asked softly.

Every nerve end was acutely aware of him, of his lean length, the tangy smell of his shaving lotion, the total masculinity of him. Her eyes were unable to rise above the dark hair visible through the partially unbuttoned silk shirt Deke wore tucked into narrow black slacks that rode low on his slim hips. "I'm fine," she murmured, scarcely audibly.

He raised her chin in a long-fingered hand that felt warm against her cool skin. "No aching muscles?"

"No."

"That's good. Didn't I tell you a nice massage would fix you up?" His hand caressed her cheek, straying up to comb through her silky hair.

Shannon jerked away like a startled, high-strung filly. "That had nothing to do with it. It was the hot bath and a good night's sleep. All the other was a waste of time."

Laughter sparked green lights in his hazel eyes. "Maybe it was for you, but I certainly enjoyed it."

Shannon gritted her teeth. "Well, you're not going to anymore! How can I get it through your head that I don't want anything to do with you?"

"Maybe when your actions match your words," Deke taunted.

To her dismay he moved closer, making her tinglingly aware of him. Her cursed memory knew every hard muscle and sinew in that virile male body. She had to will herself not to react.

His soft voice was mocking. "I find it difficult to believe I'm distasteful to you when you wrap your arms around my neck and fit that beautiful body into mine where it belongs."

"How can you say such a thing!" she gasped. "It was you . . . I didn't—"

"Shall I remind you?" He unzipped her ski jacket, his hand sliding inside to glide suggestively over her midsection. "If Mike hadn't interrupted us, you would have spent last night in my arms."

Shannon shuddered at the contact, heat igniting her traitorous body as it yearned for the fulfillment this man could bring. Drawing on her pride, she pushed him away. "You're a fine father! Jealous of your own son."

"I was the one who went to him," he reminded her.

Before Shannon was forced to reply to that undeniable truth, there was a blessed interruption. Jim appeared at the head of the stairs, briefcase in hand and wearing a business suit.

"Morning, Shannon. Deke, I'd like to go over these contracts with you one more time before I take off for Berne."

As Deke turned toward his attorney, Shannon made her escape up the stairs.

By the time she had combed her hair and washed her face, everyone was assembled around the breakfast table except Marlee, and Jim, who had gone to the airport.

"Marlee thinks she might be coming down with a cold, so she decided to stay in bed this morning," Rustin explained.

"I'm sorry," Shannon said. "Is there anything I can do for her?"

He shook his head. "I think it's just a good excuse to flake out. Her symptoms didn't develop until I suggested going skiing today." He grinned.

"Doesn't she like to ski?" Shannon asked.

"Not overly. Marlee prefers warm-weather activities."

"Why on earth did she come to Switzerland then?" Stephanie demanded.

Rustin regarded her calmly. "Because she knew I wanted to."

"I thought Marlee was more liberated than that." Stephanie's lip curled scornfully. "Don't you have any compunction at all about forcing her to do something she hates?"

"I didn't say she hates it." For the first time, Rustin's urbane charm was not in evidence. "In a good marriage each partner tries to please the other. Our last vacation was taken in the Caribbean."

"A very adult way of handling it," Jeff commented dryly.

"Are you suggesting that I'm not an adult?" Stephanie flared.

Jeff gave her a level glance. "I can't help your interpretation."

"I'm sure that after Stephanie is married she'll be happy to go anywhere her husband wants," Helene cut in smoothly, with the merest glance at Deke.

"As long as it suits her purpose," Deke teased.

Stephanie gave him a mutinous look. "I'm beginning to have second thoughts about this whole marriage bit."

"Better now than later," Jeff told her.

She whirled on him angrily. "With an attitude like that I don't suppose you'll *ever* get married. Gilt-edged guarantees aren't passed out with the license."

Jeff's eyes held hers. "The only guarantee I require is that my bride doesn't regard marriage as a state located somewhere between Camelot and Shangri-la. In real life there are real problems."

"You're fighting a losing battle, Jeff." Deke's voice was brittle. "Women expect men to be perfect."

"Isn't it nice that so many of us are?" Rustin laughed, breaking the tension.

Gretel came through the swinging door pushing a teacart laden with large platters of food. Shannon shook her head when asked to indicate her choice. "Just some toast and coffee, please," she murmured.

"That's not enough to eat," Deke said, frowning. "You should be hungry. You didn't have any dinner last night."

"I . . . I had something when I was out earlier."

"How could you? There was nothing open at that hour."

She related her meeting with the two lumberjacks, explaining that she had had coffee with them. "I thought it was awfully nice of them to share with me."

Shannon was uncomfortably aware of being the center of attention. Deke's face darkened with displeasure as she had somehow known it would, but it was Stephanie who evidenced hostility for some unfathomable reason.

"You're quite the femme fatale, aren't you, Shannon?" she sneered unpleasantly.

Shannon hung onto her temper with difficulty. "I never considered myself in that light," she answered evenly.

"That's the quality that makes you so endearing," Jeff said gently.

Shannon flashed him a grateful smile. In a short space of time they had become good friends. There was nothing romantic in their feeling for each other. Their relationship was based on mutual admiration and a sense of camaraderie.

"It's nice to know what kind of woman you're attracted to," Stephanie snapped.

"They do make a nice couple, don't they?" Helene smiled benignly on them.

"Adorable." Deke's response was almost a snarl.

Rustin glanced around the breakfast table, his expression enigmatic. "I've just had one of my better ideas, Deke. What say we rent some sleighs tonight and all go for a sleigh ride. We can end up at the lodge for dancing and midnight supper. It will do us all good to get out for a night."

"That sounds super." Stephanie's sullen face belied her words. "Deke and I can go together."

"And you can wear that new outfit we bought in Zurich," Helene agreed enthusiastically.

"I may have to fly to Berne," Deke said. "Jim is negotiating a contract with the Swiss government, and it's possible that my presence will be required." He looked at Jeff without expression. "If I do go, you'll have to come with me."

"Can I go too?" Stephanie asked eagerly.

"No, you can't." Deke's refusal was succinct. "It would be strictly a business trip."

"This is the rottenest Christmas I've ever had!" Stephanie exclaimed petulantly. "I'm sorry I came."

"You can always go home," Deke told her in a steely voice.

Helene rushed in breathlessly. "You know she didn't mean that." Turning to her daughter, Helene's small mouth pursed with annoyance. "If you don't mind your manners, young lady, I'm going to have your father speak to you when he gets back."

"Oh, for God's sake, Mother! I'm not twelve years old anymore—even if some people seem to think so." Pushing her chair back, she stormed out of the room.

Her departure brought a slight release of the unaccountable tension that had flared so suddenly, but no one was inclined to linger at the table. As they all went their separate ways, Shannon hung back for a private word with Deke, having made up her mind that her situation was impossible.

She went straight to the point. "I think it would be best if I went home."

"We've been through all that," he said impatiently.

"Why are you being so stubborn?" she cried. "Can't you see how Stephanie resents me? It's ruining everyone's vacation."

Deke's face was grim. "Then I suggest you do something about it."

"That's what I *want* to do. If I weren't here, things would settle down to normal."

"There's a less drastic way to accomplish that."

"How?" Shannon asked.

"Admittedly, Steffy is very possessive, but it would help if you stopped poaching on her property."

Shannon looked at him in outrage. What was Deke suggesting? That Shannon was the predatory female? "I wouldn't touch her *property* with a stick!" she told him furiously.

His gaze was skeptical. "Surely you can understand how she feels. Or have you forgotten those tantrums *you* threw when you thought I was paying too much attention to other women?"

Shannon clenched her fists. "For the last time—I did *not* throw tantrums. And it certainly isn't the same thing. I was married to you. If she's this jealous now, I shudder to think what she'll be like after the wedding."

A smile lightened Deke's grim expression. "Well, at least the groom knows what he'd be getting into. Love isn't blind in this case."

A crushing sense of defeat overwhelmed Shannon, making it difficult to keep the tears of humiliation out of her eyes. Deke certainly wasn't pulling his punches.

She turned away mutely, stiffening when Deke came up behind her. Folding his arms over her breasts, he drew her back against his muscled length, burying his face in the scented softness of her hair. "I'm sorry if I was abrupt with you," he murmured.

"It's all right. I understand." It *wasn't* all right, but she would have said anything to get out of his arms.

He turned her to face him. "Do you?" His hand cupped her chin, trying to force her to look into his searching eyes. "Don't play games, darling. There's too much at stake."

At the sound of footsteps Shannon pulled away hurriedly. She couldn't bear another scene with Stephanie. Why didn't the girl realize that she had won?

Shannon ran up to her room to compose herself before facing Mike. This was the most degrading thing Deke had ever done to her, warning her to stop upsetting Stephanie! She paced the floor to calm herself. Bitter laughter rose in her throat as she remembered the younger girl's words. Some femme fatale she was! She couldn't even attract the one man in the world she wanted.

Shannon stood completely still as the implications

of that thought penetrated her heated mind. *Did* she want Deke? Or was she just being a dog in the manger? Was it mere possessiveness like Stephanie's that made the thought of him and any other woman totally unacceptable?

She wandered restlessly over to the window, trying to sort out her tangled emotions. Voices below drew her attention. Rustin and Deke were going skiing with Stephanie. Her animated face was turned up to Deke's, all ill humor erased in the magic of his presence. Something shriveled up and died inside of Shannon as she watched the way he was smiling down at the younger girl, his arm protectively around her shoulders.

Shannon took a deep, shuddering breath, all her soul-searching done. Deke belonged to a past that was irrevocably over.

Chapter Seven

*A*fter Mike had eaten lunch and settled down for his nap, Shannon looked in on Marlee.

She found her propped up on two pillows, looking like an advertisement for expensive linens. The fluffy white maribou bed jacket Marlee wore was a reminder of bygone Hollywood glamour days when starlets supposedly lolled around all day under satin sheets. In keeping with that picture of luxurious idleness, the double bed was strewn with books and magazines.

"How are you feeling?" Shannon asked.

"Terrific!" Marlee stretched her arms wide, sighing happily.

"Rustin said you might be coming down with a cold."

The answer to that was a gamin grin. "Dear Rustin, he knew I was faking all along." She patted the side of the bed. "Sit down and visit with me for a while."

Shannon advanced slowly into the room. "I don't think I understand."

"It's very simple. I just felt like staying in bed and

doing absolutely nothing. That's a luxury I haven't enjoyed in ages."

"But why couldn't you just say so?" Shannon persisted. "It's your vacation; you're entitled to spend it any way you like."

"Conscience, I guess." Marlee laughed. "I'm so used to being up and doing that it feels fairly scandalous to be this lazy. Plus the fact that everyone is so *physical* here! Can you imagine the scorn I'd get from young Steffy if she knew? She already thinks we're all over the hill. We women at least," she added dryly. At the look on Shannon's face, Marlee raised a perfectly arched eyebrow. "Russ said the child was impossible at breakfast."

Shannon shrugged it off. "Everyone was a little edgy. Except Rustin. He has a marvelous disposition."

"For the most part," Marlee admitted. "Although he has his moments."

"I can scarcely believe that."

"Then you don't know very much about being married." Marlee laughed. As soon as the words were out, a stricken expression crossed her face. "I'm sorry, Shannon. That was a tactless thing to say."

"It doesn't matter." Shannon examined her fingernails carefully. "You're quite right. I wasn't a signal success at it."

They were both silent for a long moment. Then Marlee said, "I don't know what went wrong between you and Deke and I'm not trying to pry, but Rustin and I feel it's a shame. You're so right for each other."

Shannon raised her head. "We were never right for each other; that's the trouble. It should have been a torrid affair, not a marriage."

"Could you have walked away unscathed when it ended?" Marlee asked gently.

"I . . . well, maybe not, but it would have been less painful than a divorce."

"Would it? I wonder." The other woman eyed her compassionately. "And how about your son? There wouldn't have been any Michael."

Shannon couldn't envision a world that didn't include her child. Mike was the balm that soothed all wounds. When he put his arms around her neck and looked up with unquestioning love, no price was too much to pay.

"You're right, of course." Shannon drew a deep breath. "I don't know what's the matter with me this morning. With all the things I have going for me, I ought to be counting my blessings."

"True. After all, today's woman doesn't need one special man to keep her happy." Marlee's voice was casual but her eyes were sharp. "With your looks you must have to beat the men off with a stick."

Shannon thought about her arid emotional life. If only Marlee knew how wrong she was! Shannon didn't want her pity, however. "I don't really have much time for men," she said carelessly. "You're in the business world; you know how it is."

"Yes, but I have Rustin," Marlee said softly. "I couldn't do it without him."

"That's because he's special. There aren't many men like him," Shannon said somberly. "You have that rarity, a perfect marriage."

"Shannon, you surprise me. In some ways you're as unrealistic as Steffy. Do you honestly believe that perfect marriages are made in heaven?" Marlee pushed herself up straighter in bed. "Let me tell you that a lot of hard work went into mine!"

"Well, I suppose there are always adjustments,"

Shannon conceded. "But you two are ideally suited; you don't fight about every little thing."

"You're seeing the end result."

"I can't believe you and Rustin ever argued—not about important things."

Marlee raised her eyebrows. "In our early days we were known as the scrapping Stevensons. The odds were about eight to five against our lasting six months together."

"What did you fight about?"

"Everything! A phone call from my mother, the way the laundry did Rustin's shirts—you name it."

Shannon smiled. "That sounds fairly typical. Even roommates have to iron out those little differences before they can settle down in harmony."

"You're right, if that's all it was. But those weren't the things that were really bothering us. There were deep, underlying tensions between Rustin and me. He was a famous lawyer and I was a successful business woman. We were each a little spoiled by the authority we wielded. As a result, both of us went into the marriage resolved that we weren't going to let the other dominate."

That struck a responsive chord. "What's so bad about that? Marriage shouldn't make you lose your identity," Shannon stated firmly.

Marlee shook her head pityingly. "How could it possibly? You're either an individual in your own right or you're not. Deferring to the one you love doesn't make you less of a person."

"But suppose he tries to take over your whole life, what then?"

"Suppose he's only trying to share it?" Marlee countered gently.

Was that what Deke had been trying to do? Shannon wondered for the first time. In the begin-

ning they were never apart. Was he showing her off
to his friends, hoping she would like them? Did his
desire to know where she was and what she was
doing spring from a need to share her thoughts as
well as her bed? Then she remembered Cynthia
Darby, and the bubble of excitement burst.

"You were fortunate that you settled your differences before Rustin turned to another woman,"
Shannon said bitterly.

"Yes, but in that case I would have fought for him
and gotten him back," Marlee said calmly.

"You can say that because it's never happened to
you. You don't know what it's like."

"No, fortunately I don't. It wouldn't change anything, though. Pride is cold comfort in a double
bed."

Shannon suddenly realized how much of herself
she had revealed. Pinning a bright smile on her face,
she said, "Well, at least it's nice to meet someone
who has it all."

"Is that what you think? You're wrong, my dear.
You have something I'd sell my soul for."

Shannon's wide eyes were puzzled. "I can't imagine what."

"Your son," Marlee said softly. "Rustin and I
have been trying to have a baby for a long time. If
something doesn't happen pretty soon we're going to
adopt."

"Oh, I'm so sorry!"

"Don't be." Marlee smiled. "Nobody can have it
all, and I've certainly had more than my share of the
good things. Besides, maybe it's meant to be this
way. Maybe there's a little one being born right now
who needs me."

"You . . . you wouldn't give up your career,
would you?" Shannon asked uncertainly.

"I wouldn't have to. I'd certainly cut down, though, because I'd want to spend every possible moment with him—or her. They grow up so fast."

"That they do," Shannon agreed, reflecting that Mike would soon start kindergarten.

"You're lucky that you can do so much of your work at home. I can't see myself dragging young Junior Stevenson to the agency office." Marlee laughed.

"He could be your youngest model," Shannon told her with a smile.

There was determination in Marlee's voice. "Not my baby! He's going to grow up in a proper home, as a child should."

Marlee didn't realize how her words hurt. Mike had never had the proper home with two doting parents that she described. And now his life would be even more divergent from that of other children. Not only would he be uprooted every six months, Mike would go from one extreme to the other. Literally. He would travel from coast to coast, experiencing both an opulent life-style and one that was exceedingly modest. Could a small child be expected to adjust to that? But if it was too much to ask, what was the alternative?

While Shannon was wrestling silently with her problems, the church bells in the village started to peal.

"Good heavens, can it be one o'clock already?" Marlee exclaimed. "And here I am still in bed!"

"I've been keeping you," Shannon apologized.

"Not at all. I enjoyed our talk." The other woman looked at her obliquely. "Sometimes it helps to discuss things. It sort of puts matters in a different perspective."

Marlee had indeed given her a lot to think about.

Shannon sadly wished that they had met before the divorce instead of after. It seemed too late now to change anything.

She slid off the bed. "I'll let you get dressed."

"It will only take a minute. Would you be a lamb and tell Gretel I'll be right down? The poor woman has probably been waiting lunch for us."

Afterward, they went shopping in the little village. To their relief, Helene declined to accompany them. She had complained of an incipient cold all through lunch; and in her case, the symptoms were real.

Marlee was stimulating to be with. The two women discovered that their initial rapport was confirmed; they enjoyed each other's company tremendously. If nothing else comes out of this trip, Shannon reflected, at least I've made three good friends.

On their way back from the village in the late afternoon, they met the returning skiers outside the chalet.

Rustin put an arm around his wife, kissing the tip of her nose. "How's the cold, my little hothouse orchid?"

"As you expected," she said, laughing. "All gone."

"Did you have a nice rest?" he asked softly.

"A very nice one," she murmured. Their eyes held as something flamed between them.

Shannon felt a lump rise in her throat. The passion that flared between Rustin and Marlee was sweetened with love and tenderness. It was something beautiful that shouldn't be intruded upon. She turned away, stumbling because of the film of tears that blurred her eyes.

Deke's strong hand was on her arm, steadying her. "Careful. One disabled person around here is enough."

It reminded Shannon that she had been gone all afternoon. "Michael will be furious," she said ruefully.

"We'll go up to see him together." Deke kept his arm around her. "Did you have a nice afternoon?"

"Yes, it . . . it was very peaceful."

"I was going to ask you to go skiing, but it didn't seem like the right time." Deke's arm tightened, holding her close to his lean body. "I want to apologize for this morning, Shannon. I had no right to be so unpleasant. My only excuse is that finding you again has made me too possessive. I want to make up for all the time we spent apart. I tend to smother you, though, don't I?"

Stephanie had disappeared and Marlee and Rustin had gone upstairs. They were standing in the entry and Deke turned Shannon in his arms, slowly unzipping her jacket. The warm house after the cold outside was making the blood course madly through her body. Almost in a trance she unzipped Deke's jacket, her hand wandering over his ski sweater, tracing the taut muscles of his chest and shoulders.

The knuckles of his hand trailed idly up and down her cheek as he drew her closer to his urgent body. "Do you feel smothered, sweetheart?" he repeated.

She did at the moment. Shannon was drowning in the male magnetism he exerted so effortlessly over her. It would be so easy to take that one small step into his arms, to kiss the hollow in his bronze throat and hope the pulse would quicken just for her. His words echoed in her ears, bringing needed self-control.

Shannon dropped her hand and leaned back in his arms, away from the powerful allure of that potent male body. "I don't think you realize how much I've changed, Deke."

"How much?" he teased, his hands sliding below her waist to mold her hips firmly against his.

"No, that hasn't changed," she admitted honestly, trying to put distance between them. "But everything else has. I was a pliant child when I met you. I'm not anymore. I've proved that I can take care of myself."

Deke was abruptly serious. He gripped her shoulders, looking searchingly into her face. "I never doubted it for a minute. The fact that I did things for you didn't mean that I thought you couldn't do them yourself."

"Then why . . . ?" Shannon's head was in a whirl. All the things that Marlee and Deke were telling her were diametrically opposed to her own perceptions.

"Out of love," Deke said simply.

"Mommy." Michael's plaintive voice was accusing. "You weren't there when I woke up." The little boy appeared at the head of the stairs.

"What are you doing out of bed, young man?" Deke's sternness was patently fake. Taking the stairs two at a time, he lifted the child in his arms.

"I didn't have anything to do," Mike complained. "Will you play with me?"

"Mommy and I both will." Deke turned to Shannon with a smile.

They sat on Michael's bed and played games with him until Gretel appeared with his dinner tray.

"I'm not hungry," the little boy cried. "I don't want you to go."

"What makes you think we're going anyplace?" Deke scooped Shannon in his arms, sitting down in a rocker with her in his lap. "Mommy is going to read to both of us."

"Deke, please!" Shannon said in an outraged whisper, her cheeks very pink.

He subdued her struggles easily, clasping her

against his chest and pulling her head down to his shoulder. "It's good for children to see their parents show affection. Haven't you ever read any books on psychology?" Deke teased.

Not wanting to make too much of it, Shannon relaxed in Deke's arms. With an inadvertent little sound of pleasure, she fitted her soft curves to the angles of his body, letting her lips touch the side of his neck as though by accident.

"I thought you were going to read to us, Mommy," Mike reminded her.

A rumble of laughter echoed in Deke's chest. "How old do they have to be before they get some romance in their souls?"

"More than four, obviously," she sighed.

They stared into each other's eyes, the laughter drowned in a cascade of emotion that sent rivers of fire leaping from one to the other. Deke's arms tightened and his mouth covered Shannon's with a demand that stemmed from their mutual need.

"I'm not hungry," Mike announced. "I don't want any more."

Shannon pulled herself back to reality with a great effort. Dragging her mouth from Deke's, she framed his face between her palms for a long moment before getting to her feet and walking over to the bed. "You have to eat your dinner, Michael. Otherwise you won't be well enough to trim the tree on Christmas Eve."

"That's going to be your coming-out party," Deke agreed, his breathing ragged.

"Oh, boy!" Mike's eyes sparkled as he picked up his fork without further argument. "How many more days is that?"

"I'm going to take a shower," Deke murmured into Shannon's ear, his hand caressing her neck under the soft spill of hair. "See you downstairs."

Dinner was uneventful in spite of Shannon's worries after the trauma of the morning. A day of skiing had evidently smoothed over all of Stephanie's bad temper. Undoubtedly contributing to the harmony was the fact that her father was still in Berne and her mother was having dinner in bed, pampering her cold.

Stephanie even went out of her way to make amends to Jeff, taking the seat next to him and being utterly charming. Anyone who didn't know that her heart was otherwise involved would think she was interested in Jeff. His rather disapproving manner toward her was missing, too. During a good part of the meal they had their heads together, conversing in soft tones that didn't include the others.

"Is everyone ready for a romantic sleigh ride?" Rustin asked when dinner was almost over.

"I thought that was scrapped when Deke and Jeff had to go to Berne," Shannon exclaimed, only then realizing that Deke had changed his plans.

"Signing a contract can't compare to a moonlight ride with a beautiful girl," he said easily.

Shannon's excitement gave way to despair. For a moment the thought of a sleigh ride had sounded glamorous, but her enjoyment was flawed by the thought of Deke cuddling under the blankets with Stephanie.

When she returned with her black cloth coat, three sleighs were drawn up outside. As she watched the sleek black horses shaking their plumed heads and stamping their feet, steam coming from their flaring nostrils, Shannon's spirits rose in spite of herself. The curved sleighs heaped with blankets looked like relics from a romantic past. They conjured up images of jeweled countesses being tucked under ermine-trimmed lap robes before being whirled off for an assignation at some remote moun-

taintop chalet. The jingling harness bells blended
with laughing voices, making a joyous melody in the
crystal-clear night.

"Okay, everyone into the sleighs," Rustin called,
helping Marlee into the lead one.

An awkward moment developed as the other four
looked uncertainly at each other. Deke solved it by
taking Shannon's arm. "You two go ahead," he told
Jeff and Stephanie. "I forgot to give Shannon something."

To Shannon's surprise, Stephanie didn't fly into a
rage. She got meekly into the sleigh with Jeff and
they rode off.

Shannon's eyes were midnight blue as she looked
up at Deke. "What did you forget?" She was shivering in the icy air in spite of the warm tide of
anticipation running through her veins. For whatever reason, she was going to be the one with Deke
under the blankets.

He led her back into the house without answering
her question. Taking a large box out of the hall
closet, he handed it to her. "This is for you."

She looked at him uncertainly. "What is it?"

"Why don't you open it?" He smiled.

"But the others . . . they'll get way ahead of us.
Why are you giving this to me now?"

"Because it's something you need."

When she made no move to open it, he took the
lid off the box, revealing a sable coat of unbelievable
luxury. The thick, dark brown pelts shimmered in
the light of the chandelier, whisper soft, yet warm as
a down comforter.

"It's gorgeous, Deke!" she gasped. "But I can't
possibly accept it!"

"You don't have any choice." He drew her old
coat off a protesting Shannon, dropping it disdainful-
ly on the floor. "I'm going to burn that thing."

Draping the new coat around her, he framed her face in the collar. "This is the way you should look."

Shannon ran her hands lovingly over the soft fur. "This isn't fair, Deke. I'm as female as the next woman."

"So I've noticed," he said, laughing.

"Then why did you do this to me? You know I can't take it."

"It's an early Christmas present," he told her. "You can hardly refuse a present, now can you?"

"You already gave me a Christmas present." When he looked blank, she reminded him of the ski clothes.

"You must be joking! What kind of a gift is that?" He silenced her protests firmly. "I'm not going to have you catching your death of cold for a few principles that are ridiculous to begin with."

"They aren't—"

His warm hand over her mouth stilled the words. "If I'd been there when Mike was born, I would have brought you a present. This is a few years late, and nothing could equal the gift you gave me, but won't you accept it in the spirit in which it's given, Shannon?"

Quick tears sprang up, clinging to the long, dark lashes. Shannon's eyes were like dewed violets as she looked up at him. "Thank you, Deke. I think this is the kindest thing you ever did for me."

He hugged her tight, stroking her hair gently. "Do you really want to go on a sleigh ride?" he murmured in her ear.

She forced herself out of his arms. "Of course I want to go. I have to show off my new coat, don't I?"

Deke groaned. "I should have bought you lingerie instead."

Their driver was waiting patiently on the seat in back of the horses. After the robe had been wrapped around Shannon's legs, she felt delightfully warm in spite of the temperature. The only indication she had of the cold was the white puffs of breath whenever she opened her mouth.

"This is such fun, Deke. I've never been on a sleigh ride before."

He put his arms around her under the blanket, drawing her so close that she was almost on his lap. "I don't know why I always picked warm-weather vacations for us. This is so much nicer."

"Deke, please!" She nodded toward the driver. "Behave yourself."

"I'm behaving exactly as expected," he teased. "You don't think couples jounce around on these wretched things in the freezing cold for any other reason than to make out?"

"You're just not a romantic," she said severely.

"Don't you believe it," he murmured.

His hand slid inside her coat under the blanket, slipping under her sweater to cup her breast, his fingers warm against her bare skin.

"Deke, stop it!" she gasped, grabbing for his hand. All that accomplished was to trap it against her breast where his fingers dipped inside her bra, lazily caressing her hardened nipple. "Please stop," she begged, her body on fire from the indescribable sensation.

His dark head bent over her, blotting out everything except his face, which became the center of her universe. His eyes were smoky with desire as he murmured, "Later?"

"I . . . I don't know."

His thumb continued its rotation on the diamond-hard peak of her breast, his other hand starting a slow exploration of her hip and thigh. "Later?" he repeated huskily.

Shannon could no longer deny her own need.

"Yes, oh yes!" she murmured, surrendering her mouth to him.

His deep, passionate kiss left her clinging to him with every ounce of her strength. Shannon wanted him to touch her, to kiss her, to stake the supreme male claim. All barriers were down as she gave in to him completely. It was Deke who finally pulled away, his hands shaking as they gently traced the curve of her cheek.

"How is it possible that I still want you as much as the first time I saw you?" His voice was hoarse with emotion. Shannon's eyes reflected the brilliance of the starry heavens as she gazed up at him wordlessly, her mouth softly parted. Deke drew a ragged breath. "I'll never let you go!" he said fiercely, straining her against his urgent body.

No, she would never be free, Shannon realized, caught between joy and sadness. This man was as necessary to her as the heart that beat faster when he was near. Even though he might never belong to her, she would always be his. It was a sobering thought.

As Deke bent over her again, Shannon held him off with her hands against his chest. "No more, Deke. I don't think either of us can stand it."

They stared at each other for a long moment, then he rested his cheek against her hair, stroking it tenderly. "You're right, my love. When I'm with you I'm not responsible."

He held her quietly in his arms and it was like the lull in a storm. They both knew the tempestuous climax was still to come, but for now, Shannon was content just to be near him, to feel his warmth and his strength.

The sound of the horses' hooves lent rhythm to the music of the bells as they wound their way through the black-and-white world. Icicles hung from dark firs, making them look more than ever like Christmas trees decorated with crystal and cotton. Except for the gaily lit chalets nestled into the hills, they could have been alone in a primeval world, pristine and beautiful. Shannon made a sound of pleasure deep in her throat.

"Are you happy, darling?" Deke murmured.

Without having to think about it, she nodded her head

Because of their delayed start, they were the last ones to reach the lodge. The others were hovering around the entrance waiting for them.

"Did you get lost?" Stephanie demanded. "We were starting to worry."

"Until I reminded her that horses never run out of gas," Rustin teased.

Shannon's nerves tightened as she waited for the younger girl's jealousy to flare again. Strangely enough, she really did look worried rather than angry. Suddenly Stephanie's eyes widened.

"That coat, Shannon! Where did you get that heavenly coat?"

Marlee came closer to admire it. "It's magnificent."

Stephanie was prowling around her. "What is it? It isn't mink, I know that."

"I . . . it's sable," Shannon faltered, dreading the inevitable question.

"*Sable!*" Stephanie clasped her hands like a little girl. "I've never been this close to one."

"Would you like to try it on?" Shannon looked uncomfortably at Deke.

He had put her in an awkward situation. How was he going to explain the coat to Stephanie? It didn't seem to be worrying him. Deke was watching

Stephanie with the fondly indulgent look that was his usual expression with her, and Shannon's pleasure in the beautiful gift faltered.

Stephanie wrapped herself in the luxurious fur, wriggling with delight. Turning an ecstatic face to Jeff she asked, "How do I look?"

"Very nice." His response was rather restrained, considering that she did look exquisite.

Stephanie was too excited to take offense. "I'd positively kill for a coat like this!"

"It does seem to make you happy," Jeff remarked dryly.

"I'm just being honest. Any woman who says she doesn't want a sable coat is lying," Stephanie declared.

"You're the star of the show, Shannon," Rustin teased, unaware that she had no wish to be.

"You didn't tell us where you got it," Stephanie said.

"It was . . . I . . ."

"It's my Christmas present to Shannon," Deke cut in smoothly.

Stephanie surprised Shannon again. Instead of fizzing with anger, she batted her eyelashes at Deke, giving him an enticing smile. "Does it have a twin with my name on it under the tree?"

Deke laughed. "You're a pushy little minx. What gave you the idea that I was buying you a fur coat?"

She pretended to pout. "It wouldn't hurt you. You're positively wallowing in money."

"And all this time I thought you loved me for myself alone."

"I'll love you even more if you're inclined to be generous," she said outrageously.

Deke tugged her hair sharply. "Well, I'm sorry to disappoint you, but you're going to have to earn those fringe benefits—like after you've been married for a while."

Jeff jammed his hands in his pockets just as Shannon's purse fell from her nerveless fingers. They didn't look at each other as he stooped to retrieve it.

"I think we've gotten enough mileage out of Shannon's new coat, and I'm starving," Rustin announced. "Let's go to the buffet table before everything's gone."

They all headed for the dining room, Shannon and Jeff falling behind.

Swallowing her misery, Shannon gave him a determined smile. "It was a lovely sleigh ride, wasn't it?"

"Yes," he answered shortly.

"I've never been on one before," she said brightly.

"I guess it's the thing to do in Switzerland." His mind was obviously far away.

Jeff's moodiness was so unlike him that it penetrated Shannon's own preoccupation. "Is anything wrong, Jeff?"

He raised a sardonic eyebrow. "What could be wrong?"

"I don't know. You seem . . . well, different."

"No, I'm just the same—everything's the same. And what do I have to complain about? I'm young and healthy, I have a good job with a bright future. In about twenty years I might even be able to buy my wife a sable coat." The last was said savagely.

Shannon looked at him uncertainly. "Surely that isn't bothering you? There aren't many men in the world who can afford that sort of thing."

"But there are a lot of women who consider it important."

"Oh, I don't think so. Any woman who would put material things first isn't worth bothering about."

Jeff's smile was lopsided. "I'll try to keep that in mind."

It must be difficult for Jeff, Shannon reflected, having Deke as a role model. Who could live up to him? All she could do was pat his arm reassuringly.

They sat around a big table eating plump sausages and paper-thin sliced ham, accompanied by *Rösti*, the famous Swiss fried potatoes. There were beakers of German beer to wash it down.

Deke frowned at Shannon's nearly full plate. She had only picked at her food. "Don't you like it?"

She hurriedly put a forkful of sausage into her mouth. "Yes, it's delicious."

"What am I going to do with you, Shannon? You eat like a bird."

She managed a smile. "You've forgotten. I never was a big eater."

His eyes took on a darkened glow. "There isn't anything I've forgotten about you," he murmured.

Shannon was completely confused. What was Deke doing? Tonight in the sleigh she had really believed that he might still love her. Yet that little scene with Stephanie over the coat seemed to indicate that he was more than casually involved there. Was he playing them against each other? Which one did he really want—or wasn't it that important to him? Shannon no longer doubted Deke's love for his son. Would he prefer to have Shannon because it would be better for Michael—yet failing that, he was willing to settle for Stephanie?

Strains of music sounded from the lounge where a dance floor had been cleared. Deke drew Shannon to her feet. "Come dance with me."

She held back. "I don't think—"

Laughter crinkled the corners of his eyes. "I'll behave, I promise."

Deke was almost as good as his word. He held her gently, but the things he whispered in her ear made her cheeks flame.

"I hope you realize it's taking all of my willpower not to make love to you here and now." Tiny lights flickered in his tawny eyes as he looked down at her. "I keep imagining that you're nude in my arms and I want to kiss that tiny birthmark on the inside of your thigh where the skin is so soft and white."

"You promised!" she gasped.

"And I'm keeping it," he teased. "Just look around you at the others and then tell me that I'm not being a pillar of rectitude."

It was true. Many of the other couples were glued together, making no secret of their feelings. The exception was Jeff and Stephanie. Their brief period of good fellowship had evidently come to an end. They were arguing again, this time in earnest. Stephanie's face was flushed and Jeff's mouth was grim. As Deke steered Shannon by them, she caught a fragment of their conversation. They were too angry to lower their voices or even care if they were overheard.

"You're just using that as an excuse," Stephanie cried.

"It was pretty indicative," Jeff grated. "Why won't you just admit that it would never work?"

"Because you don't want it to," she accused.

"And neither do you—not really."

"I do! How can I convince you, Jeff?" Stephanie was almost in tears.

Jeff was unmoved. His face looked as if it were carved from granite. "Grow up, Steffy."

Shannon looked up questioningly at Deke. He

shook his head slightly, guiding her off the floor. "Never get in the middle of someone else's argument."

When the evening was over they walked back to the chalet. The horses had long since gone to their warm stables. The wind had come up and the stars were obliterated.

Rustin glanced up at the overcast sky. "Looks like we might get some snow tomorrow."

"I hope so," Marlee said. "I love to watch it fall."

"From a soft couch by a blazing fire," her husband teased.

"It's the only civilized way," she told him. "If people were supposed to slosh around out there, they would have been born with skis on their feet."

"Then they could never sleep on their stomachs," Deke pointed out.

Jeff and Stephanie were taking no part in the banter. They were forced to walk together since the other two couples were strolling arm in arm, but Stephanie didn't even pretend that it was anything but distasteful. For his part, Jeff ignored her.

When they were back at the chalet, Deke walked Shannon to her room. This was the moment she had both feared and looked forward to. She had no doubt that Deke would press his suit one more time. The others had gone their separate ways, and they were alone in the quiet hall.

With her hand on the doorknob she turned to him. "Thank you again for the beautiful coat, Deke, and for a lovely evening."

He leaned against the doorjamb, blocking her way. "I'm going to be cad enough to remind you of your promise in the sleigh."

Long eyelashes swept her flushed cheeks. "I don't know what you mean."

"Don't you?" A tapered forefinger raised her chin. "Then why are you trembling like that, my love? It can't be fear, so it must be expectation."

"No! I . . . no," she finished lamely.

"You've never been able to lie to me, Shannon." His hands slid down her sides, molding the curve of waist and hip before trailing across the flat plane of her stomach. She shivered at the intimate contact, and he curved his hands around her bottom, drawing her close to his hard loins. "What do I have to do to get you to admit you want me?"

"I do admit it!" Shannon gasped, her arms going around his neck, fingers twining in his thick, dark hair.

With a growl of triumph deep in his throat, Deke's mouth covered hers, his tongue exploring the warm recess that received him eagerly. Shannon was lost in a wave of sensation as Deke's hands and lips built a storm in her body.

Without removing his arm he drew her into the darkened bedroom. In the dim light coming from the window, his eyes glowed like phosphorous. The tiny buttons at her neck gave way as he slowly unfastened them.

"I've been wanting to undress you all night," he murmured huskily. "Now the dream will become a reality. It's going to be even better than before, my darling."

Shannon's eyes darkened to cobalt blue, her breathing quick and shallow. Would it be better? There was no doubt that Deke could transport her to heaven, but it was such a risk. Once he had her body again, he would own her completely.

Her hand captured his disquieting fingers. "Deke, wait! I have to have time to think."

He bent to kiss the shadowed valley between her

breasts, his lips sliding over to touch one sensitive nipple. "That's always been your trouble, sweetheart. Why don't you listen to your body instead?"

It was a great temptation. With a herculean effort Shannon stepped out of his reach. "Please, Deke, if you care anything at all about me, give me tonight to think it over."

The hands that had been reaching for her dropped as he looked at her searchingly. "You're really serious, aren't you?"

"Yes." She wrapped her arms around her shaking body. "So much has happened today. Maybe I've been wrong about everything—I just don't know. That's why I have to have time to sort it all out."

Deke was silent for a long moment. When he spoke, his voice was very quiet. "Every instinct tells me to take you right now before you erect foolish barriers between us. But I won't do it. God knows I want you, Shannon, but when you come to me it has to be without reservations." There was a steely quality to the words. He turned away then, his tall figure blending into the darkness.

Shannon's body reproached her so bitterly that she almost ran after him. Yet Deke said he wanted her without reservations, and she had many to resolve.

It took almost all night. Just before morning Shannon made her decision. She could no longer deny her love for Deke, and rejecting him was merely self-flagellation. Marlee was a very wise lady; she had shown Shannon the error of her ways. This time her marriage would be built on trust. And as for Stephanie—she would find out that she was in for the battle of her spoiled life!

Shannon fell asleep with a smile on her face.

Chapter Eight

Shannon overslept the next morning. At least that's the way she put it to herself, although there was no reason why she had to get up. It was a luxury she couldn't accustom herself to. No early-morning alarms, no cooking to get started on, no breakfast for Michael.

Michael! She was neglecting him shamefully. Shannon swept aside the covers, running for the bathroom.

After a quick shower she pulled on a pair of fawn-colored wool pants and Marcia's red cashmere sweater. A brief look out the window had partly confirmed last night's prediction. It wasn't snowing, but the skies were a leaden gray. The sparkling blue of yesterday was gone, at least temporarily.

After brushing her long, shining black hair until it crackled with vitality, Shannon tied it back with a scarlet ribbon, merely to keep it off her face. She didn't know that with her clear blue eyes and translucent skin devoid of makeup, she looked very young and very vulnerable.

Shannon's headlong rush into her son's room was

checked by the unexpected sight of Deke. He was sitting beside Mike's bed, and the two were deep in conversation.

"Mommy!" Michael's fervent greeting never failed to warm Shannon's heart.

"Good morning, darling. I'm sorry I didn't get here sooner. I . . . I'm afraid I overslept." She was aware of Deke's eyes on her, yet she couldn't force herself to look at him. This wasn't the place to tell him of her decision. Her pulse started to skip around erratically at the thought of what it was.

"I'm glad one of us got some sleep," Deke said sardonically.

Shannon shot a nervous glance at him, alerted by the irony in his voice. There were deep lines grooved alongside his nose, evidence of the restless night he alluded to. Shannon's heart swelled with love and hope. Deke did care for her! She hadn't been alone in her suffering. Deke's body had cried out in protest, too, making sleep impossible. He didn't look too friendly at the moment, but when they had a chance to talk, everything would be wonderful.

"Have . . . have you and Michael been having a nice visit?" she asked.

Deke nodded. "Poor kid. It must be boring for him having to lie up here in bed all alone."

Shannon stiffened. Was Deke suggesting she neglected him? That was scarcely fair, since this was the first morning she'd missed. "Mike isn't used to having someone entertain him every minute," she explained. "He's very self-sufficient."

Deke's amusement was sardonic. "At four?"

"What's wrong with that?"

"Just about everything. At his age, 'self-sufficient' shouldn't even be in his vocabulary. What a child of four needs is a stable home environment and lots of playmates."

There was no doubting Deke's criticism this time. "He *has* a stable home!" Shannon said hotly. At Deke's skeptical look, she added, "And plenty of playmates, too. Mike goes to nursery school. You like it at Jack and Jill, don't you, darling?" she appealed to the little boy.

Michael's attention was on a wire Slinky he was shifting from one hand to the other. "Sometimes," was his indifferent reply.

"I'm overwhelmed by his enthusiasm," Deke said mockingly.

Shannon clenched her fists in frustration. "He *does* like it, he's just being difficult for your benefit. You know how children are."

Deke gave her a level look. "No, that's the problem. I don't know how children are, but I intend to find out."

It sounded like a veiled threat. Shannon couldn't believe that she had walked into this room almost in a state of euphoria such a short time ago. Why was Deke being so hateful?

"You certainly got up on the wrong side of the bed this morning," she told him resentfully.

That caught Mike's attention. "Did Daddy fall out of bed?" he asked his mother.

"Your mommy wouldn't know," Deke told him dryly.

"So that's it!" Shannon's eyes sparkled with anger. "Don't you think you're a little too old to be acting like a frustrated schoolboy?"

"Much too old." His eyes held hers until Shannon's fell before the challenge. "That's why I've decided to act like a man from now on."

Her chin came up. "Thanks for the warning."

"You have nothing to fear from me, Shannon." Deke's voice was deceptively soft. "You can wreck your own life quite effectively without my help."

"I don't *want* your help. I don't need it now and I didn't need it in California. I just thought I did."

Mike looked up then, his eyes sparkling with animation. "Daddy told me all about California. He says the sun shines all the time and I can go swimming in my own backyard."

"I notice you didn't mention the smog," she said tartly.

"I was sure you would do it for me."

"What's smog?" the little boy asked.

"It . . . well, it isn't important," Shannon told him.

"That's what *I* thought," Deke murmured.

Before Shannon could make a sharp rejoinder, Mike tugged at her hand. "You know where Daddy's going to take me? To Disneyland! He says I can shake hands with Donald Duck and—" The little boy checked himself, showing a puzzled face to his father. "Ducks don't have hands do they, Daddy?"

It was only a little thing, but it stabbed Shannon like a knife. Mike had always come to her for everything; now in just a short space of time, he was turning to Deke.

"They aren't exactly hands, but there's a kind of flipper thing you can shake," Deke was explaining.

Mike found the substitution satisfactory, taking up his saga again. "And we're going to go on all the rides, and then we're going to go to Marine World."

"Not all in one day." Deke laughed.

"No, but *next* day." Mike nodded his head confidently. "Daddy says they have whales and sharks and everything there," he told his mother.

Shannon decided that if she heard "Daddy says" one more time, she was going to scream. "It looks like you plan to spoil him thoroughly," she said tautly.

"Marine World is considered educational," Deke

answered mildly. "They conduct tours for school-children."

"You know what I mean."

Deke's tone was level. "No, I'm afraid I don't. Were you hoping his stay with me would be so unpleasant that he wouldn't want to repeat it?"

"I was hoping—" Shannon stopped, aware that the unmistakable tension between herself and Deke was bringing a cloud to their son's small face. "I think this is something we can discuss later."

"When? You can't put *everything* off, Shannon," Deke said sarcastically. "I'm going to have my son—with or without you." Rising to his feet, he leaned down and ruffled the little boy's hair. "See you later, tiger."

Michael watched him go with a troubled look on his face. "Is Daddy mad at you, Mommy?"

"No, of course not, darling." To get his mind on something else, she suggested a game of Chutes and Ladders.

Mike was soon immersed in it, leaving Shannon free to review this latest encounter with Deke. As she shook the dice and moved her little marker around the board, she puzzled over his behavior.

How could a man change that quickly? Last night he had been a tender and importunate lover; today he was the autocrat from the old days. The velvet glove was certainly off the steel fist. Deke had all but served notice that he intended luring Michael away from her.

Had her plea for time last night crystalized his decision? Had he given up hope of wearing her down, and was he now going to use plan B? Her wariness had been justified, hadn't it? That's what her common sense told Shannon. It was difficult to convince the rest of her.

"It's your turn, Mommy," Michael complained.

There was no one around when Shannon got downstairs sometime later. All of the large rooms were empty, even the kitchen. The only sounds came from the den. Since she certainly didn't want another encounter with Deke, Shannon wandered into the living room, where a cheerful fire was blazing in the large fireplace. She was staring moodily into the flames when Marlee and Rustin came clattering down the stairs.

"Gracious, Shannon, you look like a lost soul," Marlee observed.

Shannon forced a smile. "I guess it's just one of those days."

"Yes, the weather's rotten. That's why we decided to take in a movie," Rustin said. "Come with us."

When she declined, they tried to convince her to join them; but Shannon knew she was too jumpy to sit still.

After they had gone, the silence closed in once more. She was all alone with thoughts like little demons intent on poking her where it would hurt the most. When a log broke with a hissing shower of sparks while Shannon was staring out of the window, she almost jumped out of her shoes. It was then she decided to go upstairs and get a book to read.

As she was passing Helene's bedroom door, the older woman called to her.

"Do come in and chat for a bit, Shannon."

There was no way to get out of it, although it was the last thing Shannon wanted. She was incapable of being rude, however, no matter how little the woman deserved her consideration.

"Well, how are you getting along, Helene? It's too bad about your cold."

If the other woman noticed that the pleasantry was forced, it didn't seem to bother her. She was lying propped up in bed against a mountain of pillows. There was a box of tissues next to her, a stack of magazines, a plate of cookies, a half-filled cup of tea and just about everything else necessary for her comfort. It didn't seem to be enough, though. Helene's face above the lavish bed jacket was pinched with discontent.

"I can't seem to shake off this wretched cold, and my cough keeps me up all night." She gave a few delicate hacks to prove the point. "Not that anyone in my family cares. Jim's off to Berne, and Stephanie's out enjoying herself."

Shannon couldn't help saying, "You seem to have everything you need."

"I certainly do not! I could starve to death until that Gretel brings up my meals. I can't imagine why Deke puts up with her."

Reflecting that Helene could only benefit from going for a week without food, Shannon fought to keep the amusement out of her face. "I believe she has a lot to do. There are only Gretel and Paul to take care of all of us."

That didn't mollify Helene. "I had no idea Deke lived so modestly here. It's certainly different from his life-style in Beverly Hills."

Shannon thought of the rolling lawns and formal gardens with the staff of gardeners to take care of them, of the private maid he had wanted to hire for her until she had totally rejected the idea. "That's true," she murmured.

Helene looked at her sharply. "He's not . . . uh . . . frugal, is he? So often in their private lives these millionaires are a little eccentric and nobody actually knows about it."

Is he cheap? Shannon translated. Helene was so transparent it was laughable. And if she wasn't the world's stupidest woman, she was up there among the contenders. That it is in poor taste to pump an ex-wife for pointers which might be useful to his future one never even occurred to her. An imp of Satan influenced Shannon's answer.

"I wouldn't call Deke any more eccentric than your average tycoon. Of course he is a little kinky, but that rather goes with the territory, doesn't it?"

"Kinky?" Helene's expression was startled.

"You *do* know what the word means?"

"I'm not sure," Helene said hesitantly.

"Aberrant sexual behavior is the way psychologists describe it, I believe."

"You're joking!" Helene gasped.

"Oh, nothing as extreme as a Marquis de Sade complex. Deke isn't into pain. You don't have to worry about whips and chains and all that ugly black leather. He does have other . . . um . . . rather unusual appetites, though."

"I had no idea," Helene whispered. "Is that why you—"

"I wouldn't like to say," Shannon murmured, letting her eyelashes fall demurely.

"No, of course not." The older woman's face was an ugly, mottled red. "We really shouldn't be talking about this."

"You're so right. Why don't we talk about something more pleasant? Stephanie for instance. Such a lovely girl. I'm sure you're going to miss her dreadfully when she gets married."

Helene seemed preoccupied. "Yes, of course." Rallying herself she said, "To tell you the truth, Shannon, I'm feeling quite weak suddenly. Would you mind if we postponed our little chat?"

"Certainly not. You really are looking quite washed out. Can I get you a cup of tea?"

"No, nothing."

"A little sandwich?" Shannon persisted. "I make a divine *croque monsieur.*"

Helene appeared to be gritting her teeth. "I'd just like to be left alone if you don't mind."

Shannon seemed surprised. "Of course, Helene. Why on earth didn't you say so?"

Shannon could barely restrain her laughter until she got out of the room. You could say all you wanted about turning the other cheek, but revenge was still sweet. She had taken a great deal from Helene, but today evened the score. Shannon didn't dare dwell on what Deke would do to her if he ever found out. Whatever it was, it was worth it. For the first time today, she had been in command.

Shannon didn't fool herself that she had discouraged Helene's matchmaking proclivities. Diminishing her pleasure was reward enough. She had no doubt that after the woman pulled herself together, she would find some way of assuaging her conscience about sacrificing her daughter on the altar of her own greed and ambition. It was enough to have tarnished her joy.

Shannon's high wasn't destined to last. A short time after she had settled down before the fire with her book, Jim arrived home from Berne.

With much stamping of feet and complaints about the cold—and just about everything else in Switzerland—he swept into the entry. Shannon reflected that he and his wife were well matched.

She went back to her book, but after a while the warmth from the fire enveloped her and the words on the paper ran together. Her sleepless night took its toll, and Shannon dropped off to sleep. She awoke to find Jim and Deke standing over her.

"I'm sorry to wake you up, Shannon, but we'd like to have a little conference," Jim said.

What could they have to talk to her about?

Shannon's disoriented mind wondered. Then recollection returned, and she remembered her outrageous talk with Helene. A quick look at Deke's face wasn't reassuring. It was completely expressionless.

Because she was still somewhat fuzzy, Shannon said, "It was only a joke."

Jim frowned in perplexity. "What?"

"I think maybe we should postpone this," Deke said quietly.

"I don't agree. There's no time like the present," Jim said with his usual lack of originality.

Shannon got to her feet. Her hair had come loose from the ribbon and was cascading over her shoulders. She pulled it back, preparing to restrain it in its former severe style. Deke lifted his hand involuntarily, then let it drop to his side.

Shannon squared her shoulders. "All right, get it over with. I know I shouldn't have done it, but she had it coming to her."

"What are you talking about?" Jim demanded peevishly.

Caution overtook her. "What are *you* talking about?"

"Let's go into the den where we won't be disturbed," Jim said.

Shannon preceded the two men, feeling as though she were going before a firing squad. Anger gradually superseded guilt. Helene had asked for everything she got. If she was stupid enough to believe such a wild story, that was her problem, not Shannon's.

"Sit down, Shannon," Jim said.

She was about to refuse on general principles before she realized how childish that was. But she couldn't help saying mutinously, "If you expect me to apologize, you can save your breath."

Jim looked at her in carefully controlled exasperation. "You're being completely irrational for no reason that I can discern."

"You never were too swift on the uptake," Shannon answered flippantly.

Jim turned to Deke, his breathing hard. "Can't you talk to her?"

Surprisingly, there was laughter in Deke's eyes. "Not when she's in this mood."

Jim turned back to Shannon, his manner ponderous. "Deke gave me to understand that Michael was your first consideration, Shannon. In light of that, I find your present behavior inexplicable."

She caught her breath. "What has this to do with Mike?"

He looked at her in surprise. "Everything. What did you think we wanted to talk about?"

"I thought you . . . oh, never mind. Just tell me."

"Well, there are a lot of things that have to be taken into consideration, as I'm sure you're aware."

"Like what?" Ripples of apprehension were traveling up her spine.

Jim made a steeple of his fingers, leaning back in his chair. "You and Deke were legally married for two years, am I correct?"

"You already know that. What does it have to do with anything?" she demanded.

"Please, Shannon, it's best that we proceed in a logical fashion," Jim said in his best pontifical manner. "Now, when the marriage was dissolved you didn't receive any alimony."

"I didn't want any," she informed him distantly.

"You weren't entitled to any," he corrected.

Deke stirred restlessly. "Jim, you don't—"

"Please, Deke. Let me handle this. It's what you pay me for." Jim took up the questioning in a dry, emotionless manner. "You do realize that your leaving Deke constitutes desertion?"

Shannon looked straight at Deke. "Perhaps I felt he had deserted me," she said distinctly.

"Ah, but not according to law," Jim pointed out triumphantly. "The law clearly states that the partner who leaves the—"

"To hell with your law!" Shannon pushed her chair back furiously. "Okay, I left Deke. Is that what you want me to say? Those are the bare facts, all right, although it doesn't tell the whole story."

Deke's anger was better controlled but equally vibrant. It wasn't directed at Shannon, however. "This isn't what we were going to discuss, Jim. Why are you raking up the past?"

"Trust me." The lawyer was not the least bit ruffled. "It's best to set things straight for the record. That way difficulties are avoided."

"*What* difficulties?" Shannon was almost choking with rage. "There was never a question of alimony. I never wanted anything from Deke and he knows it."

"That pride of yours is as monumental as it is ridiculous!" Deke towered over her, his lean body taut with emotion.

Shannon refused to be intimidated. Raising her chin, her eyes blazed into his. "Maybe to you; not to me."

"Can we all please try to stay calm." Jim sighed. "The reason I brought up the matter of alimony is that very often women refuse it in a fit of pique or whatever, only to change their minds at a later date. I was only trying to protect my client."

Deke seemed about to explode; but before he could say anything, Shannon declared, "All right, you've made your point. If it will ease your mind, I'll sign a paper saying I won't ever ask for anything. No! As a matter of fact, I *demand* to sign it!"

Deke caught her wrist in an iron grip. "Shannon, I won't let—"

She twisted away from him. "Stay out of this and let your lawyer *protect* you."

"Very wise advice," Jim stated, ignoring his client's incipient apoplexy. "I think that takes care of the matter of alimony. Now we must discuss Deke's will."

It sounded so portentous that some of the fight went out of Shannon. "His will?"

Jim peered at Shannon disapprovingly. "I must inform you that he insisted on drawing it up in this manner against my express counsel."

"Just get to the point, don't editorialize," Deke growled.

"Yes, well," Jim proceeded reluctantly. "Under the terms of said will, half of Deke's estate will go to Michael. Since the child is his only heir, this is understandable."

When the pause lengthened, Deke said harshly, "Get on with it."

"The other half of the estate will go to you, Shannon."

It took a moment to sink in, then she reacted violently. "No! You can't do this to me!" Her startled eyes went to Deke. "I won't take it. I . . . I'll give it to charity."

Deke shrugged. "Suits me."

"This is all very premature," Jim reminded her. "Deke is a young man in the prime of life. He can expect many happy years, God willing. In fact his will might conceivably be revised in the ensuing years due to changed circumstances—a possible remarriage, and perhaps more children." The prospect made him distinctly happier.

Shannon caught her lower lip between small white teeth as she realized that was exactly what would happen. Her overreaction was stupid and pointless. She turned toward the door, tears misting her eyes.

"Wait, Shannon, we aren't through yet," Jim called.

What more could they possibly put her through? she wondered; then she asked the question in a different way.

"We've gotten the past and the future out of the way, now we have to settle the present," Jim told her.

"I don't understand. What is there to settle?" Shannon asked dully.

"I take it that you and Deke between you have come to an agreement on joint custody." Jim shook his head. "Most irregular. These things are best left to attorneys."

"This doesn't concern you, and I'd appreciate it if you'd butt out," Deke told him coldly.

"I'd be remiss in my duty if I failed to get it all down on paper," Jim insisted. "You don't know what an emotional issue child custody can be."

Shannon smiled bitterly. "Tell me!"

Jim raised his eyebrows at Deke as though to say, See what I mean? "As I understand it, the child is to spend six months with each parent."

"His name is Michael," Shannon said tightly.

"Yes, of course. Well, is that correct?"

"It's what Deke blackmailed me into."

Deke's eyes narrowed. "Would you have given him to me if I hadn't?"

"You know damn well I wouldn't!" she cried passionately. "He's *mine!*"

"And mine, Shannon," Deke said softly. "We made him together—out of love, no matter what came after."

It wasn't fair of him to remind her. Shannon's shoulders slumped as she turned away.

"What we have to work out now is the time-period

he is to spend with each parent," Jim continued as though there had been no interruption. "At the present it's no problem, but when the child—when Michael—goes to school, there will be difficulties. It would be unfair to expect him to attend two different schools in the same year, as I'm sure you will agree."

The enormity of the problems facing her were just beginning to be borne in on Shannon. "Yes, I suppose you're right," she faltered.

"If you'll allow me, I'll try to work out something equitable and get back to both of you. The only remaining consideration is something that may not have occurred to either of you. I assume that your paramount concern is the well-being of your son?"

They both nodded. On that at least, they were agreed.

"Well, let's suppose Michael settles in, one place or another." Jim's voice was deceptively casual. "Just for the sake of argument, let's say that he's completely content in one particular home. He has his friends, perhaps a pet; he's doing well in school."

Shannon sprang to her feet. "Now I see where all this is heading!"

"You have to face facts, Shannon," Jim advised her. "You did agree that his happiness was your prime consideration."

"He *is* happy—with me," she declared. Turning to Deke she cried, "Aren't you ever satisfied? Do you always have to have it all?"

"Shannon, I swear to you—"

"Getting emotional won't solve anything." The lawyer's dry voice was completely uninvolved.

"I ought to fire you," Deke grated. "I never told you to bring up anything like that."

"Still, it's something you should both think about," Jim insisted. "He's too young right now to choose, but the day may come when he decides that he wants to remain with one parent. I think Shannon should sign a paper giving up custody if it turns out to be in the child's best interests. . . . And you too, Deke, naturally," he added as an afterthought, his own conclusions already drawn.

Before Deke could answer, Shannon drew herself up into a tense tower of fury. "Listen to me carefully, both of you, because I'm not going to repeat myself. Michael is my child and I will never give him up." Each word was separate and distinct in spite of her choking anger.

"Believe me, that wasn't—" Jim began.

She didn't let him finish. "I know about all the tricks you lawyers practice, all the fancy jargon—the whereases and to wits—but it won't work. I'll fight you and I'll win!" She turned scornfully to Deke. "Did you honestly think you could buy me off by putting me in your will?"

"Shannon, the only reason I—"

She interrupted him also. "You can take your will and your alimony, and you can set up a fund for homeless chipmunks as far as I'm concerned. All I want is my son. Keep your money. You're going to need it, because if you try to take Mike away from me, you're in for the longest court battle of your life."

Jim remained unruffled. "You're upsetting yourself needlessly, my dear. No one's trying to take advantage of you. I just thought it would be sensible to anticipate all eventualities. If we discuss this calmly and in good faith, there won't be any problems in the future."

"Good faith?" She glared at him in outrage. "Coming from you those sound like dirty words!" Whirling around, she ran from the room.

"Shannon, wait!" Deke called.

Jim stepped in front of him, blocking his path. "Let her go, Deke. She's only bluffing. She doesn't have the money for a court fight. After she's calmed down, she'll realize it and be more amenable to reason."

"Get out of my way, you blithering idiot!" Deke's face was contorted with rage. When the other man tried to restrain him, Deke savagely pushed him aside.

Shannon's headlong rush took her into the hall. Without conscious thought, she reached into the front closet and grabbed her ski jacket. The only thing that penetrated her pain and anger was the need for flight. She had to escape from Deke's house; from his evil, invidious scheming.

By the time Deke disentangled himself from Jim and dashed into the hall, it was empty. Taking the stairs two at a time, he raced up to Shannon's bedroom. Finding that vacant too, he streaked to Mike's room, stopping on the threshold to try to compose himself.

Deke made himself ask the question calmly. "Has your mother been here?"

The little boy had just awakened. He stopped knuckling the sleep out of his eyes when something in his father's voice alerted him. "What's the matter, Daddy?"

"Nothing, son." Deke forced a smile. "I was just looking for Mommy."

The child's face was apprehensive. "What happened to her?"

"Not a thing. She's fine."

In spite of Deke's efforts, his tension was transmitted to the child. "I want Mommy. Where is she?"

"Don't worry, Mike. I'll go get her."

After leaving the room, Deke's pace quickened. He ran down the stairs, noticing for the first time that the front door was slightly ajar.

"Oh, Shannon, where are you?" Deke cried despairingly.

Chapter Nine

Shannon had no objective when she ran out of the house, just a primal urge to run until she dropped. The world around her was colorless. Leaden gray skies; pine trees that looked almost black; dirty, slushy snow underfoot. It was all part of her hopeless mood.

Her mind rejected all conscious thought. Later she would have to think about Deke's duplicity, his betrayal, but not now. She was too wounded at present. In the interest of self-preservation, her mind cut off, mercifully became a blank. Even her body cooperated. Shannon didn't feel the biting cold that seeped inside her down jacket. There were mittens and a knitted cap in her pockets, and she put them on more out of habit than because she felt any discomfort.

When her breathing became labored and she developed a stitch in her side, Shannon slowed down to a trot, still heading away from the chalet. She was grateful not to meet anyone along the way, and when her flight had taken her as far as the lift, Shannon realized why. All the little gondolas were clustered together at the top under a tarpaulin. A chain at the bottom bore a sign: Lift Closed.

It must be one of the many holidays Europe is noted for, Shannon thought indifferently. Turning away she headed down the edge of the smooth slope, concentrating on putting one foot in front of the other. As she trudged through the packed powder, Shannon gradually became aware that it was snowing.

White flakes were floating down like frozen tears. She lifted her face to the gray sky, her own tears starting to flow as she began to function once more. Her numbed mind switched on. Shannon had never been a quitter.

After standing completely still and meditating for a while, she turned back, starting to retrace her steps. Nothing was ever solved by running away. At least all the cards were faceup now. She knew the lengths Deke would go to in order to get his son. But he knew that she wasn't going to be a pushover. She had meant every word she said—she would fight for Michael, and Deke must know it.

The snow was coming down more heavily now, swirling around her like a white shroud. She put her head down against the wind, hurrying her footsteps. Suddenly she collided painfully with a solid object. Putting out her hands to ward off whatever it was, Shannon encountered a tree trunk. Now that she was on top of it, she could see that it was one of the tall firs that dotted the area beyond the piste. But how had she gotten here? She had been walking back up the slope.

Fear started to unwind its ugly coils. She shouldn't be anywhere near the forested area. Wait. Don't panic, Shannon told herself. It was very simple. She had merely veered off to the right. If she walked straight across, she would be back on the slope and headed for home.

Adjusting her direction, Shannon started for what she thought was the ski run. When she bumped into another tree, she fought down rising apprehension. You just wandered deeper off the path than you realized, she told herself. If you don't get excited, you'll find your way out.

The trouble was that she was trapped in a white world that had no top or bottom; there were no boundaries or markers. Shannon was reminded of the game of blind man's bluff, where you were blindfolded and whirled around until you were disoriented. Then the other players called your name, teasing and taunting while you tried to fasten onto something familiar. Why was she thinking about that now? This wasn't a game. Something warned her that she was in a battle for her life.

After wandering about for what seemed like hours, Shannon leaned against a tree, trying to assess the situation calmly. She was lost in a blizzard with very little chance of finding her way out on her own. Hadn't she read somewhere that people in a predicament like this tend to wander around in a circle? Therefore it was pointless to continue. She was only wearing herself out. The deepening snow made every step a major effort. It was nearly knee-deep now, clinging to her legs and holding her back with diabolical determination, almost as though the elements demanded a human sacrifice. . . . No! This was no time to get fanciful, or she would never survive.

Think! Shannon urged herself. It might be fruitless to continue, but she couldn't stay here. The biting cold was stiffening her limbs. Soon she wouldn't be able to move. But which way was the path to safety? *Which way?*

Thrusting her hands deep into her pockets and burying her chin in the collar of her jacket, Shannon tried to still the shudders that were racking her slender body uncontrollably. There was a ski patrol; they would find her. But the lift was closed. They wouldn't expect anyone to be out here on whatever holiday this was. Deke? He wouldn't know where to look for her, either—if he even wanted to.

No, that wasn't fair. In spite of all he had done to her, Shannon knew he would come to her rescue if it were humanly possible. Only it wasn't. She had sealed her own fate. Take care of our son, Deke, Shannon whispered aloud, the sad words dissipating in the rushing wind.

Her hands clenched into little fists inside her pockets as she wondered how long it would take her to die. At least it wouldn't be painful. She had heard that right before you froze to death you felt quite warm. Everything in her being rejected the idea violently. She clutched tightly at something hard, only recognizing it when it bit into her palm: the silver whistle Jeff had given her the day they went skiing.

A stab of hope went through Shannon as she raised it to her frozen lips. It was a one-in-a-million chance, but at least it was a *chance!* After the six short whistle blasts died away she stood very still, listening to find out whether she would live or die. The howling wind was her only answer, gleefully declaring its victory. Shannon tried again—and again and again and again. It was no use. Stubbornly she kept on, no longer expecting a response but defying the elements that held all the odds. She would not go gently.

When the response came, Shannon thought she was imagining it. No, surely those were three blasts! Eagerly she blew her whistle again, and this time there could be no mistaking the answer. Somewhere out there was salvation. The next few minutes were a siren song, with Shannon calling and a will-o'-the-wisp following her direction.

When a tall, dark figure glided out of the white curtain which re-formed in back of him, Shannon's heart leaped into her throat. He was dressed completely in black, from the hood that covered his head to the black gloves on his hands. Had the Prince of Darkness come for her personally? She shrank back as a hoarse cry issued from the apparition's mouth.

"Shannon, thank God I've found you!"

"Deke!" Was she already dead and dreaming?

He gathered her against his hard body and Shannon knew she was alive. Deke held her so tightly that her ribs threatened to crack, but it was an injury she would gladly have sustained. She held onto him just as determinedly, kneading her hands into his parka until she could feel the straining muscles across his back. Questions would come later; right now she needed to be close to him, to absorb some of his strength.

Deke buried his face in her neck, murmuring incoherently. His hand traveled from her shoulder down the length of her arm, wrapped more tightly around her waist, seemed to be trying to reassure him that she was real. Finally his words began to make sense, although they were uttered in broken phrases.

"So worried about you . . . don't ever, *ever* . . . what would I do if anything happened . . ." He pulled himself together with an effort, holding her slightly away so he could look at her. "Are you all right? You're not hurt, are you?"

Her face was so stiff that it hurt to smile, but she did it anyway. "I'm fine now that you're here."

"We've got to get you in out of the cold." Deke's

voice was decisive. He was once more in command of himself. "Put your feet on the backs of my skis and your arms around my waist."

Shannon's original euphoria was fading as she realized the danger they still faced. "We could never get up the hill that way."

"Just do as I say."

"No, Deke, it wouldn't work. It's not going to help matters to have both of us die out here."

His cold lips touched hers briefly. "Neither one of us is going to die, sweetheart. We have too much to live for."

She wanted to believe him. Nothing had ever defeated Deke before, but even he couldn't perform miracles. "You'd better go for help." Shannon tried to keep the terror out of her voice, fear so abject that it threatened to strangle her. "I . . . I don't mind waiting here alone as long as I know help is on the way. It's better than trying to get up the hill and maybe failing."

"We aren't going up. You're right, we'd never make it. We only have a short distance to go—to a shelter not far from here. Now, do what I told you. Put your arms around my waist and try to lean most of your weight against my body."

When she was in position, Deke used his poles to push off while Shannon clung to him for dear life—knowing that was literally true. Their progress was necessarily slow, hampered not only by her added weight on the skis but by the blizzard howling around them.

Although Deke had told her the shelter was not far away, Shannon began to wonder if he'd said it only to comfort her. Time seemed as frozen as the world around them. It had no beginning and no end. Shannon felt as though they had been struggling on for days. The thought even occurred to her that they might not make it.

It didn't carry the terror that had invaded her earlier. Shannon rubbed her cheek against Deke's back, the shifting muscles reassuring her. At least they were together. The momentary pressure of his arm against hers told her he sensed her emotions.

When the dark shape of the shelter loomed up out of the blankness, Shannon was almost afraid that it was a mirage. No, that was only in the desert, wasn't it? That blessed, warm place of sand and sunshine. Shannon recognized dimly that relief was making her lightheaded.

Her arms were locked so tightly around Deke that he had to help her remove them. Then he kicked off his skis quickly, throwing open the door and helping her inside.

"I'll get a fire going. Just hang on, honey. The worst is over," he assured her.

The shelter was a rough one-room shack with a fireplace, a bed heaped with blankets in one corner and a small wooden table and two chairs. On some long shelves were canned goods, a few dented pots and pans and various boxes and cartons of food. Other than a braided rug in front of the fireplace, those were the complete furnishings. It was strictly an emergency shelter, with only the things necessary to sustain life; but it looked like a pasha's palace to Shannon.

Deke was kneeling on the hearth, piling up logs from the well-stocked bin next to the fireplace. He had pushed back his hood, revealing temples that were powdered with snow. As Shannon stared down at him, she had a picture of what he would look like in ten years or so. Deke would be even more handsome and virile than he was now, if that was possible.

He turned to smile at her, the smile fading to concern as he noticed how she was shivering. "Get out of those ski clothes and come close to the fire." After she had done so, he went to the bed and picked up a blanket to wrap her in. His arms tightened for a moment as he held her swathed body in his arms, then he pushed her gently down onto the rug. "You'll be warm in a few minutes."

She nodded wordlessly, gazing up at him with trembling lips.

Deke drew a sharp breath. Jamming his hands in his pockets, he went to sit on the hearth, a careful distance away. "How could you do such a foolhardy thing, Shannon?" he asked in a low voice.

She pulled the blanket down so her arms were free. Holding her cold hands out to the flames, she avoided looking at him. "I just got . . . lost."

"But to run off into a blizzard!" Words failed him.

"It wasn't snowing when I . . . when I left."

"I didn't even know you'd gone out. I looked all through the house first."

"How did you find me, Deke?" Shannon recognized it for the miracle it was.

"When I realized you'd actually gone out in this weather, I came after you. The only trouble was that I went up in the hills above the chalet first. That's what delayed me. When you weren't there, I thought of the slopes. It didn't seem possible that you'd come here, but it was the only other place I could think of. *Why*, Shannon? Why in God's name?"

"I didn't know there was a holiday this close to Christmas," she said defensively.

"What are you talking about?"

"The ski lift was closed. I assumed it was because of a holiday."

Deke groaned. "It was closed because of the blizzard. The weather bureau warned that a storm was coming, so nobody was allowed out on the slopes."

"I didn't know," she said in a very small voice.

Deke mustered a smile to cover the anxiety that had carved deep lines in his tanned face. "Well, you're safe now; that's all that matters."

The trouble was, it *wasn't* all that mattered. It's funny how imminent tragedy can make everything else seem unimportant, Shannon reflected. Yet when the crisis was passed, existing problems re turned to assume their former status.

The fact remained that Deke had tried to do an underhanded, devious thing to her. He was seeking to wrest custody of Michael from her, and that was something she would never permit. It was going to be awkward to bring it up right now on the heels of his saving her life, but the one thing really had nothing to do with the other. And nothing would be gained by postponing the confrontation. At least the ordeal she had been through had sobered her.

Shannon set her trembling chin firmly. "Deke, we have to talk."

"Why don't I make us some coffee first? It will help thaw us both out."

Shannon hesitated. Actually she was dying for a cup of coffee, and a couple of minutes more wouldn't matter. She started to unwind the blanket. "All right, I'll make some."

He pressed her back firmly, securing the covering once more. "I said I'd do it. You stay right where you are."

She looked at him in amazement. "You've never done anything in a kitchen in your whole life."

"Then it's time I started, isn't it?" He smiled. "I'm not getting any younger."

She watched as he filled the battered coffee pot with water, but when he started to pour in coffee directly from the can, she stopped him. "Wait! You don't pour it in the water, you put it in that little basket. And you measure it."

He looked surprised. "Does it make a difference?"

"Of course it does." Shannon struggled to her feet. "Deke, please let me do it."

He surrendered the pot reluctantly. "You could tell me how."

"I don't feel up to a lesson on cooking right now," she said crisply.

He watched her deft movements with admiration. "You really do know how to cook, don't you?"

She laughed, the first natural laugh since this whole nightmare started. "Making coffee is scarcely a *cordon bleu* effort. More than ninety-nine percent of the population know how to do it. The remaining one percent encompasses people who don't drink the stuff and rich men like you who have always had someone to do it for them."

"You could teach me."

Her hands stilled momentarily. "That would be a switch, wouldn't it? Me teaching *you* something."

"I would be willing to learn, Shannon." His eyes held hers for a long moment, Shannon's falling first.

Once more she was confused. Had she ever met Deke halfway? Or had her dependency been her own fault? A willingness to accept the strength he offered and a reluctance to give anything but her body in return?

"Let's have something to eat," Deke said casually, sensing her tension and seeking to dispel it. "I'm starving. Playing hero is hungry work."

Shannon turned gratefully to the shelf of food. "Well, let's see. You have a gourmet choice of beans and Vienna sausages or canned spaghetti."

"Beans and franks, by all means."

While Shannon opened the cans and emptied their contents into a saucepan, Deke set the table. Since it was completely dark outside now, he lit a number of candles, putting them into saucers and distributing them around the room. The small cabin took on a festive air, aided by the dancing red and gold flames from the fireplace.

Shannon hadn't realized how hungry she was or how satisfying a simple meal could be. "I certainly hope my clients don't ever discover that hot dogs can be as delicious as caviar or smoked salmon."

Deke regarded her steadily. "You really enjoy your work, don't you, Shannon?"

"Yes, I honestly do. Of course it has its bad moments, but cooking is rather creative. The mixed blessing is that people consume your masterpieces. I wonder how Picasso would have handled that," she said, laughing.

Deke continued to regard her with an impassive gaze. "You should have told me that you felt a lack in your life."

"I didn't know it," she said simply.

"You know I would have helped you to accomplish whatever you had your heart set on."

She fiddled with her spoon, unable to look into his searching eyes. "It means more because I accomplished it all by myself."

"That's very important to you, isn't it, Shannon?"

She looked up then, knowing that this was the time for absolute truth. "Try to understand, Deke. I was so young when I married you, and you must admit you were pretty overpowering. You were older, rich, successful. I couldn't imagine why you married me."

"Oh, my darling—"

"No, let me finish," she said in a little rush. "I was both immature and insecure. I loved you wildly,

Deke, and I was terrified of losing you. But a little part of me resented your dominance. I didn't want to be the child you took care of, I wanted to be the woman you were in love with."

The candlelight was reflected in his eyes, turning them molten. "Didn't I treat you like a woman?"

"Only in bed."

"I'm sorry, Shannon. I never realized." His warm hand covered hers.

"I know." She sighed. "I don't blame you anymore, Deke. I see now that it wasn't anybody's fault. It's just the way it happened."

A log broke in the fireplace, sending up a shower of orange sparks. While Deke went to tend the fire, Shannon removed their dishes. When he returned, looking at her with an unfathomable expression, her nerves tightened. The full import of their situation dawned on her. They were marooned here together for the night, two people who had once loved each other—one of whom still did. Shannon knew how vulnerable she was to this man. She must rally all of her defenses against him.

Turning to the food shelf, she selected a package of cookies. "How about a Peanut Fudgie for dessert?" she asked brightly. "Not exactly *gateau Saint-Honore*, but a lot less trouble. The little elves at Mama's Cookie Factory whipped these up."

"Shannon." Deke's warm hands fastened gently on her shoulders.

Moving deftly away, she sat down at the table. "I'm sorry I can't offer you a pony of Napoleon brandy, which is what these cry out for."

He accepted her rejection with good grace, entering her mood with ease. "I don't mind; it was the absence of wine with dinner that disturbed me."

"You're so right. We should have had a nice zinfandel, or perhaps a Petite Sirah. Something that made a statement without being too audaciously bold."

Deke nodded his head consideringly. "Witty, yet not presumptuous."

They both laughed at the pretentious language used by all too many wine connoisseurs. Then their eyes met and the laughter died.

Deke captured her hand. "There's so much we have to discuss, Shannon."

Shannon drew a shuddering breath "One thing, Deke—Michael."

He sat back in his chair, his eyes narrowing. "Don't you think we have something even more important to settle first?"

"That's the difference between a mother and a father."

Deke sighed. "All right, Shannon. We'll do it your way."

Her voice shook with intensity. "How could you, Deke? How could you try to take Michael away from me completely?"

"Do you really think I would do a thing like that?"

"You can't deny it after the things your . . . your stooge said to me."

"I never told him to discuss anything but the will."

"*I don't believe you!*"

His face paled. "I'm sorry to hear that."

Shannon refused to be softened by compunction. "If the situation were reversed, you'd feel exactly as I do."

"No, Shannon," he said softly, "that's where you're wrong. I would never credit you with a deliberate act of cruelty." His clear eyes were regarding her steadily.

She wouldn't back down. "Then you admit it was cruel."

Deke's mouth tightened. "I asked Jim to be

present at that little conference because it's important that you know the terms of my will in case anything should happen to me."

The idea made Shannon even colder than she had been in the snow. "Don't be silly," she snapped. "You're a young man."

"Accidents occur." He shrugged. A hint of laughter curved his firm mouth. "If I should come to a bad end as you perhaps expect, I want you to know that you and Mike are taken care of. Just in case you're breaking your back to keep up a college annuity for him or something like that."

"It's understandable that you provided for Michael, but there's no reason to include me," she faltered.

He started to say something, then checked himself. "I have no one else to leave it to," he said carelessly.

The money meant nothing to her, but it was shocking even to think of a world without Deke. Shannon sprang to her feet and began pacing nervously. "All of this is beside the point. What we have to settle between us is that damn paper Jim wanted me to sign. There isn't enough money in the world to make me do it! With that in your hot little hand you could convince any judge to give you full custody. After all, how can a mere mother be as beneficial as a swimming pool and a pony and a mansion in Beverly Hills?" As her agitation increased, Shannon twisted her slim fingers together.

Deke watched her silently, his face an expressionless mask.

"Well, aren't you going to deny it?" she demanded. "Aren't you going to say something?"

"Not until you get it all out of your system."

"I never will! Oh, Deke, how can you do this to me?" Her voice broke.

He stood up then, taking her in his arms and holding onto her when she tried to struggle away. "Shannon, I don't want to take anything away from you. I want to give you things, but you won't accept them."

"Bribes," she said scornfully, trying to sustain her anger. Deke's circling arms were sapping her strength.

His hand tangled in her long, black hair, pulling her head back so he could stare down into her eyes. "You don't really believe that."

"How can I help it?"

Deke's warm mouth touched the soft skin just below her ear. "Because you know I would never willingly hurt you," he murmured.

Shannon tried to hold him off, but she found that her hands were spreading across his shirt front, feeling the hardness of his chest. "You have before," she whispered.

His lips traveled down the white column of her neck, pausing to kiss the pulse that was thundering in the hollow of her throat. "Never on purpose. If you had only told me, Shannon. If we had only talked things out."

His drugging kisses were drawing the very soul from her body. "It's too late for that now," she gasped.

"Is it, darling?" His eyes held hers hypnotically as he drew her slowly closer, molding her hips to his, her entire body to his lean length.

A flame of desire enveloped Shannon, sending a shudder through her. Deke pressed his advantage, curling his hand around her breast, his fingers going unerringly to the hardened nipple. When his mouth covered hers, Shannon's lips parted helplessly, allowing him to invade her.

"This is all I want to take from you, my love." His

breath mingled with hers as he lifted his head a fraction, his lips sliding tantalizingly over hers in a feathery caress.

He moved his body sensually, their thighs joining and parting. She could feel the hard thrust of his desire, and her body flamed into answering passion. When his hand slipped under her sweater, smoothing her silky skin, Shannon moaned in mingled ecstasy and protest. She mustn't let him do this to her. Deke could seduce not only her body, but her will. In another minute she would be completely his, welcoming him into her very soul.

With a violent shudder, Shannon tore herself out of Deke's arms. She turned her back on him, staring into the fire and fighting down the answering flames within.

"I know what you're trying to do, and it won't work." Her breathing was labored.

"I think it's obvious what I'm trying to do." He chuckled, a low male sound of triumph. "I want to make love to you."

Shannon clenched her fists hard, hoping the pain of her raking nails would counteract the waves of desire that were turning her liquid inside. "You'll do anything to get your own way, won't you?"

"It isn't a hardship," he teased.

Before she could move, Deke came up in back of her, drawing her against his rangy body. His arms went around her waist and his hands spread out over her flat stomach, touching, caressing, moving down to the juncture of her thighs. When she drew a gasping breath and made a frantic grab for his hands, they moved to cup her breasts. His palms slowly outlined their round firmness, his fingers capturing the pointed tips that traitorously longed for unveiled contact.

"Stop it, Deke," she moaned.

Obediently his hands dropped to her waist, but only to grasp the edge of her sweater. He drew it over her head and Shannon raised her arms to help him, giving up the struggle. How could she deny the raw need that reduced her body to a demanding void screaming for fulfillment?

After removing her bra Deke turned her in his arms, his eyes brilliant. "Let me look at you, my love. I can never get enough of your beautiful body."

He lowered her gently to the rug, lying down beside her and feasting his eyes on her loveliness. His fingertips trailed feather-light caresses from her collarbone to her navel, which he bent to kiss. Shannon twined her fingers in his crisp hair, drawing his head up to hers. His mouth left a fiery path as it traveled up her flawless skin, stoking the passions underneath. He stopped to kiss each rose-tipped breast, touching the peak with his tongue until she arched her body with delight.

"That's right, darling, give in to it." Deke's eyes were a blaze of green and gold. "Tell me how much you want me. I have to hear you say it."

She moved against him in mindless delight. "I need you, Deke, more than I've ever needed anyone." Shannon no longer cared that she was baring her soul. It was true. If he didn't make love to her soon, she would surely be consumed by the urgent desire he had aroused.

Her fingers fumbled in their haste to unfasten his shirt. She wanted to touch that splendid male body, to feel his hair-roughened chest pressed against her. Deke's desire equaled Shannon's. Tearing off his shirt he clasped her in his arms, groaning in satisfaction at the inexpressible feeling. Raining kisses over her face and neck, he murmured tender endearments.

When he had built her tension almost to the breaking point, Deke slowly removed her slacks. Shannon shifted her legs to help him, shuddering as his hand lingeringly caressed the soft skin of her inner thigh. He stooped to kiss the spot before quickly stripping off the rest of his clothes. In the light from the fire his body gleamed like that of a Greek god, perfectly formed and dominantly masculine. Shannon's breath caught in her throat, and she held out her arms to him.

Deke's possession was fierce and yet gentle, meeting a like reception in Shannon. Their bodies fought a duel that they both would win. They advanced and retreated until the ecstasy was too exquisite to be borne, and then they were propelled to the very summit of sensation.

Shannon was wrapped in a mantle of peace as she slowly made the descent to earth, cradled in Deke's arms. She turned her head, putting her lips against the bronzed column of his throat, totally fulfilled by the man she loved.

"Sweet Shannon," he sighed. "I've missed you so."

She awoke sometime in the middle of the night to find herself in bed, her body fitted to the contours of Deke's. He must have carried her there after she fell asleep. In the dying embers from the fire she studied his face, its strength apparent even when he was asleep and vulnerable. His chiseled mouth was relaxed without being slack, those all-seeing eyes covered by thick, black lashes that lay on his high cheekbones.

There was no doubt that she loved this man passionately and completely, but that didn't solve any of the problems between them. He would always be able to talk her into his bed because that was where she wanted to be. There was only one thing he would never talk her out of. Was Deke really scheming to take her son away? Or should she believe him when he said he would never willingly hurt her? She wanted so desperately to believe him, but it was such a risk. The old doubts reared their disquieting heads, and Shannon shifted uneasily, trying to move out of Deke's arms so she could think rationally.

His eyes opened at her first movements and his arms tightened. "Where do you think you're going, woman?" he growled.

"I . . . I didn't mean to disturb you."

"It's too late for that." He nibbled delicately on her ear. "You bother me when you're done up to the eyebrows in a ski suit and goggles, so how do you think I feel when your deliciously nude body is snuggled up against mine?"

"You know what I meant," she muttered.

"And you know what *I* mean," he teased.

His fingertips trailed lightly down her back to the base of her spine. Shannon involuntarily arched her body into his, then recoiled from the intimate contact. "Deke, stop it!"

"You used to like it." He trapped her legs with one of his, drawing her close enough to feel the heat he was generating.

"I still—I mean, I can't think when you do that."

"It isn't required," he murmured wickedly.

She brought her knees up, levering her body a blessed few inches from his. "This didn't change anything, Deke. We still have to have a talk."

"Now?" He couldn't believe she was serious.

"It's as good a time as any."

"I can prove you're wrong." His fingertips traced a sensuous pattern on the soft skin of her thigh.

Shannon forced herself not to react. "I don't deny that you can distract me, but you can't put me off forever."

Deke sighed deeply. "All right, Shannon, what is it you want to talk about—as if I didn't know."

"I want your assurance that you won't try to lure Mike away from me."

"What good would that do? You don't believe anything I say anyway."

"Well, you could . . . I don't know . . . yes, I do! You could sign a paper, like you wanted me to do."

"All right."

His capitulation without any argument came as a surprise. It was so easy that Shannon had a sudden inspiration, an idea that came to her out of the blue. Hiding her inner excitement, she put her arms around his neck, snuggling close and twining her fingers in the dark hair that covered his chest. "Thank you, darling, I knew you'd be reasonable." She bent her head to trail her lips across his shoulder, missing the sardonic look in his eyes.

"I aim to please."

"I know. You've always been so good to me." Her hand disappeared under the covers, touching him with quick fluttery motions. "You didn't realize how much it would hurt me to give up Mike for six months out of the year."

"You think it would be more equitable if you kept him full-time and I just visited when I can?" His judicious voice sounded as if he were considering it.

Triumph flooded Shannon. She had to fight to keep her exultation from shining through. "It would be less upsetting for Mike, at least for the next few years," she murmured, even managing to sound faintly regretful. As a consolation she slid her leg between his, letting her breast rest enticingly against his arm.

"Tell me, Shannon, exactly what is the difference between what you're doing now and what you accused me of trying to do to you?" His crisp words were like a pitcher of cold water over her.

"Wha . . . what? I don't know what you mean."

"You're trying to seduce me to get what you want. But when you thought I was doing the same thing, it made me a monster." She looked at him with shamed comprehension as Deke continued inexorably. "I love my son, Shannon, no matter what you think. I'm willing to share him, but I'm not willing to give him up. I missed the first four years of his life. That can't be helped, but at least I'm going to be part of the rest of it."

She had drawn away as each word seemed to batter her shrinking flesh. Deke was right. What she had tried to do was unconscionable. "I'm sorry," she murmured.

"Do you expect me to believe you?"

Her startled eyes flew to his stern face. "I didn't really mean to keep him away from you," she pleaded.

"That's what I told *you*, but you weren't willing to give me the benefit of the doubt."

Shannon's eyelashes swept her flushed cheeks. "I see what you mean. I guess if they had a prize for jumping to conclusions, I'd make the longest leap." She started to get out of bed. "I don't blame you for hating me."

"I wouldn't go that far." His hand fastened around her wrist, drawing her back. Wrapping his arms around her, he rolled her beneath him, pinning her to the bed with his hard length. "It was just an object lesson, sweetheart. Do you think someday you might learn to trust me?"

Deke's mouth closed over hers before she could reply, his kiss deepening as his body quickened at her fervent response. Nothing could stem the tide of feeling that always rose up in answer to his slightest touch, no matter what had gone before. Shannon moved in throbbing pleasure beneath him, all conscious thought suspended before the magic this man could weave, the total engagement of all her senses. The driving force of his passion carried her to uncharted heights. Shannon clung to him while they rode the wild storm together and returned to earth in each other's arms.

In the calm that followed, Deke stroked her cheek gently. "We could make a go of it this time, Shannon," he murmured.

"Do you really think so?" she whispered wistfully.

"I really do. This time we have something extra going for us—We have Mike." He kissed the tip of her nose. "We both care about him, and we both know he'd be better off living in one place with two parents. How about it, Shannon?"

"I . . . I'll think about it."

Long after Deke had fallen asleep with his head on her breast, Shannon mulled it over. If only Deke had said, Marry me, Shannon, I love you so much I can't live without you. But he hadn't. His major argument was that it would be good for Michael. She ought to be glad, but her heart cried out for his love, not just his passion, and concern for his son. Looking down at Deke's beloved face, she wondered if she could settle for that. The alternative was so terrible that she didn't even want to think about it. With a deep, shuddering sigh, Shannon closed her eyes.

Chapter Ten

It was cold in the cabin when Shannon awoke the next morning. She groped for Deke's comforting warmth, feeling desolate when she found herself alone in bed. She sat bolt upright, tortured by the thought that last night had been all a dream. When she saw Deke kneeling before the fireplace, Shannon relaxed.

"Good morning, lover." Deke looked up and smiled. "Stay in bed until I get the fire going. I'll have it warm for you in a jiffy."

She hugged her knees under the covers, watching his deft movements. In his hip-hugging black pants and dark shirt, he looked very lean and masculine.

When the flames were leaping merrily, he came over to sit on the edge of the bed. "How do you feel this morning?"

"I feel wonderful." Her eyes met his steadily in spite of the flush that colored her cheeks.

"Me too," he murmured, his hand moving under the covers to caress her sleep-warm body. "With the slightest encouragement I could take off my clothes and get back in bed with you."

It was a temptation that Shannon resisted reluctantly. "Now that it's daylight, won't someone be coming to rescue us?"

"Don't you think it's too late for anyone to rescue you?" He chuckled, kissing the sensitive spot at the back of her neck.

She shivered deliciously, reaching up to tug at his hair. "Don't be a cad. A gentleman never reminds a lady of the previous night's dalliance."

"Then I'm no gentleman, because I'm going to remind you of it often—and graphically."

She peered provocatively through long lashes. "Is that a threat or a promise?"

His eyes darkened with emotion. "Very definitely a promise. One that I'm going to fulfill right now."

As he pressed her back against the pillows and her arms went around his neck, there was a shout in the distance. Giving her a rueful look, Deke went to the door as Shannon started to scramble into her clothes.

Snow from last night's blizzard was piled high against the front door, making it impossible to open from the inside. After a few tries Deke went to the window to look out. The skies were still leaden but the snow had stopped. Three men in full ski equipment with first-aid kits strapped around their waists were approaching the cabin.

"Here comes the ski patrol." Deke turned toward Shannon with a twisted smile. "The honeymoon is over, love."

It *had* been like a honeymoon. Shannon was reluctant to leave this place where she had experienced such bliss. The outside world didn't exist for those enchanted hours. She could pretend that everything was the same as it was in the very beginning when she was the most important thing in

Deke's life. Would she ever be again? A premonition of disaster lifted the hairs on the back of Shannon's neck.

The men were pounding on the door now. "Anybody in there?"

After Deke's answering hail, there was the sound of digging. In a short time the door was forced open and they were back in the everyday world. While Deke banked the fire, Shannon folded the blankets and straightened the room. Just before the door closed behind them, she swept the cabin with a wistful look. As though he understood, Deke's arm went around her and he squeezed her shoulder.

The ski patrol had brought a toboggan, standard procedure in case anyone was injured. Shannon was tucked under blankets, and the trip back was accomplished with ease.

Someone must have been keeping vigil at the window, because when they approached the chalet, the door flew open. After that there was utter chaos.

Everyone crowded around them, all talking at once, but Stephanie's reaction was the most violent. She was almost hysterical. Elbowing the others out of the way, she threw her arms around Deke, laughing and crying at the same time.

"Deke, you're safe! I can't believe it! I was so worried."

One arm circled her waist while he patted her back reassuringly. "There was nothing to worry about, honey."

"How can you say that? You were gone all night and I was going out of my mind imagining the worst."

"You know you can't get rid of me that easily," Deke said fondly. "It takes a lot more than a blizzard to do me in."

Shannon felt a chill that had nothing to do with the temperature. They might have been long-lost lovers, meeting after an unbearable separation. Everybody else in the room seemed to be forgotten.

"Don't joke about it, Deke." Stephanie's arms tightened around his neck and she started to tremble.

"We were all pretty worried," Rustin said gravely.

"What actually happened?" Marlee asked. "When we got back from the movies, all we could find out was that you went out."

"I'm sorry everyone was upset," Deke answered.

"Naturally we were." The situation had even been grave enough to get Helene out of bed. She was hovering disapprovingly, dressed in a quilted satin bathrobe. Every now and then she dabbed delicately at her nose with a tissue, as though to remind the assemblage that she had gotten out of a sickbed. "It was really quite thoughtless of you to stay out all night without letting us know." Her eyes flicked to Shannon and then away.

Stephanie turned on her mother like a virago. "Don't you understand anything? Deke could have been injured. He could have been lying out there freezing to death and nobody was doing anything about it."

Helene looked taken aback. "Well, really, we—"

"I tried to get them to go look for you but they wouldn't," the young girl cried passionately.

"There was nothing they could do in the darkness," Deke soothed.

"They could have *tried!*" Tears streamed down her pale cheeks. "You don't know what I went through."

"Hey, calm down, little one. I'm here now, safe and sound."

"Oh, Deke, if anything had happened to you I would have died." Sobs racked her slender body and Deke tightened his hold, murmuring comforting words.

Shannon retreated until her back was against the door. The poignant scene being enacted before them was all too revealing. In the drama of the moment, Deke had forgotten her very existence.

"I think the child ought to go upstairs and lie down," Jim said. He had been on the fringes looking on.

"No!" Stephanie clung like a limpet. "Don't leave me, Deke. I want to be sure you're really here."

"Don't worry, honey, I'm the most substantial ghost you'll ever come across." He lifted her easily into his arms, smiling down at her. "Come on, let's put you to bed."

Some of the tension went out of the room with their departure.

Marlee came over to Shannon. "Poor Shannon, with all the racket Steffy was making, no one even got a chance to ask if you were all right."

"I'm fine," she answered steadily.

Noting the pinched look on her face, Rustin commented, "You look like you could use some rest, too. Why don't you scoot upstairs to bed?"

"Nobody actually said what happened." Helene was regarding Shannon suspiciously.

"Explanations can wait," Rustin said sharply.

Jim took the hint, taking his wife by the arm and leading her away.

"Can we do anything for you, Shannon?" Rustin asked. "Do you want Marlee to go up with you?"

She gave him a wan smile. "No thanks. Fortunately, I'm ambulatory."

That produced an awkward moment. Shannon

had only meant to reassure the Stevensons, not allude to Deke's carrying Stephanie up the stairs. After a moment's hesitation they both left her alone. Only then did Shannon notice Jeff watching her with concern. He had been a witness to the whole traumatic scene, although he had taken no part in it. Now he came toward her.

"You look a little dazed, Shannon. Would you like to talk about it?"

"There's nothing to talk about. We got lost in the blizzard, Deke found a shelter, and we had to wait until morning for them to dig us out." She carefully avoided any further details.

Jeff left it at that, giving her a reassuring smile. "I told them not to worry. If you were with Deke you'd be okay."

"They weren't worried about *me.*"

"Oh, come on, Shannon. Of course we were."

"Stephanie too?" she asked sardonically.

"Well, she can be a little dramatic. But I will admit she was scared silly. You know how she feels about Deke."

"And now we all know how he feels about her."

Jeff gave her a startled look. "Surely you aren't suggesting—"

"It's all right," Shannon cut in. "Deke is a free agent; he doesn't have to answer to me for his actions. Actually, he never did," she added bitterly.

"You're jumping to all the wrong conclusions, honestly you are. Steffy overreacts a good part of the time. That's what she was doing this morning, and when she gets that way Deke indulges her."

Shannon regarded him steadily. "Which one of us are you trying to convince?"

The first shadow of uncertainty entered his face. "It couldn't be," he murmured, almost to himself.

How could there be any doubt? The way Deke gathered the girl in his arms, the look on his face as he smiled down at her . . .

Suddenly Shannon felt inexpressibly weary. "For Deke's sake I hope Stephanie isn't merely in love with love," Shannon said wistfully.

"That's what I've always—" Jeff broke off abruptly. "You've been through an ordeal, Shannon. Why don't you put it all out of your mind for now?"

"Everything will look better in the morning, you mean? It *is* morning." She gave a deep sigh. Jeff meant well, he just didn't know what he was talking about. "You're right though. I am tired. I think I'll go up and take a hot bath."

As Shannon went up the stairs she thought to herself, It isn't morning, it's midnight. The bell has tolled for Cinderella and the prince has gone back to his princess. He had made his choice in front of everyone.

"Mommy!" Michael's drawn-out wail carried a note of alarm.

Shannon was smitten with guilt. She should have gone to him long ago. "I'm coming, darling."

He threw his arms around her neck, his small body trembling. "Where have you been?"

She rocked him in her arms, smoothing his hair gently. "I'm here now, baby."

"I called you and you didn't come, and Daddy didn't come either."

"I know," she soothed. "We . . . we had to go someplace."

He turned reproachful, tear-filled eyes on her. "I was scared, Mommy."

"There was nothing to be afraid of, darling. Remember when Daddy and I went to Zurich for the day? You weren't frightened then, were you?"

"N . . . no." He sounded doubtful, aware that there was a difference, yet unable in his child's mind to pinpoint it.

"Well, there you are." Shannon gave him a bright smile.

His clear eyes were still troubled. "Why was Steffy crying?"

Shannon realized he was feeling all the tension in the house. It presented her with a dilemma. She had always answered his questions honestly, but how could she explain what had happened without making him more insecure?

Choosing her words carefully, Shannon said, "Stephanie stayed up all night. This morning she was very tired and she didn't feel well."

"Did her Mommy punish her?" Mike asked gravely.

"Not exactly." Bitter, hurtful laughter welled up in Shannon's throat. Far from being punished, Stephanie was being rewarded for her vigil. Was Deke still sitting by her bed comforting her—or was he lying alongside her? Shannon closed her mind to the painful thought. "Stephanie has to stay in bed today just like you."

That distracted him. With his mother beside him, safety had been restored to his world. "I can get up tomorrow," Mike said gleefully. "It's Christmas Eve and I get to trim the tree and hang up my stocking for Santa Claus and everything."

Christmas had never seemed bleaker to Shannon, but she mustered a smile. "That's right. You've been a very good boy and I'm sure Santa Claus will be pleased."

His eyes went past her to the door. "Daddy, do you know what day tomorrow is?"

"I sure do, son." Deke's hand rested lightly on Shannon's shoulder.

Twisting deftly away she slipped off the bed, going to stand by the window.

"Can we go out in the woods and chop down a tree the way you promised?" the small boy asked excitedly.

"You bet." Deke's voice was abstracted, his eyes on Shannon.

"Will you come with us, Mommy?"

She turned then, her smile strained. "I think not, that's man's work."

Michael nodded importantly. "Me and Daddy can do it all by ourselves."

"Daddy and I," she murmured automatically, conscious of Deke's eyes probing her face.

"Is anything wrong, Shannon?" he asked. "Don't you feel well?"

"I'm fine," she answered coolly.

He cupped her chin in his long fingers, forcing her to look at him. "Don't try to kid me. I know when something's bothering you."

She pulled away, angry that his touch could still make her pulse race. "Your concern is somewhat belated."

Deke frowned. "What do you mean?"

"Shouldn't you be with Stephanie? She might wake up and have hysterics again if you're not there holding her hand."

He gazed at her impassively. "I should think you'd have a little compassion. The poor kid was a nervous wreck."

"So I noticed."

A muscle worked at the point of Deke's jaw, but he kept his voice even. "All right, so maybe Steffy does overdo it a bit. What was I supposed to do?"

"Exactly what you did. I thought it was very romantic the way you carried her up the stairs. The poor thing could never have made them on her own." Shannon was appalled to hear the shrewish things that were coming out of her mouth, but a core of anger deep inside was driving her on.

"Shannon, even you can't—" Deke's furious words ground to a halt as he became conscious of Mike watching them with big, round eyes. Clamping his hand around her wrist, he turned to his son with a smile that was more like a grimace. "Mommy and I need to have a talk, Mike. We'll be back a little later."

His fingers were as tight as a handcuff, resisting all of Shannon's efforts to break his grip. Shoving open her bedroom door, he pushed her inside, slamming the door in back of them.

"Okay, what's this all about?" he demanded tightly.

"You have no right to drag me around like a slave girl. Let go of me and get out of my room!"

"Not until you tell me why you're acting this way. And just in passing let me say that after spending the night in my arms, this touch-me-not attitude of yours is a little ludicrous, to say the least."

"How dare you!" She clenched her fists. "I should think you'd be ashamed to remind me of last night."

His equally angry face glared down at her. "Are you trying to imply that I forced myself on you?"

She couldn't quite accuse him of that, but Shannon refused to back down. "You seduced me and that's the same thing. You made love to me against my will."

"Both times?" he asked derisively.

Her eyes fell before his mocking laughter. "I don't want to talk about it. Please go."

"Not on your life! We're going to thrash this thing out here and now. It's Cynthia Darby all over again."

"You have a lot of nerve to bring *her* up!"

Deke raked impatient fingers through his thick, dark hair. "I will never understand this irrational jealousy of yours."

"You flatter yourself. Maybe I was jealous once, but that was light years ago. I no longer have the slightest interest in what you do—or with whom you do it."

"I can scarcely believe it." Deke shook his head. "All of this because of an excitable kid."

Shannon gritted her teeth. "I don't want to hear any more about suffering Stephanie. I can't really get worked up over her Victorian vapors, but since you obviously can, I suggest you go back to her."

Deke's eyes narrowed dangerously. "Maybe I'll do exactly that."

"Good! I wish you would, because I've had about as much of your company as I can take." All of her anger and misery combined into a tight knot in Shannon's stomach. She looked for something that would hurt him as much as he had hurt her. "To put it bluntly, your manly charms no longer turn me on."

His smile was unpleasant. "Are you sure about that?"

"Would you like me to have it notarized?" she flared.

His arm snaked around her waist, drawing her against his hard body.

Shannon's defenses came up immediately. "What do you think you're doing?"

"Just proving a point."

His head came down and his mouth took possession of hers in a kiss that was punishing. Shannon gave a small moan as her teeth were ground against her lip. She struggled, but Deke's grip was inexorable. His body savaged hers in the same way as his mouth. Grinding her hips against his, he made her aware of every hard masculine muscle and bone. Still she resisted. Her lips were tightly clamped together, resisting the onslaught of his tongue.

Suddenly he changed tactics. The hand holding her head moved to her neck, gently massaging the taut muscles. He lessened the bruising pressure of his mouth, tracing the outline of hers with his tongue. When she turned her head he explored the intricate curves of her ear, breathing warmth that invaded her whole body.

Shannon drew in her breath, turning her head back in an effort to escape the blatant sensuality of his mouth; and Deke took the opportunity to enter her parted lips. It was a sexual encounter such as she had never experienced—suggestive, promising, arousing. She trembled in his arms, clutching at his shoulders in an attempt at sanity that gradually slipped away.

His hands slid slowly down her back, pressing her breasts against his chest, then moving down to mold her hips against the juncture of his thighs. A current of electricity charged Shannon's body, arching it into his in a desperate need for more intimate contact. Her arms went around Deke's neck and her eager fingers combed through his hair, tracing the perfect shape of his head.

He moved against her in a slow, circular motion. "Tell me again that I don't appeal to you."

She didn't even hear him. Her lips were pressed against his throat, her fingers moving blindly to the buttons of his shirt. When Deke's hand covered hers, staying her motions, she looked blindly up at him.

He repeated his request, adding, "Although I warn you, I'll find it difficult to believe."

Her eyes focused slowly as his mocking words

registered. Shannon's heated blood chilled and a long shudder passed through her body. Pulling herself out of his unresisting grasp, she stared at him. How could he do a thing like this to her?

"Get out," she whispered. "Get out and stay out."

Deke raised a sardonic eyebrow. "Your every wish is my command." He paused at the door, sweeping her with an insulting look. "If you should change your mind and have need of my . . . services . . . you can ask Stephanie where to find me."

After the door had closed softly after him Shannon started to tremble uncontrollably. Wrapping her arms tightly around herself, she leaned her forehead against the wall. "Damn you, Deke Masterson," she groaned. "Damn you to eternal hell fire!"

After a long time Shannon went into the bathroom and ran a steaming tub. Her whole body ached as though she had been running for a long time. The hot water gradually eased her tension, but nothing could erase her degradation.

How could she even have considered marrying this man—because that was what she had decided in the small hours of the morning. It was bitterly ironic. After she had ironed out all her doubts about their past relationship and faced the future with such bright hopes, she had lost him to another woman. Deke couldn't be that cruel if he cared anything at all about her. That practiced assault on her emotions was unforgivable.

Shannon tried to summon up the energy to hate him, but she was too exhausted. She crawled into bed, emotionally and physically drained.

It was late afternoon when she awoke. Looking at the clock, she couldn't believe the time. Not that there was really anything she had to do except get through each remaining day. Maybe now Deke would let her go home after Christmas.

With a sigh Shannon got out of bed, shivering after the warmth of the covers. Going to the closet, she took out a blue velvet caftan, the color of her eyes. It had gold braid around the wide sleeves and long hem. After drawing a brush through her silken hair and putting a bit of pink gloss on her soft mouth, Shannon lifted her head proudly. If Deke thought she was going to slink around like some broken little reed, he was mistaken.

She went first to Michael's room, surprised to find Gretel's husband, Paul, there. He and the little boy had their heads together over something.

When he spied her, Mike said, "Paul is making me a billy goat."

"Mr. Biedermann," Shannon reproved gently.

"He *told* me to call him Paul."

"It is true. We are not formal here," the caretaker said.

"Then I think 'Uncle Paul' would be better, don't you?" Shannon asked. She was rewarded by a flashing smile from the older man.

"Oh yes, I like that," Mike cried. "Look what Uncle Paul is making me."

There was a piece of newspaper on the bed to catch the scraps from a block of wood Paul was using to whittle out a small figure. Shannon was appropriately admiring, standing over them to watch for a while. They were too absorbed to notice her, so after a short time she quietly left.

Shannon wandered downstairs feeling tense and jumpy, afraid that she would run into Deke. It was an occurrence to be avoided like the plague, yet she refused to give him the satisfaction of thinking she was sulking in her room.

The downstairs was quiet except for some sounds from the kitchen, but Shannon didn't feel like a cozy chat with Gretel right now. If the older woman chose to extol Deke's virtues again, Shannon wasn't sure that this time she could manage to be polite.

The late afternoon twilight had fallen, filling the large, deserted living room with shadows. It was depressing, although the ever-present fire was crackling on the hearth. Shannon picked up a magazine that had been left on the couch that faced the fireplace with its back to the room. Lying down with a pillow under her head, she began to leaf listlessly through the pages. At the sound of voices in the hall, she lifted her head, hoping it was Rustin and Marlee.

When she heard Stephanie's clear tones Shannon's jaw clenched. But before she could get up and leave, she realized it would be awkward. Jeff was with her and they were evidently having a heated argument. Stephanie's voice was raised in anger.

"You have a lot of nerve saying a thing like that to me, Jeff Collins!"

"I notice you aren't denying it," he said grimly.

"I wouldn't give it that dignity."

"That's a cop-out and you know it, Steffy."

"You're a fine one to talk." She almost choked on her indignation. "You and all those lame excuses."

Jeff seemed to be hanging onto his temper with difficulty. "I wasn't trying to get out of anything, if that's what you're implying. I was merely pointing out to you that your decisions are usually motivated by your whim of the moment—which isn't necessarily what you want the *next* moment."

"Well, thanks a lot, pal. It's nice to know you think I'm immature."

Shannon had no idea what they were arguing about, but they appeared set to continue in this vein for hours. Why hadn't she made her presence known before it was too late? Jeff's next words riveted her attention.

"All I said was that display over Deke this morning was a little much, under the circumstances."

Shannon made a mute gesture of protest. Jeff shouldn't fight her battles; it would only get him in bad with Deke—besides being useless.

"*Any* display of emotion is suspect as far as you're concerned," Stephanie practically shouted.

"I think you know better than that."

"No, I don't! You allow your emotions to take you just so far, and then you stop and examine them for flaws and imperfections. Why can't you believe your heart like Deke and I do?" she cried passionately.

In contrast, Jeff's voice was icy cold. "I'm beginning to wonder exactly how you do feel about Deke."

"I've never made any secret of loving him," she said defiantly.

"That must have delighted his wife," he remarked sarcastically.

"She's his *ex*-wife now," Stephanie corrected. "Shannon never made him happy, and Deke's happiness is all I care about."

Shannon could almost see them standing toe to toe, glaring at each other.

"How about Mike? Would you toss him in the scrap heap too if he didn't please your idol?"

Her voice softened for the first time. "Mikey is a darling. It's going to be fun having him around."

"Another role for you to play, Steffy? Just you and Deke and baby makes three? Never mind that the boy has a mother all the way across country, crying her eyes out for him."

Stephanie's voice was troubled. "I'm not a mon-

ster, Jeff. I've always liked Shannon. I only said
those things because you made me so angry."

Jeff refused to accept the tentative olive branch.
"Just lately I seem to be doing that more and more.
Perhaps it would be better if we tried to avoid each
other for a while."

"That suits me fine!" she flared. "And while we're
at it, why don't we make that forever?"

"If that's what you want," Jeff said coldly.

"It's obviously what *you* want."

They were like two squabbling children. Shannon
could almost have laughed if she hadn't been so
heartsick—and if it weren't so serious for Jeff. How
did he think he was going to avoid coming in contact
with Deke's wife when he was at the house so often
out of necessity?

"Don't try to put words in my mouth." Jeff was
quietly furious. "You aren't as guileless as you look,
are you?"

"What are you talking about?" she demanded.

"You engineered this whole argument very clever-
ly."

"Are you out of your mind? *You're* the one who
started it with your nasty accusations."

"Just be sure and send me an invitation to the
wedding," was Jeff's parting shot as he strode out of
the living room, almost colliding with Marlee.

"Maybe I'll do just that if you behave yourself,"
Stephanie shouted after him. "Better yet, you can be
best man!"

"What on earth is wrong with Jeff?" Marlee
asked, turning to look after him with a puzzled face.

Giving her an outraged look, Stephanie swept by
without answering.

Shannon slowly swung her legs to the floor, feeling
emotionally battered. It was bad enough to have

been an unwilling witness to their argument; to hear Stephanie spell out her plans was shattering.

"Oh, hi, Shannon. I didn't see you," Marlee called. "What's been going on in here?"

"I . . . they . . . I'm not sure."

Marlee raised her eyebrows, lowering herself gracefully into a chair. "We're all used to Steffy's explosions, but Jeff is usually so even-tempered."

"Yes, he is." This was the first time Shannon had ever seen him ruffled, and she felt guilty about it.

"I guess Steffy could make even Job lose patience after a while." Marlee grinned. "I hope she marries a very strong man."

Shannon stood up abruptly. "There's something I forgot," she mumbled, making a hasty exit.

As Shannon turned down the upstairs corridor to the blessed solitude of her own room, she saw Stephanie and Deke standing at the end of the hall outside his bedroom. He had his hands on her shoulders, looking down at her indulgently as she twisted a button on his shirt.

Shannon had eavesdropped enough for one day; she especially wanted to avoid overhearing any tender exchange between these two. But as she turned to go back downstairs, Deke spied her over Stephanie's head. Without removing his hands, he looked at Shannon in sardonic understanding. A flush of anger spread over Shannon's delicate skin and she lifted her head, proceeding unhurriedly to her room.

"Deke, I can't take this thing with Jeff anymore," Stephanie was saying. "Can't you do something about him?"

He patted her back. "Don't worry, honey. It's all going to work out."

Shannon closed her bedroom door, leaning against it while anger and pain savaged her body like a pair of sharp knives. How could Stephanie do a thing like that—run to Deke with tales about Jeff just because he dared to criticize her?

As volatile and spoiled as the girl was, Shannon would never have expected anything as vengeful as that from her. And why didn't Deke wait to hear Jeff's side of the story? How could he comfort Stephanie in that fatuous way, promising her he would take care of any unpleasantness? Would he actually fire Jeff?

Maybe love hadn't made him blind, Shannon reflected bitterly, just feebleminded! Didn't loyalty count for anything? Her slender figure sagged. She of all people knew the answer to that. Deke was a marauding male animal who took what he wanted and walked away from the remains without a backward glance.

It was a fact she'd better learn to live with.

Chapter Eleven

The weather changed for the better on the morning of Christmas Eve. Skies were blue once more and the sun shown brilliantly, turning the landscape into a field of diamonds.

Shannon heard Michael's excited voice in the hall almost before it was light. Turning to look at the clock, she groaned—not even seven yet. A smile curved her generous mouth. She really couldn't blame him. The poor child had been incarcerated for most of his vacation.

Shannon paused in the act of pushing back the covers when she heard Deke's deep voice. "Ssh! You'll wake Mommy."

"She always gets up early at home."

"Well, this morning we're going to let her sleep. How about if I make your breakfast?"

"Do you know how to cook, Daddy?"

"Well, that depends. What do you usually eat?"

Having recently witnessed Deke's culinary ability, Shannon stifled her laughter. He could pour milk out of a bottle, though, and cereal out of a box. Mike was in no danger of starving. Shannon's laughter sobered as she faced the fact that Deke could provide for their son adequately, in one way or another.

She pulled the covers back up to her chin, reluctant to face the day, yet with a curious sense of anticipation invading her. There was something about Christmas after all. By the time she had showered and dressed in a wool skirt and a white blouse with a lace collar under a lavender angora sweater, Shannon was definitely in a holiday mood. Her yuletide spirit lasted until she got to the breakfast table.

Only Stephanie, her mother and Jeff were there. Deke and Mike had gone into the woods with Paul to select a Christmas tree, and the Stevensons weren't down yet. Shannon wondered why Helene had bothered to come to breakfast, since she did nothing but complain.

"I don't know when I'm going to get over this dreadful cold," she grumbled. "I had no idea Switzerland has such ghastly weather."

"You've led a sheltered life, Mother," Stephanie observed sardonically.

"Hardly," Helene responded sharply. "You'd think your father would be concerned, but no, suddenly he decides to go home and leave me in this outpost of civilization."

Shannon was startled. Why *had* Jim left right before Christmas? Had Deke told her the truth? Was he really angry with his lawyer? More likely, a business deal had demanded Jim's attention.

"You could have gone with him," Stephanie reminded her mother.

The peevish lines in Helene's face relaxed. "I wouldn't think of insulting Deke. Especially at a time like this," she added coyly.

Jeff slammed his fork down with a clatter, and

Stephanie inquired sweetly, "Is there something wrong with your waffles?"

His eyes dueled with hers. "They're a little too rich for me."

"Maybe Gretel would give you some dry toast in the kitchen. I'm sure it's against your principles to mingle with the guests."

"Don't be ridiculous, Stephanie," her mother frowned. "Deke is very democratic."

Shannon felt as though her nerve ends were on the outside of her skin. Between Jeff and Stephanie's abrasiveness, and Helene's stupidity, she wished she were a million miles away.

Shoving her chair back, Shannon said, "If everyone will excuse me, I think I'll go for a little walk."

Jeff put his napkin down, rising at the same time. "I'll join you. I could do with a bit of fresh air."

Stephanie's eyebrows rushed together. "Go right ahead. I'll just wait here for Deke."

Helene nodded approvingly. "And maybe we can start making some plans, dear."

After putting on their ski jackets, Shannon and Jeff escaped into the clean world outside. Inhaling the crisp, dry air deeply, they walked along without speaking. By tacit consent they turned up into the hills, avoiding the village. The powdery snow crunched satisfyingly underfoot, and as they climbed higher, Shannon felt her taut nerves relaxing.

"It's beautiful country, isn't it?" she commented at last.

"Yes, it transcends all human pettiness," he replied soberly, making oblique reference to the tension back at the chalet.

Shannon hesitated for a moment, looking for the right words to phrase her reassurances. "Deke is an honorable man; I'm sure he would listen to reason."

Jeff turned a quizzical look on her. "You think I have something to worry about?"

"No, I really don't. You're very . . . very capable."

"That's a strange way of putting it, but thanks anyway." He smiled.

"I honestly don't think that he would try to replace you."

"I don't either, really. I know Steffy is just bluffing, so why am I worried?"

Shannon's heart sank. She had a vivid picture of Stephanie working her wiles on Deke. Jeff would be shocked to discover the extent of her revenge. Well, there was time enough for him to face that later. She didn't want Jeff's Christmas to be spoiled. "I don't think she would do anything she'd regret afterward."

Jeff looked tortured. "If I could only be sure of that."

"Maybe if you just . . . sort of went along with her. Stephanie is young, but she'll grow up like all the rest of us. With a little careful handling she won't insist on having her own way."

"There's nothing I want to believe more," Jeff said slowly. Suddenly his face lit up. "So why the devil don't I? I've been an absolute idiot, fighting her all the way. When you can't beat 'em, join 'em, I always say." Throwing his arms around her, he gave Shannon a big hug.

Shannon had a terrible feeling that Jeff was heading for a fall, but his high spirits swept her along. It was Christmas, time for goodwill on earth; surely all problems could be laid aside for two days.

Deke and Michael had returned with the tree in their absence. It was a towering pine that almost touched the ceiling.

The little boy's face was flushed with excitement. "I got to pick it out all by myself, Mommy."

"You did a good job, darling. That's the most beautiful tree I've ever seen."

A slight cloud tempered his delight. "Daddy says we have to wait till this afternoon to trim it."

Deke's eyes met Shannon's over their son's head. They smiled, all the rancor and bitterness of last night temporarily laid aside in this sweet kind of sharing. "Well, that's sort of traditional," she told the little boy. "It isn't really Christmas Eve yet."

"But what am I going to do all day?" he wailed.

Shannon realized how long time could seem to a child. Minutes turned into hours. "I'll tell you what. If Gretel will let us use her kitchen, we'll bake Christmas cookies. Would you like that?"

Gretel was happy to oblige, and Mike was soon gleefully engaged in helping his mother measure and mix. To Shannon's surprise, Deke accompanied them.

"I'll keep him busy," she murmured. "You can do something you'd rather do."

"I can't think what that would be."

She gave him a surprised look, her cheeks flushing at the intensity of his regard. Shannon was too busy now, though, to puzzle over Deke's ever-changing attitude. Mixing up a big ball of dough, she rolled it out on the wide, wooden table. Gretel had provided some cookie cutters, which Shannon gave to Mike, instructing him how to use them.

The little boy's efforts were awkward but his enthusiasm more than made up for it. Shannon allowed him to do it by himself, giving unobtrusive help only when necessary. Their heads were bent over the dough and they were both unaware of the melting look on Deke's face.

When the first tray of misshapen cookies came out of the oven, Deke and Michael devoured most of them while they were still hot.

"Mmm." Deke licked a crumb from the corner of his mouth. "I can see why you're such a big success."

Shannon smiled. "You're not a very critical audience."

Little lights danced in Deke's laughing eyes. "Take it from a connoisseur—these are even better than the Peanut Fudgies made by Mama's little elves."

Shannon flushed a bright rosy pink, gripping the mixing bowl hard. It was painful to think of that night in the cabin. Deke's last reminder of her vulnerability had been brutal. Why was he reverting to his former engaging manner? The hateful man from last night might never have existed. Was it all an act put on for Michael's sake? Shannon sighed. It was probably just an excess of Christmas spirit such as she had experienced this morning.

When the last scrap of dough had been rolled, baked, admired and consumed, Gretel took over.

"I'll clean up," Shannon protested, but the older woman wouldn't allow it.

"You go play with the boy." She beamed at all three of them, her matchmaking heart delighted by the charming picture of domesticity they presented.

Paul came in the back door, letting in a chill blast of air and the sound of frenzied barking. "I think your friend is calling you," he told Mike with a twinkle in his eyes.

"Brandy!" the little boy shouted. "Can I go outside and play with him?"

"I'll get your jacket," Deke offered.

He returned with Shannon's and his own also. Gretel's joy was unbounded as she watched them leave.

As soon as they stepped out of the door, they were confronted by the largest dog Shannon had ever seen. His broad, comical face surmounted a wooly brown and white body that was wriggling with pure glee. After licking Mike's entire face with a tongue almost as broad as the child's hand, he turned his attention to Shannon, putting his huge paws on her shoulders.

"Down, Brandy!" Deke commanded, coming to Shannon's rescue as she staggered under the dog's weight.

"I had no idea he was such a monster." She laughed, trying to avoid the pink tongue that was intent on washing her face.

"He isn't a monster; he's my dog," Mike informed her, sinking both hands into the soft fur. "Can we take him home with us when we go, Daddy?"

"I'm afraid not."

"Why not?" Mike demanded.

Deke hunched down in front of the little boy. "Because he's used to these mountains and forests. Brandy wouldn't be happy in a fenced yard."

Michael's attention was diverted for the moment. "Do you have a yard with a big fence like they do at play school, with swings and a teeter-totter?"

"Well, we don't have those right now, but we can get them."

The child's eyes gleamed with rapture. "And I can play on them?"

"You sure can."

Sensing that he was on a winning roll, Mike looked at his father beguilingly. "And can we get another dog as long as Brandy can't come with us?"

Shannon hadn't said a word during this exchange, but her body had stiffened like a marble statue. She couldn't fault either of them. Michael was only a child; naturally he was interested in immediate pleasures. And how could she blame Deke for providing them—she would herself if she could.

Deke sensed her distress. Reaching out, he grasped her hand, squeezing it reassuringly, but she pulled away. She didn't want his pity. Mike was entitled to the things Deke could give him and she would just have to learn to live with that.

"We'll talk about it later. How would you like to take Brandy for a walk?" Deke asked, deftly changing the subject.

They strolled through the gentle hills above the chalet with Michael between them, holding onto their hands. The huge Saint Bernard ran ahead of them, doubling back on his tracks to be sure they were following. Occasionally, in a fit of exaltation he would spring on Deke or Shannon, bestowing lavish affection. In some instinctive way the dog knew not to fling himself at Michael. His sheer exuberance lifted Shannon out of her depressed mood.

They all had lunch together, and Mike's presence lightened what might have been a disastrous meal. Stephanie and Jeff still weren't speaking. In fact, her barbed remarks made everyone uncomfortable, although Jeff was careful not to respond to them. His set face was at such odds with his usual cheerful demeanor, however, that everyone sensed the effort that went into his restraint. Shannon's heart sank. Jeff had been so willing to meet Stephanie halfway, and she wasn't even giving him a chance.

Helene was another irritant. With her usual disregard for anyone else's feelings, she made constant tactless remarks. Her main topic of conversation, though, was a complaint about her husband's defection.

Her discontented voice was like a fingernail on a

blackboard. "Jim knew I wasn't feeling well; I don't understand how he could go off and leave me like this. And at Christmastime, too! Couldn't you have persuaded him to stay, Deke?"

Deke's face was impassive. "I believe Jim did what he knew was best."

His phraseology was unusual, but Helene didn't pick up on it. "I certainly think after all these years I'm entitled to a little more consideration." She eyed Deke apprehensively. "I do hope this won't affect our . . . future relationship."

Deke's expression gave nothing away. "Our future relationship is already settled."

Shannon's eyes dropped to her plate, not wanting to witness Stephanie's triumph. The younger girl's reaction was unexpected.

"Oh for heaven's sake, Mother, stop politicking. If Dad loses Deke as a client you're not going to starve to death."

Helene looked shocked. "I'm sure that Deke wouldn't . . . I mean, under the circumstances . . ."

Deke deftly changed the subject. "Anyone for skiing this afternoon?"

"Me! Me!" Mike crowed.

"No, not you, tiger." Deke ruffled his hair. "You have to take a nap so you'll be bright eyed and bushy tailed when it's time to trim the tree."

For the first time, Mike didn't accept his father's edict without question. Pushing out his lower lip he said, "Why do I have to? Everybody else is going skiing."

"Not everybody," Deke corrected. "I'm sure Mrs. Deighton is going to take a rest just like you."

Michael's disdainful face told how much that impressed him. Helene had gone out of her way to make overtures to him whenever it occurred to her, but he saw through her false, sugary manner with the uncluttered perception of the very young. "Is Mommy going?"

"Yes, Mommy is going," Deke said without consulting her.

Shannon waggled her fingers in back of Mike's head. "No, I'm not. I'll read you a story before your nap," she said to placate the little boy.

"You go ahead, Shannon. I'll do it. I don't have anything else to do," Stephanie said somberly.

"I was going to ask you for a favor," Deke put in smoothly. "Would you mind going into the village with Jeff and picking up some supplies? There will probably be people dropping by all evening."

"He doesn't need me," she said shortly.

"Oh, but he does." Deke smiled. "Haven't you ever watched men in a market? They pick up anchovies and pickled mushrooms, and forget the bread and milk."

"Why can't Gretel go?" Helene asked sharply. She didn't like the way this was progressing—Deke off skiing with Shannon while her daughter did menial chores.

"Gretel has her hands full preparing Christmas dinner," Deke said easily.

"I'll be glad to go," Stephanie said, "but I don't need Jeff."

"I'm afraid you do," Deke told her. "We're low on soda and mixes—all that stuff that's too heavy for you to carry."

Although both Stephanie and Jeff looked as though Deke had proposed self-immolation at the very least, neither saw a way to get out of it. As luncheon broke up they went out of the room together, keeping a careful distance while studiously avoiding each other's eyes.

"Okay, woman, this is it," Rustin said to his wife. "You've exhausted all your excuses. Today you're going skiing."

She gave him an impish grin before turning to Michael. "Come on, Mikey, I'll race you up the stairs. With luck I'll sprain my ankle before I get to the top."

As Shannon prepared to follow, Deke caught her hand. "Come skiing with me. You don't have to read to Mike."

"It isn't that. I want to wrap some packages for him while I know he's safely out of the way."

"Can't it wait?" He linked his arms loosely around her waist, a slow smile curving his firm mouth. "If we're lucky another blizzard might come up."

Shannon put her hands on his forearms, feeling their muscular strength. For a terrible moment weakness overcame her as she remembered going to sleep with her cheek against his hair-roughened chest while Deke cradled her body against his.

Trying to ignore the ripple that went up her spine, she gave him a bright smile. "You just want to show off with some more of that trick skiing."

"I hope that isn't my only claim to fame."

He was drawing her closer, a flame kindling in the depths of his eyes as they captured hers, reminding her inexorably of his other talents. Shannon held him off with her palms against his chest, commanding her body not to seek out the male contours that would eliminate all will to resist. Help came unexpectedly.

"Mommy, are you coming?" Michael called down. "You said you'd read me a story."

"Right away, darling," she gasped, practically running for the stairs.

Deke's amused chuckle followed her. "See you

later, Shannon." It carried a promise that was a
threat to her peace of mind.

After Michael was settled down she went to her
own room, a little calmer but not much. The exploits
of the Hardy Boys had failed to take her mind off
Deke. He had the knack of keeping her constantly
off base, and she had to try and figure it out once and
for all. He was being so sweet to her today. Was he
playing her against Stephanie? And if so, why? The
girl was obviously madly in love with him, so he had
no need to try and make her jealous.

Shannon stopped dead still in the middle of the
room. Was it possible that he had been trying to
make *her* jealous? The implications of that idea
made a wild happiness well up in her breast. There
could be only one reason for that. Deke really did
want to marry her! Never mind the reasons. She
would *make* him love her again. There was an
undeniable spark between them—a spark?—make
that a roaring flame of desire. Surely that was
enough to start with. Shannon hugged her shivering
body with an excess of pure joy as her whole life
turned around.

If only he were here right now! To still the longing,
Shannon forced herself to do what she had stayed
home for. Ferreting out all of Michael's gifts from
their secret hiding places, she wrapped them lovingly
in bright foil paper and satin ribbons.

With her arms full of packages, Shannon went
downstairs to put them under the tree. They made a
bright splash of color under the stately pine that
would rival them in brilliance once it was trimmed.
Thinking everyone else was out or otherwise occupied, Shannon jumped at a sound behind her.

"Helene, you startled me! I thought you were
resting in your room."

"I'm tired of just lying around in bed." The older woman's voice was petulant. "That's all there is to do in this godforsaken hole. I haven't been out of the house since I got here."

That wasn't strictly true, but Shannon wasn't inclined to argue with her. "Why don't you take a walk down to the village and browse through some of those darling little shops?"

"Big deal! All that tacky, touristy stuff—Rodeo Drive it isn't," Helene said scornfully, referring to the exclusive shopping street in Beverly Hills. "I wouldn't waste my time."

Shannon was fast losing the scant patience she possessed. "Suit yourself." She shrugged, turning back to her task.

"You hear such glamorous stories about winter vacations in Switzerland." Discontent etched unflattering lines in Helene's carefully tended face. "I could tell them a few things. If it weren't for Stephanie, this whole thing would have been a washout."

Since the girl had scarcely spent a willing five minutes with her mother, Shannon raised an incredulous eyebrow.

Helene didn't notice. For the first time some animation relieved her bored expression. "To think of my little girl getting married."

Shannon stiffened. "Aren't you being a bit premature? I thought she said she was *thinking* about it."

"Oh no, it's all settled."

The room suddenly tilted alarmingly. Shannon gripped her knees hard. "How do you know?"

"A mother can always tell," Helene informed her smugly.

Shannon let out the breath she had been holding. "Perhaps you're mistaken. She could have made that announcement to shake you up a little bit, or . . . or just to get some attention."

Helene's vapid eyes suddenly hardened. "I hope you're not going to be difficult about this, Shannon. You had your chance at Deke and you failed. It isn't fair to stand in the way of someone else's happiness."

"Is that what you're interested in, Helene? Stephanie's happiness—or your own?"

"You have no right to say a thing like that to me! You're just jealous," the older woman flared spitefully. "Anyone can see how much in love those two are. You saw it yourself yesterday morning."

Shannon's face paled, but she held onto herself. "We were all a little upset at the time."

"Maybe that's what it takes to bring things to a head," Helene said with satisfaction.

"Did Stephanie actually *tell* you she was getting married?" It was torture, but Shannon had to hear her say it. A quick death to her hopes was preferable to this slow dying.

"In a way." Helene's eyes sidled away from Shannon's. "She had that certain look on her face. I don't want you to think that I condoned what they were doing in her bedroom all that time. I know morals are laxer than they were in my day, but I would certainly have marched right in there if I hadn't known that they were . . . um . . . sealing their bargain."

Nausea rose in Shannon's throat at the thought of Deke making love to Stephanie, caressing her body, lowering his head to . . .

She sprang to her feet. "I always knew you were a hypocrite, Helene; I just never knew how big a one. Too bad you don't have more daughters to sell off—you could make a fortune!"

"I'll let that go, Shannon, because I know you're upset." Helene gave her a sharp look. "There's nothing you can do about it, though."

"What makes you think I want to try?"

The other woman was unconvinced. "If you'll consider this calmly you'll see that you could actually benefit by it." Helene was unperturbed by Shannon's icy contempt. "Michael is a darling little boy, but newlyweds need time to themselves. If you bow out gracefully I'm sure Stephanie could convince Deke to let the boy remain with you. He would probably be quite generous about support, too."

Giving her a look of withering scorn, Shannon said, "Unlike you, Helene, I don't use my child for bargaining purposes."

The kitchen door banged loudly, announcing the return of Jeff and Stephanie, their lilting voices preceding them. They came into the living room continuing a laughing discussion.

Through her misery, Shannon perceived that they had made up their differences. She was happy for Jeff; it would make things a lot easier for him.

"It's such a glorious day out," Stephanie caroled. "What are you two doing holed up in here?"

Jeff reached out and pulled her long hair teasingly. "It's below zero outside."

"Well, it *feels* glorious." She twirled around with her arms in the air. "Everything does today."

Helene regarded her daughter indulgently. "Why don't you go comb your hair before Deke gets home?"

Shannon slipped quietly out of the room. She walked carefully up the stairs, feeling curiously fragile, as though at any minute she might shatter into a million pieces.

Deke and the others returned by the time Michael got up from his nap, and in the resulting confusion of trimming the tree, Shannon's unnatural quiet went unnoticed. Almost. Several times she looked up to see Deke watching her. He seemed on the point of saying something, but she made sure there was no opportunity.

Actually, Michael kept her busy. He kept demanding specific ornaments from among the multitude of shimmering globes, and then needed help in hanging them. As soon as one red, or green, or gold ball was hung precariously on a branch, he was ready for the next one. It didn't matter that they were all bunched together in one spot, leaving great bare patches on the rest of the tree. Mike's shining eyes as he considered his handiwork told that he thought it was perfect.

Stephanie was almost as excited as the little boy. She was up and down the step stool, hanging tinsel on the upper reaches, animation on her face as she called to everyone to admire her efforts.

When the last bauble had been put in place, Michael's stocking was hung with much ceremony.

"Are you going to hang yours too, Steffy?" Mike asked her.

"I was going to, but I couldn't find one big enough for a sable coat," Stephanie laughed, slanting a provocative look at Deke. "And besides, your daddy said he wasn't going to buy me one anyway."

A strange calm descended on Shannon as she heard the low, teasing response that was meant only for Stephanie's ears.

"Maybe I'll get it for you after all—for a wedding present," Deke said.

Shannon went through the rest of the afternoon in a daze. She helped pack away the empty ornament boxes in a big carton, supervised Mike's early dinner in the kitchen and returned to have a Christmas Eve drink with the others—all without anything penetrating the protective shield she had drawn around herself.

Only one incident pierced her armor. It was when Stephanie lifted her glass, her cheeks hectic with excitement, although it had to be only her first drink. "Quiet, everybody, I have something to say." After she had their full attention, her mouth curved in a secret smile. "At precisely midnight I'm going to make an announcement."

When Helene's triumphant eyes met hers, Shannon looked away.

Jeff shook his head indulgently. "Only our Steffy would make an announcement that she was going to make an announcement."

Deke chuckled. "This is her moment, Jeff. Let her make the most of it."

Shannon started blindly for the door, only to be stopped by Deke's hand on her arm. "Where are you going, Shannon?"

She looked at him blankly. "I don't know." Where did you go to hide when you felt like a mortally wounded little animal?

"What's wrong, honey?" His strong face was full of concern. "Something's been bothering you all evening."

Shannon felt hysterical laughter welling up inside of her. Clenching her hands tightly, she managed to stifle it. What could be wrong? I can't wait to hear another woman announce her engagement to my husband, she wanted to tell him. But Deke would only remind her that he was her *ex*-husband. As Helene said, she had her chance and she failed.

Shannon managed a bright smile, although she couldn't meet his eyes. "Everything's just dandy," she said, turning back into the room.

The rest of the evening was a blur. A buffet had

been laid out in the dining room and everyone helped himself to sandwiches and coffee. Carols played on the hi-fi and people stopped by to deposit packages under the tree, staying for a drink afterward. It was all very festive.

Shannon wandered through the throng, talking and even smiling while a part of her stood off at a distance—the part of her that was racked with pain.

Finally the grandfather clock in the hall started to toll midnight. When the last stroke died away, Stephanie went to stand by the punch bowl, beckoning to Deke, "Will you do the honors, darling?"

He smiled down at her radiant face, bending to kiss her cheek. "It would be my pleasure." Deke filled the little crystal cups, handing one to each person.

Stephanie stood in the middle of the floor, tall, beautiful and confident, "We'd like all of you to join us in a toast to blessed wedlock. Jeff and I are getting married."

Amid the chorus of good wishes, the only two people in the room who didn't react were Shannon and Helene. They were both rooted to the spot.

Helene recovered first. "Did you hear what you said, Stephanie? You said Jeff when you meant *Deke!*"

"No, Mother, I said exactly what I meant." She held out her arms and Jeff moved into them, holding her with a tender intensity that ignored everyone else in the room.

"You're out of your mind! I won't let you do this." Helene tried to pull her daughter away by force. "Deke is in love with you; he wants to marry you. Do you know what you're throwing away?"

Stephanie turned to her mother, keeping one arm around Jeff's neck. Her young face was contemptuous. "Sometimes I actually feel sorry for you, Mother—you live in a world all your own. Don't you know that Shannon is the one Deke wants? He always has."

"You're wrong!" Helene cried. "I don't believe—" One glance at the look on Deke's face stilled the impassioned words.

The truth was written in his eyes as they held Shannon's. He moved toward her, a little smile around his mouth. Shannon remained pinned to the spot.

"Don't look so shocked, darling." He ran his hands up her arms under the wide sleeves of the caftan, and she shivered involuntarily. "You knew it all along."

"No, I didn't. I—"

He folded her in his arms, kissing her trembling mouth.

"Deke, please! The others . . ."

He turned an amused glance on their interested audience. "You're right. This is something that demands privacy." Tugging her by the hand, he led her toward the stairs.

"Where . . . where are we going?"

"Well, it's too cold outside for what I have in mind, so I thought my bedroom would be the logical place."

Shannon was too confused to protest. Surely this was a dream! There were a million questions swirling around in her head, but Deke refused to answer any of them until they reached his room.

The master suite was spacious, almost apartment-sized. Deke led her to a big chair, sitting down and pulling her onto his lap. "First we'll get the preliminaries over with. Will you marry me?"

"I don't know, Deke. There are so many—"

His mouth cut off her protest. Gently forcing her

head onto his shoulder, his lips trailed a path of fire
from her earlobe down the length of her throat,
nibbling at the delicate slope of her shoulder. His
hand went inside the wide neck of her caftan,
curving around her bare breast and slowly
smoothing the creamy skin.

"Please, Deke, that isn't fair."

"Will you marry me?" he murmured, his fingers
capturing the rosy nipple and stroking it lingeringly.

"I'm not sure. I—"

He slid the gown off her shoulders, running
his fingertips lightly up and down her body until
she arched toward him, aching for closer contact.
Bending his head he kissed her breast, his tongue
making languorous circles that lit flames in her entire body. His hand wandered in a slow, erotic pattern, caressing and arousing. When it reached the
juncture of her thighs he raised his head, his eyes
lit from within by molten passion. "Will you marry
me?"

"Yes! Oh, yes!" she cried.

"When?"

"Now," Shannon gasped.

"That's exactly what I had in mind," he said with
satisfaction.

In one swift movement Deke swept her into his
arms and carried her to the bed. Flinging his own
clothes aside he joined her, covering her soft body
with the hard male contours she longed for. Shannon
flamed into life beneath him, intensifying his already
throbbing desire. Their union was immediate and
compulsive, their need for each other so consuming
that it couldn't be held off.

Deke clasped her body to his while they struggled
toward the ultimate release that occurred for both of
them in a tidal wave of pure sensation. The first
crashing waves eventually subsided to ripples and

then into calm, leaving complete satisfaction in their wake.

Much later Shannon stirred in Deke's arms. "We really do have to talk, you know."

"If you say so." He positioned her closer in his arms, nibbling suggestively on her ear. "Although, personally, I think this is more fun."

Shannon turned her head so she could look into his face, drinking her fill of its rugged strength. "I thought you were going to marry Stephanie."

That got his attention. "You didn't!" he exclaimed incredulously.

Shannon's eyelashes veiled her troubled eyes. "She always did say she loved you, and that morning after the blizzard you . . . you went to her."

"Only because she was hysterical." He cupped Shannon's chin in his hand, forcing her to look at him. "Listen to me, my one and only love. Stephanie is like a kid sister to me." It was what Jeff had tried to tell her. This time, hearing it in Deke's quiet voice she knew it was true.

"I know she's difficult sometimes," Deke continued. "But underneath she's a warmhearted human being. She was really terrified when she thought some catastrophe had taken place. I'll admit I was annoyed at you for not being more understanding, but I thought you were just miffed over an imagined neglect. It never occurred to me that you could be jealous of her as a woman."

"Her own mother thought that you and she . . . that when you were in Stephanie's bedroom . . ."

Deke gave an exclamation of disgust. "That woman ought to be committed! You didn't believe her?" When Shannon didn't answer immediately Deke chuckled, a low, male sound deep in his throat. "There is only one woman who could make me rise to those heights after the night we spent together." His hand trailed erotically over her thighs. "You demand a man's best, my little sex kitten."

She looked up at him provocatively. "Are you complaining?"

His hand moved higher. "I asked you to marry me, didn't I?—that night in the cabin among other times."

Shannon remained silent. That was the fact that hurt: that he wanted her more for Michael's sake than his own. She knew now, though, that she would take Deke on any terms.

He touched her cheek gently. "What is it, sweetheart?"

Her blue eyes darkened to navy pools. "It doesn't matter, Deke. You've been honest with me. From the very beginning I've known that you wanted me back primarily because of Michael. But I'm willing because I love you so much that I think I'd die if I had to give you up now." She gave him a gallant little smile. "And maybe someday you'll love me a little bit, too—not just want me."

Deke groaned, crushing her against his hard body until she felt bruised. "My darling angel, what have I done to you? Don't you know that I love you more than life itself? Don't you realize that I kept dragging Mike into it because I hoped your sense of duty to him would make you come back to me? Of course I love my son, sweetheart, but I love you even more."

It was like a miracle. Shannon was afraid to believe that all her dreams had come true—until she looked into Deke's eyes and saw the unmistakable love that shone just for her. He held her quietly while she became accustomed to it.

Shannon finally stirred, rubbing her cheek against

Deke's chest. "I'm so ashamed of the things I accused you of. Jim thought of all of those things on his own, didn't he?"

Deke's muscles flexed angrily. "I told him to get his damn tail out of here if he knew what was good for him." He scowled in remembrance. "I might still fire him."

"You can't fire your kid sister's father," Shannon teased.

Deke grinned. "Truthfully, I'll be glad to turn her over to Jeff. She's quite a handful."

Shannon shook her head. "I was absolutely stunned tonight when she announced their engagement. They didn't even seem to *like* each other."

Deke laughed. "Jeff and Steffy have had a stormy courtship. They're madly in love with each other, but Jeff has always wanted to wait till she finished college to get married. He was afraid that because Steffy is so young she doesn't really know her own mind. He's also very defensive about the fact that he can't give her all the things she's accustomed to, so he had the mistaken idea that they should wait until he piled up a little nest egg."

"I wonder how she got him to change his mind?"

"I guess I can take part of the credit." Deke chuckled. "Steffy came to me almost in tears, and I promised her I'd take care of it. I sent them off together, knowing they were bound to make it up once they were alone."

So that was the explanation for that scene where Shannon thought Stephanie was trying to get Deke to fire Jeff! She vowed never to jump to conclusions again.

Deke pulled her closer, bending his head to kiss the hollow in her throat. "I don't know why Jeff bothered to resist," he murmured. "A smart woman can get the best of a man any day."

Shannon put her arms around his neck, looking meltingly into his eyes. "Oh, I don't know. Men aren't so dumb. I'll bet you know exactly what I have in mind right now."

His mouth closed over hers, parting her willing lips. He not only knew, he had the same idea.

Silhouette Special Edition. Romances
for the woman who expects a little
more out of love.

If you enjoyed this book,
and you're ready
for more great romance

...get 4 romance novels FREE when you become
a Silhouette Special Edition home subscriber.

Act now and we'll send you four exciting Silhouette Special
Edition romance novels. They're our gift to introduce you to our
convenient home subscription service. Every month, we'll send
you six new passion-filled Special Edition books. Look them
over for 15 days. If you keep them, pay just $11.70 for all six. Or
return them at no charge.

We'll mail your books to you two full months *before they are
available anywhere else.* Plus, with every shipment, you'll receive
the Silhouette Books Newsletter absolutely free. *And with
Silhouette Special Edition there are never any shipping or handling charges.*

Mail the coupon today to get your four free books—and more
romance than you ever bargained for.

────────── **MAIL COUPON TODAY** ──────────

MORE ROMANCE FOR
A SPECIAL WAY TO RELAX
$1.95 each

2 ☐ Hastings	23 ☐ Charles	45 ☐ Charles	66 ☐ Mikels
3 ☐ Dixon	24 ☐ Dixon	46 ☐ Howard	67 ☐ Shaw
4 ☐ Vitek	25 ☐ Hardy	47 ☐ Stephens	68 ☐ Sinclair
5 ☐ Converse	26 ☐ Scott	48 ☐ Ferrell	69 ☐ Dalton
6 ☐ Douglass	27 ☐ Wisdom	49 ☐ Hastings	70 ☐ Clare
7 ☐ Stanford	28 ☐ Ripy	50 ☐ Browning	71 ☐ Skillern
8 ☐ Halston	29 ☐ Bergen	51 ☐ Trent	72 ☐ Belmont
9 ☐ Baxter	30 ☐ Stephens	52 ☐ Sinclair	73 ☐ Taylor
10 ☐ Thiels	31 ☐ Baxter	53 ☐ Thomas	74 ☐ Wisdom
11 ☐ Thornton	32 ☐ Douglass	54 ☐ Hohl	75 ☐ John
12 ☐ Sinclair	33 ☐ Palmer	55 ☐ Stanford	76 ☐ Ripy
13 ☐ Beckman	35 ☐ James	56 ☐ Wallace	77 ☐ Bergen
14 ☐ Keene	36 ☐ Dailey	57 ☐ Thornton	78 ☐ Gladstone
15 ☐ James	37 ☐ Stanford	58 ☐ Douglass	79 ☐ Hastings
16 ☐ Carr	38 ☐ John	59 ☐ Roberts	80 ☐ Douglass
17 ☐ John	39 ☐ Milan	60 ☐ Thorne	81 ☐ Thornton
18 ☐ Hamilton	40 ☐ Converse	61 ☐ Beckman	82 ☐ McKenna
19 ☐ Shaw	41 ☐ Halston	62 ☐ Bright	83 ☐ Major
20 ☐ Musgrave	42 ☐ Drummond	63 ☐ Wallace	84 ☐ Stephens
21 ☐ Hastings	43 ☐ Shaw	64 ☐ Converse	85 ☐ Beckman
22 ☐ Howard	44 ☐ Eden	65 ☐ Cates	86 ☐ Halston

Silhouette Special Edition

87 ☐ Dixon	102 ☐ Wallace	117 ☐ Converse	132 ☐ Dailey
88 ☐ Saxon	103 ☐ Taylor	118 ☐ Jackson	133 ☐ Douglass
89 ☐ Meriwether	104 ☐ Wallace	119 ☐ Langan	134 ☐ Ripy
90 ☐ Justin	105 ☐ Sinclair	120 ☐ Dixon	135 ☐ Seger
91 ☐ Stanford	106 ☐ John	121 ☐ Shaw	136 ☐ Scott
92 ☐ Hamilton	107 ☐ Ross	122 ☐ Walker	137 ☐ Parker
93 ☐ Lacey	108 ☐ Stephens	123 ☐ Douglass	138 ☐ Thornton
94 ☐ Barrie	109 ☐ Beckman	124 ☐ Mikels	139 ☐ Halston
95 ☐ Doyle	110 ☐ Browning	125 ☐ Cates	140 ☐ Sinclair
96 ☐ Baxter	111 ☐ Thorne	126 ☐ Wildman	141 ☐ Saxon
97 ☐ Shaw	112 ☐ Belmont	127 ☐ Taylor	142 ☐ Bergen
98 ☐ Hurley	113 ☐ Camp	128 ☐ Macomber	143 ☐ Bright
99 ☐ Dixon	114 ☐ Ripy	129 ☐ Rowe	144 ☐ Meriwether
100 ☐ Roberts	115 ☐ Halston	130 ☐ Carr	
101 ☐ Bergen	116 ☐ Roberts	131 ☐ Lee	

SILHOUETTE SPECIAL EDITION, Department SE/2
1230 Avenue of the Americas
New York, NY 10020

Please send me the books I have checked above. I am enclosing $_____
(please add 75¢ to cover postage and handling. NYS and NYC residents please
add appropriate sales tax). Send check or money order—no cash or C.O.D.'s
please. Allow six weeks for delivery.

NAME _____

ADDRESS _____

CITY _____ STATE/ZIP _____

Available Now

A Hard Bargain by Carole Halston

Adam Craddock desperately wanted to buy a valuable piece of
Alabama beachfront. And once he met the owner Whitney
Baines, he knew he wanted her every bit as much!

Winter Of Love by Tracy Sinclair

Even though Shannon and Deke's marriage had dissolved in
divorce, their love never did. And through their son Michael
they would be brought together again, this time, forever.

Above The Moon by Antonia Saxon

When the sky fell in on their perfect world, Kay and Alan were
devastated. But out of their sadness came the strength to build
a new life, with love that would last forever.

Dream Feast by Fran Bergen

Glenn Reeves was a developer who wanted to build a dream.
El Paseo was a part of that dream, but only the owner
Janet Howe, could make his dream complete.

When Morning Comes by Laurey Bright

Claire Wyndham saw Scott Carver as a playboy, a reckless
traveler of the world, a despoiler of hearts—her own included.
Now that he'd taken her heart, should she give him
her soul, also?

The Courting Game by Kate Meriwether

It would have been a routine case if Courtney Ross' adversary
had been anyone except millionaire Blaz Devlin.
In his embrace she realized she might lose the case,
and her heart, as well.